Praise for *Sorry*

'Gail Jones' sixth novel is an elegantly written lament for lost opportunities, both for its characters and a wider, national failure.'

The Age

'One of the most interesting and talented novelists at work in Australia today.'

The Sydney Morning Herald

Praise for *Dreams of Speaking*

'If a good novelist makes us look at everyday subjects in new ways, then Jones is an excellent one, and *Dreams* takes flight, skipping from descriptions of sound waves to cellophane with bravura flair.'

TIME magazine

'Jones is an extraordinary writer no matter what genre she is working in, and often breaks new ground in her treatment of her subject matter, but this novel strikes the most successful balance I've seen in her work so far between intellectual complexities, on the one hand, and simple narrative seductions, on the other side.'

Australian Book Review

T03633354

Praise for *Sixty Lights*

'Wonderfully written passages . . . it's when Jones's ability as a stylist comes together with her intelligent and intensely visual imagination that her fiction becomes truly illuminating.'

The Sydney Morning Herald

'There is an intelligence and honesty to her writing that brings the characters powerfully to life.'

The Age

'Jones's imagery is evocative . . . wonderful turns of phrase.'

The Bulletin

Gail Jones is the author of two short-story collections, a critical monograph, and the novels *Black Mirror*, *Sixty Lights*, *Dreams of Speaking* and *Sorry*. Thrice shortlisted for the Miles Franklin Award, her prizes include the WA Premier's Award for Fiction, the Nita B. Kibble Award, the Steele Rudd Award, the *Age* Book of the Year Award, the Adelaide Festival Award for Fiction and the ASAL Gold Medal. She has also been shortlisted for international awards, including the IMPAC and the Prix Femina. Gail holds a Chair in the Writing and Society Research Group at the University of Western Sydney.

Black Mirror

GAIL JONES

VINTAGE BOOKS
Australia

A Vintage book
Published by Random House Australia Pty Ltd
Level 3, 100 Pacific Highway, North Sydney NSW 2060
www.randomhouse.com.au

First published in Australia by Picador, Pan Macmillan Australia, in 2002
This edition published by Vintage in 2009

Copyright © Gail Jones 2002

The moral right of the author has been asserted.

All rights reserved. No part of this book may be reproduced or transmitted by
any person or entity, including internet search engines or retailers, in any form
or by any means, electronic or mechanical, including photocopying (except
under the statutory exceptions provisions of the Australian *Copyright Act 1968*),
recording, scanning or by any information storage and retrieval system without
the prior written permission of Random House Australia.

Addresses for companies within the Random House Group can be found at
www.randomhouse.com.au/offices

National Library of Australia
Cataloguing-in-Publication Entry

Jones, Gail, 1955–.
Black mirror.

ISBN   978 1 74166 854 4 (pbk).

A823.3

Cover image by Getty Images
Cover design by Sandy Cull, gogoGinko
Typeset in 13/15pt Perpetua by Post Pre-press Group, Brisbane
Printed and bound by Griffin Press, South Australia

Random House Australia uses papers that are natural, renewable and recyclable
products and made from wood grown in sustainable forests. The logging and
manufacturing processes are expected to conform to the environmental regula-
tions of the country of origin.

10 9 8 7 6 5 4 3 2 1

For my parents

As a painter might see it:

The rain has made her luminescent and she is a pillar of shine.

She pops open her umbrella, holds it close above her, and is transformed to a domed shape, darkly vertical. The air is suddenly pale; it bears the appearance of onion skin.

How translucent the sky is. How awash and water-coloured.

For some reason this is the way she imagines herself, as a modernist composition in a hypothetical artwork, caught in the possibilities of the elements and their visual trickery. And later, when Victoria is dead, she will remember how on this day of their very first meeting she was so distracted she became soaked before she recalled her umbrella, and how as she stood catching pneumonia and feeling her legs swept by water from passing cars, she saw an apparition of herself there, sodden, aesthetic, saturated with questions.

Beneath the vegetable sky this young woman seems lost. But she is merely stalled by her own nervous and chilly apprehensions.

She says her own name, Anna, in a watery whisper. *Anna. Anna.*

For Victoria, however, the same moment is the ribbon of a movie she is endlessly unspooling. This screen, its slick flickerings, a new face represented.

She can see the wet woman crossing the road, moving in a diagonal towards her house, and the redundant umbrella, darkly bob-bobbing, and the slow cars, and the leafless trees, and the backwards stretch of the grey road; and she can see the sky, which today is unusually shot and illuminate; it reminds her of a pool of spent semen, glistening mother-of-pearl.

For some reason Victoria can also see herself as though filmed, in the sly act of gazing. She is a profile in winterlight, a woman not entirely visible, and obscurity releases her face from time. She could be any age; she could be fifty or twenty-one. And for some reason it occurs to her:

I am waiting for this visitor so that I can tell my story and die.

THE KISS

What is a kiss?
A divagation, everything collapses.

(André Breton questioning Susanne Muzard)

With Kiss. Kiss Cross. Cross. Criss. Kiss
Cross. Undo lives' end.

(James Joyce, *Finnegans Wake*)

1

Let us say that her memory is like peering into a night-dark tunnel and waiting for the circle of gold up ahead.

She was born in a large house, *Kathleen*, named after somebody's mother, and it is both immemorial and vague — portals, columns, a white space hollowed out which must be, she supposes, the grand entrance hall — and she remembers sounds, ringing sounds, ricocheting in its emptiness, and a spine of thin pale light slanting on a bright chequered floor, and a pair of chairs with curly legs upon which nobody sat, and an indefinable atmosphere of cold and constraint; yet with these few details *Kathleen* remains merely an incomplete entrance, as though time has confiscated the rest of the house and left it blurred into history. But as she thinks about it now, as she rests her mind in this entrance, what disturbs her is not the dreamy incompletion of the vision, but complete and clear words spoken in a woman's voice, saying *flame tree* in response to some forgotten question, hanging there — this is how she considers it — like a streamer of smoke exhaled from shadows in a black-and-white murder mystery, smoke waving at the slightest disturbance of the air as someone moves with a rustle of heavy clothes across a corner of the room: it could be a grass-stained child or a corpulent father; or it could be a mother, a lost mother, shaped like an hourglass in grey bombazine and silk and traced only by these stirring, barely-there words.

Perhaps it is a fantasy, this voice, but she cannot relinquish it. And the simple phrase *flame tree* — it may have been her mother — is the distant gold coin that she secretly aims for.

Victoria leans her cheek on the window pane and breathes at its cold surface so that she covers over the dull London view and the semen-coloured sky and the wet woman approaching her door from the street below. How can she speak her own life when so much exists as unspeakable images, wound filmic and narcissistic in this old, old head? Her past is not another country. It is her homeland of lost things. She inhabits the entrance to *Kathleen* like a prodigal daughter.

Your mother was an hourglass, her nurse would say with admiration, and the child, denied a face, saw only a shape perpetually emptying.

Victoria pinches at the loose crepey skin of her neck, and remembers thumbprints that years ago bloomed there, purple as pansies, when a drunken man tried to strangle her in a Paris park. Now she presses against her own throat as if to mime: don't say anything; resist this compulsion.

Kathleen. Flame tree. How can she tell such things?

Her memory, she knows, is distended in darkness. Nor does she believe in the consoling dazzlement of something rushing into vision.

Anna Somebody: she has already forgotten the name. I will not say too much, Victoria decides. I will sound sensible. Wise. Entirely plausible. And that young woman will be re-made Anna-chronistic: I will plunge her into my time rather than be made to feel old.

Victoria is afraid of meeting her biographer. Her fingers move lightly at the base of her throat. Sequins of dew are forming where her breath had been.

Before the window, waiting, this is what returns: a winter (when was it, 1942?), a bruised-looking sky, her own fall into tearfulness.

It was during the Occupation of Paris that Victoria saw a woman throw what she thought was a baby into the Seine. It was a bundle in a tartan rug — the load apparently heavy, the shape infant-imprecise — there were fringes, she thinks, or a tasselled border; in any case, she remembers seeing a woman throw a bundle into the river. Victoria paused for a second or two in a kind of dumb perplexion, then ran down the stone steps towards her, shouting. The woman stood still, transfixed, staring at the water; she did not respond to shouts, nor did she turn to look. Victoria remembers an olive felt hat with a peacock-feather decoration: it seemed somehow incredible that a person in a hat like that could hurl a possible baby. The women stood together for what must have been only an instant — it was near quiet Quai de la Tourelle, it was December and windy, one or two people slowed or paused in their rugged-up walks to observe — and Victoria was at once shouting, trembling and peering into the water. There was no sign of the bundle. The River Seine was pale yellow and peaked with the wind. A bell rang somewhere in melancholy resonations. The façades of the Île St Louis held up their sombre blind windows.

In her memory there was no hesitation at all; she leapt into the river. It was astonishingly cold and Victoria thrashed about heavily, groping before her. One of her shoes dislodged, so she kicked the other away, and felt her handbag, which until then she must have instinctively clutched, release and spiral down-wards into yellow oblivion. For a moment she apprehended her own death-by-water approaching: shoes, garments, a self becoming liquid. For a moment she was tempted to cease thrashing and join the baby; and there she was, suddenly still, wondering which French verb form — *sink, sank, sunk* — would describe a willed dissolution, a corrupt fantasy of effacement.

The surface of her skin was freezing and Victoria was aware of both the intensities and the solitude of her body. There was a slapping sound of waves against the stone embankment and her own amplified breathing.

There was water wrapping her face, a swaying necklace of bubbles, and a grainy vision before her within which no baby was evident.

With her eyes open under the water Victoria was reminded of something; she remembered diving in the Swan River as a lonely child. It was warm then, and balmy, and the water was sun-lit. She would look up through pleats of wavy illumination to see brown jellyfish the size of fruit-bowls pulsating above her, light caught semicircular in their fleshy domes. Now, in the current of tenseless recollection, she half expected to see a baby-face heave jellyfish-like into view.

Ten minutes, and nothing. No drifting lit shape. No glimpsed floating hope.

She was clutching at the stone bank, pained by cold, when someone very strong stretched down to claim her. A man, perhaps forty, with a five o'clock shadow, seized her under the armpits and hauled her dripping from the water. Victoria remembers that his gloves were completely soaked, and that he wiped her nose, which was streaming, with the end of his woollen scarf, as though tending a small and errant child. The woman in the hat had in the meantime disappeared.

Victoria sat down by the Seine and in her humiliating confusion simply wept and wept. She wept for the baby as if it had been her own. She wept for Occupied Paris, and its many barbarities; she wept for her lover,

Jules, who was missing, assumed dead. She wept too for private things — her lost hourglass, the *flame tree*. All those irretrievable bundles that had sunk, or caught in tunnels, or washed away. The shadow-faced man became embarrassed. He looked down at his wristwatch, constructed an excuse, and hurried off in the direction of Notre Dame.

Rain began falling in faint blown skeins. The stone face of the Île St Louis darkened.

Still more immersion, Victoria thought. *Still more immersion.*

If Picasso had appeared he would have recognised his *Crying Woman*: a figure all angles and distortion, jigsawed by tears, a woman whose inner violence had left her faceted and prised apart. Victoria touched the surface of her own face and found it bevelled and acute. She had fallen into effigy, into teary abstraction.

On her bed, a foreigner in Paris, alone, misplaced, looking up at the rusty Rorschach of her water-stained ceiling, she listened to noise echo in dim zigzags up and down the dank stairwell and in the food-scented, dirty, unlighted corridors. Sometimes she rose for ersatz coffee or a lump of hardened cheese. If she thought of it she paid the boy in a nearby apartment a few ration cards and a kiss to bring her a demi-baguette, which she consumed with the detachment of one who has forgotten the function of food. Once he brought her some tiny oranges — a gift from his mother — and

Victoria left them beside her bed, five perfect baubles, so that she could marvel at the occurrence of colour in her life. In the morning the oranges were frozen solid. She thawed them segment by segment, vaguely pleased to have a modest and important task to perform.

She sobbed and she slept. She was woeful, blank. Outside sirens sounded and once she heard gunshots and exclamations, issue, sharply resounding, from an adjacent street.

In the unheated room her breath was a feather before her. *I am this frail,* she thought. *This insubstantial.*

And when at last she re-joined the world of the living, rising up with the same mysterious lack of volition with which she had earlier sunk, Victoria was so thin she imagined herself translucent. Upraised veins marbled her glassy skin. She was toppling, unstable, barely alive. She reached for the windowsill to support her as she looked down at the still-there world, the bicycles, the flapping banners, the strolling men in grey uniforms, and her two hands, blue stars, were unrecognisable.

Some time later she would see again the olive and peacock-feather hat. It was like seeing a monstrance held aloft, aglitter in a dim church. She tracked the woman to her home and one night confronted her, pushing her through the doorway of an apartment building with aggressive insistence. Light poured down on them both from a small iron lantern. Their features were distorted by stencils of diamond. *At this hour, in this Occupation,* Victoria remembers thinking, *everyone's face is patterned with distortion.* Nevertheless she was surprised that the woman seemed not to recognise her. She forced her upstairs, pleased to have induced fear.

In one corner of the room was a narrow bed, neatly tucked and covered over with tea-stained lace, but on every other surface, messily strewn, were pieces of cloth, ribbons, feathers and beads. Simplified models of the human head, of burnished oak and teak, were lined against the window like puppet decapitations, and in the air hung the sweet wet-wool odour of newly pressed felt. This was the room of a milliner: finished and half-finished hats were piled against the walls.

The woman put down her small cargo of parcels and turned to face the intruder.

My name is Marie-Claude, she announced directly. Do you want to buy a hat?

When Victoria thought about it later, even years later, she recalled that the woman Marie-Claude was at once persuasive and poised. She conceded that, yes, she had been by the Seine at Quai de la Tourelle, and yes, she had hurled a bundle in a tartan rug. It had been her husband's clothes, she said, weighted with a few books. He had been a member of the Resistance, a hero, she added, and had died after torture by the Nazis in the offices at Rue Lauriston. His body had not been recovered. It was burned somewhere. Gone. I threw away his things, she said, because their existence appalled me. I could not sell them or give them away; I just wanted to fling them where they would be lost.

She had taken up a hat as she spoke and was stitching carefully: a trail of spherical jet beads composed an elaborate arabesque. Victoria watched the rhythmical lift and fall of her sewing, her concentration, her skill, the pretty inclination of her head, and decided that Marie-Claude must be telling the truth. The milieu produced a photograph of her husband and held it between her knees. The image was of a middle-aged man with a quizzical look, as though his eyeglasses were faulty or maladjusted; he was a scholar, perhaps, or a postman, or an office worker.

Victoria put her arm around Marie-Claude as a sign of her understanding. She kissed her warm cheek, relieved by the gift of an explanation.

In a recurring dream Victoria is diving in the Seine with an orange lantern, anxiously searching for an anonymous baby. She dives to the bottom of the river and sees there scissors, mirrors, corsets, cameras; she sees hatters' models, bobbing, as if underwater creatures, and trails of peacock eyes, iridescently staring. Her orange lamp finds each sunken object in turn, but among the *objets trouvés* there is no found baby.

The water becomes immensely heavy. She feels herself begin to run out of air. And this recurrent dream always concludes the same way; it always concludes with drowning. It closes with Victoria's vision of her own body, naked and deadly pale, floating facedown in furrowed black water. She still clutches at the lantern which is almost extinguished. It contains the merest of lights, shaped like a diamond.

2

In the meanly simplifying genre of art-catalogue biography Victoria May Morrell was born in Melbourne, Australia, in 1910, daughter of a wealthy businessman and an Irish beauty. She moved to the West Australian goldfields at the age of three, and grew there, precocious, destined to be an artist, but for a short stint at boarding school in the south-west city of Perth. She left Australia, never to return, at the age of twenty, moving first to London and then to Paris, where she worked on the fringes of the Surrealist movement. She established a reputation as a painter of dreams, producing paintings which were described by one reviewer as *bewildering and shocking*. Her work was largely forgotten in the fifties and sixties, but a revival in the late seventies led to a retrospective exhibition which both consolidated her fame and established her as something of a cult figure in the London art scene — *She now lives the life of a recluse in Hampstead, London.*

This version registers none of the strangeness of Victoria's life. There is no hourglass, flashing. No river-plunge. No dream. It is like reading about someone else, someone already dead, someone obliterated in Parisian dark by twin purple thumb-marks.

When Victoria opened the door she put her thumbs beneath her chin and extended her fingers in a gesture she would later describe as shutters of astonishment.

Ah! she said. The Australian biographer at last!

Anna was charmed by this greeting and the appearance of the woman, who, unlike her photographs, was multicoloured, discomposed and vigorously animated. Upon her head she wore a crown of long black feathers, which quivered as though still expressing a will to flight, and about her shoulders hung a robe of crimson silk, full and somewhat cardinal, extending to the floor. Ropes of amber beads clacked on her chest; her lips were painted and her eyes startling with a definition of kohl.

Swans, Victoria announced. In your honour I am wearing swans.

She tweaked a feather, winked and smiled.

Anna stood in the rain, waiting to be admitted. Her umbrella produced a circular veil of raindrops, closing her up in a wet parenthesis. It was one of those taut peculiar moments in which strangers, having passed the flurry of effusive first greeting, are halted before each other, in a pause of true estrangement. Perhaps, thought Anna, she will not admit me.

Perhaps she considers me too young, too realist. It was a pause such as occurs before lovers' declarations.

Well? said Victoria. What are you waiting for? Kiss me now. On the lips.

Anna tilted the water, leaned forward to the face, and placed a kiss soft as a dream and moist as sex on the aged and expectant lips of Victoria.

Her arrival in Paris, 193–:

Monsieur Marcel Duchamp answered the door. He peeped, flung it open, then flew his hands to his face in the sweeping gesture of a magician who has that very instant puffed something strange into existence.

Ah, voilà! L'Australienne!

His thumbs were joined beneath his chin and his fingers outstretched in twin shutters of astonishment. The smile was enormous and the tone one of foolish exaggeration.

L'Australienne!

Victoria felt herself suddenly endowed with symbolic accessories: bounding kangaroos, vistas of orange earth, spectral stringy eucalypts, empty dead centres, any number of odd and arresting Antipodean inversions. The mantle of Australianness descended upon her, as though an invisible parasol had collapsed, leaving her drenched in novelty. She stood there bedraggled, pre-empted by nationhood. Duchamp lunged from the doorway, seized Victoria by the wrist, and led her into the drawing room.

He chanted: *L'Australienne! L'Australienne!*

They were all conducting a kind of séance. From the entrance to the drawing room Victoria felt herself lean inwards in anticipation of the life she wished to discover. She could hear incoherent mutterings in several languages, could smell the stale emanations of candles and cigarettes, could sense her own bashful elation at announced admission — since no one had yet detected her black-swan trespass or noted the measure of her insignificance — and she was filled with artistic ambition and a will to impress. Faces turned in her direction, lighting up for an instant like spangles flung into shadow, but then turned away again, just as quickly, preoccupied with the proceedings. The room was pink-coloured from light filtered through drawn scarlet curtains; it made her think, said Victoria, of blood pressed thin on a glass slide. There were golden candles here and there, on ledges and tables, and replicated unevenly on a glass-topped cabinet, but over all was the impression of an organic pinkness. She breathed deeply and imagined her lungs blooming with pigment, so that inside her chest became a vase of pink hydrangeas.

(*You see how serious I was? How bent on Surrealist transformation?*)

Everyone was there. Breton, Ernst, Desnos, Man Ray, women of extraordinary beauty clad in feathers and furs whose names she did not yet know (one was Gala, perhaps, another Dora, Jacqueline) and they sat at an oval table upon which were scattered letters of the alphabet, symbols and cards. André Breton was busy invoking the spirit of the Marquis de Sade: his eyes were closed and from his mouth came strange intonings:

Oh *corpus delicti*, body
dismembered and remembered
no crystal, but worms,
no necktie but excrement in vertical rivers,
the absence of butterflies,
brain . . .

Here someone took up the letter J and shouted: *Juteux*!:

— brain a juicy jungle
swung through with monkeys —

Brioche!:

— a brioche curled upon itself
tasty convolutions, without butterflies.
hollows intolerable: the banker, the taxidermist.
Gloved hands, handless gloves,
razors invading —

Duchamp took up an A and eyed Victoria mischievously.

L'Australienne!

— Noir et noir et noir et noir, Breton sang.
Black and black and black and black,
black is the body continent
at which we force frontiers,
black the juicy jungle, the tasty convolutions,
the monkeys, the monkeys,
the razors invading . . .

Victoria ceased to listen. She was suddenly ashamed and flushed with embarrassment. Her gloved hand

burned against her face. She remembered a desert
hawk, its whole face sharp, diving fast through the sky
towards some cowering creature, and the mushroom
of dust as it speared its prey. Then the peculiar silhouette of two beings uprising, its diminishing shape, its
wingbeat, its swift arcing away. Whatever recalled this
little death stayed as the colour of her cheeks.

noir et noir et noir et noir

Surely they could all see it: the stranger rosy with
discomfort. A man peered over rimless spectacles in
which twin candle flames were reflected. Words
everywhere dispersed and disassembled. Faces
gleamed with alien light. Three porcelain cats, dis-
tinctly bourgeois, seemed to regard her from the
ledge above a gaping fireplace. At the end of the table,
now a vast expanse of dark green felt, sat a young
woman with frizzy hair and bee-stung lips, Simone-
someone-or-other, who acted as secretary to the
chants and invocations. Victoria saw her pen inscribe,
upside-down, the mysterious word *corps*. The hand-
writing was copperplate and there was a netted
shadow of hair filaments lying, with a perceptible
quiver, across the perfectly formed letters.

(*You cannot imagine*, said Victoria, *how red that room
appeared*.)

Did Duchamp introduce her?

Only, Victoria thinks, as *L'Australienne*. It was years
before some of them called her Victoria. She thought
of having a map of Australia tattooed on her forehead,
so that it would be too unSurreal and literal-minded

21

for them to call her by her emblem. Disbelieving in nations they still wanted an Australia.

(*It is the same with Africa. All of Europe*, Victoria added, *wants an Africa.*)

After the séance they drank bowls of Kir Royale. Scarlet rose-petals floated on the surface of each drink. People stood around the room peeling petals from puckered lips and flicking them away. A man in a quilted smoking jacket lined with silver braid, a rich man, perhaps, or a figure of importance, spat out a mouthful of petals so that they adhered to a pink lampshade; he proclaimed: *An explosion of bloody flowers, set off by gentle anarchists!* And soon everyone was spitting. One of the women pasted two dripping petals on the cheeks of another, and there was a short epileptic burst of applause.

How did it happen, her presence there, witnessing this theatre? How had she come across the ocean, yearning for mother-England, and ended up in this red drawing room, clenching her gloved hands, anxious for approval and known only as a nation? The details remain spot-lit in her old woman's memory: the scattered alphabet, like blown litter, across the broad green table, a woman's hand in the act of forming the word *corps*, the pink standing lamp of spat rose-petals, the man with candles for eyes, her generalised confusion and disorientation.

Words of English came drifting above the crowd. Victoria looked up from her Kir and saw the painter

Leonora Carrington, sashaying towards her in a polka-dotted dress. She had a rose-petal stuck to the centre of her forehead and walked directly to Victoria, said Hallo Australian with a fake Indian accent and a sideways shake of the head, then kissed her on the lips. Victoria was close enough to see the streaks of her pale makeup and feel the electricity of her long black hair. She is my age, realised Victoria, and so much more confident. There was a scent of patchouli oil and sexual fluids. Someone wound up the gramophone and saxophonic jazz rose quaking into the room. Leonora took Victoria by the wrist, an emissary with floral lungs from the land of *noir*, and led her forward to meet the Surrealist maestro, Monsieur Breton. He removed a petal from his tongue and inspected it critically on the tip of his index finger. Then he announced:

We are all Australians.

All bodies are black.

And Victoria thought to herself — quite unSurrealistically — *Neither statement is true.*

3

Somewhere in the past you will find Anna in girlhood, in the blazing goldfields, awaiting Visions.

She likes to sit on the verandah at twilight, watching the moonrise. She peers into mauve-coloured air and sees boys skidding their bikes beneath dark shadows of jacaranda which release blooms and whispers on waves of desert breeze. Dust arises from wheels, performing wheelies. There will be a dog-fight somewhere, a few blocks away, and the sound of batteries crushing ore further off in the distance. Lights randomly switch on, in beady spots and rectangles. The triangular shapes of poppet heads can be glimpsed against the sky. Insects whirr: moths and mosquitoes. There is the smell of mutton cooking and an echoic clatter of plates and pans. Her father, who must work night-shift, is moving about in the kitchen, preparing their dinner. Soon Anna will be summoned inside by her name; she will shift from the mauve into the lemon light, and they will sit together, facing each other, listening to the droning wireless so neither is obliged to talk. Chops. Mashed potatoes. A silent cleaning-up. Father leaves for work; Anna returns, padding on barefeet, to the open verandah, and watches the dark unfurl its patterns of planets and stars.

Sometimes Anna likes to pretend she is invisible: this way she can follow her father into the mine. She watches him pack his crib — a slab of bread, left-over meat and a thermos of tea — then sits on the crossbar as he cycles away into the night. The wind is cold on her invisible face and she leans forward affirmatively, like a racer on a circuit. The bike swerves through streets, a show-off, a skite, leaps gullies, circles poles, recklessly accelerates. It travels as though flying, past pubs and shacks, past the Methodist church, and the primary school, and the falling-down Mechanics' Institute. It speeds down the brothel road, just for fun, and red lights stream away and scarlet women wave. Other shift workers are also on bicycles, ped-alling hard to produce a twinkling headlight, and they converge in a kind of neat and synchronous solidarity, an asterix that only a racing child notices.

Ahead Anna will see the gold-mine curve upwards to greet them. It has looped strings of lights, like a giant ship, and seems to shudder with mechanical noise and activity. These sounds are imprecise but somehow appalling. There is a screech as the metal cage is slowly lowered and a series of internal growls and below-surface rumblings. Invisible Anna stands there in the cage with the miners, and descends and descends. Blind dark sweeps over her: she imagines this is like death. But she will have a lamp on her head that will cast a small moon into the blackness before her; and as she follows her father down a corridor deep into the earth, as she experiences tunnel-vision and earth-smell and scary enclosure, the little moon governed by her head rests and slides on his back. He recedes, held into being by her fragile projection. In her imagination the tunnel is so low that he must bend his head like a cyclist.

It is as though she has been there. It is as real as her two hands.

At home on the verandah, visible Anna tucks her knees up under her chin and languidly — naughtily — unpicks the hem of her dress. She trails kinky thread, like a girl in a myth. She is thinking: *Twelve hundred, he is at level twelve hundred.* When she moves into the house, she sees glowing in the dark the phosphorescent lime-green of numbers on the wireless, and uses this eerie beacon, which her father habitually leaves, to navigate towards her bedroom without turning on a light. With the sound of the wireless somewhere behind her, blaring ABC, and the smell of mutton still in the air, and the night cold swiftly descending, Anna touches the outline of her bed, slides into it hoping for dreams, and thinks of the mysterious word *moonstruck*. *Moonstruck at twelve hundred.*

———

In the blazing goldfields little Anna is just another thin sandy child in a hemless cotton dress, covered with the flower print of a blossom wholly unknown to her; she is just another scallywag miner's daughter. Her home is monumental and there is a scale to things that is certainly inhuman: even if she were God looking down, the poppet heads above the mines would seem outsized, the grey slag dumps, like ancient monoliths, would be too massive and solid, and the miles and miles of railway sleepers laid across the red dirt, a ladder horizontally to travel on, a reaching promise of other places, would be too repetitious and too extensive. Once a teacher drew railway lines on the blackboard to illustrate the principle of converging perspective and Anna thought: *Yes, that is it, that is exactly what I know*.

In her precocity she recognised recession as the shape of desire. She knew too the principle of correspondence, that even the vaguest feeling finds shape in a common thing. This knowledge reassured her; every thing possessed design, every ordinary thing possessed design and meaning. On the blackboard the white lines were her own personal geometry.

Perhaps it was the flatness of the desert that made structures and shapes so dominant. Perhaps it was the illusions. Where the vaulted sky wavered, solid fabrications seemed impressive. Here the waltzing wind disturbed everything but steel.

Once, when she was seven, Anna saw a black cat fly in a blur past the window of her school. It spun upended and squealing in a gusty cylinder of air. Other children burst into laughter and ran for a better look; but Anna was immobilised: this *marvellous* thing. The tin walls of the school room suddenly rocked and banged — as though the whole world was alarmed and shaken by what was yet possible.

She began to anticipate such events; she began to look.

She waited for dust storms the way other children waited for Christmas. To see it again: a cat spun dizzily in a whirlpool of air. The world restless, upset, susceptible to dislodgement. Or to see, better still, the atrocity she had heard of: a man from Broad Arrow had been decapitated in a dust storm by a piece of flying tin; his lost head, they said at school, was still out there, spinning. Such a lonesome idea. And such a *marvel*.

Anna also wishes to be God, with a swooping view; this is another form of invisibility she likes to practise. She will be high enough to see the neat curve of the globe, then she will zip through space, to the enamelled blue sky, and sweep above the desert plain with its saltbush and sandalwood; she will survey the mines with their steel poppet heads, and the makeshift houses, and sheds with rusty rooves of corrugated iron; she will breeze through smoke winding upwards from the campfires of prospectors, she will follow the straight gravel roads and the crooked dry creeks, then she will settle, the holy spirit as a barefooted girl, on the scorching earth.

This is no self-importance; it is simply the route of her imagining. Anna would rather be spirit than body. Her tiny shape frustrates her. In a child-way she intuits this by wishing herself translated into speeding thin air.

On Sunday mornings hymns travel the town as Anna does: metaphysically. Although they no longer go to church, she loves the fragments and melodies of blown-away song and in her head sings the hymns of the Methodist church.

(He's got the whole wor-ld in his hands,
He's got the whole wor-ld in his hands . . .)

But in the house her father, Thomas Griffin — people call him Griffo — is a man who has become almost entirely silent, and Anna believes that in his skull no hymns enter and no sound ever plays. He is a man closed in on himself like the fists of a miner he once saw, crushed under a cave-in and clenched in final anger, still holding the damp wilted stub of a dead cigarette.

On this particular Sunday, Griffo gathers what they need for a rabbiting excursion. He pours black sugared tea into a metal flask, and cuts fat wedges of bread which he wraps in oiled paper. And as a special treat, and mindful of the need to indulge his motherless daughter, Griffo includes in the picnic a can of condensed milk. He packs these items in the same crib box he takes nightly into the mines. Anna can detect the slight self-consciousness of his gestures, the mark of a man still unused to the preparation of food. From her position lying with her cheek on the grainy kitchen table, she feels a certain meanness and condescension: she knows her father has forgotten the jam, but will not move to tell him. Griffo's silence, and their poverty, impose an economy on language. There is the condensed milk, of course, but Anna is weighing up in her stomach how tasty it would have been to have two doses of sweetness. Just last year her mother was offering jam on a spoon. She sees it now, a shiny mound of brown gelatine, a glistening jewel held up to her face, an offering, a love-gift, with a smile hovering behind. It was new fig jam, smelling of sugar. They had traded, she recalls, tomatoes for figs.

Together father and daughter set out on the bicycle, with Anna balanced on the crossbar, her twiggy arms braced. They ride out past the edge of the town and enter the scrub territory of small mining claims, where many shafts are ruined and long abandoned. Scattered about are windlasses, metal buckets and bits of broken-down machinery, all eaten and corroded by blistery rust. Sometimes there are lonely old men with flyblown beards, picking away at the earth. They have scabby hands, bent shoulders and mystically patient dispositions. And sometimes one will call out: Eh! Griffo! Eh! and Anna's father answers back with a silent wave. He used to be a laughing man, this bloke, this bloke they call Griffo, Ern's boy of course, poor Ern who was hurt. People round here remember a different Griffo.

Poor bugger, they say, missus pissed off, left im high an dry, an with the kiddie too . . .

Anna's invisibility enables her to hear such things. She watches the old fossickers and listens to their thoughts, and knows they describe in their own ways the varieties of forsakenness.

But now Anna and her father are working together, checking the traps. Of a dozen traps, ten are full. They release the bodies of the rabbits and gather each one into a hessian bag. The small corpses are limp and warm, some punctured by the narrow jagged teeth of the traps, and all carry the stench of wasted blood. Flies in lazy dozens stir around their work. Anna has flies in her eyes and can see them clinging in massed groups on the back of her father's shirt. She does not mind the trapping, but she hates the lingering flies. Sometimes she strikes at them, shooing, and they rise up in ominous clouds. She carries smokebush to wave at them, and to hold off the bloody-death smell.

When they pause for their small meal, in the thinnest slice of shade, Griffo unpacks and portions the food with slow and deliberative movements; then suddenly he says:

She's not coming back, you know.

He kicks at the ground with the toe of his boot, setting off tiny detonations of dust. Then he squats and shifts four thick slices of bread into alignment.

I know, Anna replied. (Although she hadn't.)

It is a shocking moment because Griffo begins to

weep. He is almost immediately embarrassed and wipes his teary face with the back of his hand; then he spits into the dust, as if to spit out his tearfulness. It is the only time in her life Anna ever sees her father cry, there, with ten dead rabbits, on a hot Sunday morning, and the lingering tunes of blown hymns still playing in her head, and the pestering flies, and the dank smell of musty hessian, and the stronger pungent smell of fresh animal blood, and the anomalous taste of condensed milk, infantile and syrupy, still delicious and sticky around the corners of her mouth.

She leans forward and kisses her father lightly on the cheek. He flinches and looks away.

Riding home they catch sight of a pack of wild camels which buck away into the far blue distance, screaming. Their forms rock and jerk, like something wounded.

Anna listens to her father's breathing as he pedals the bicycle. She holds the bag of bloody rabbits close to her chest. A stain appears on her dress: she rubs it with spit but it does not seem to fade or disappear.

At home father and daughter perform the ceremony of skinning, up the back, in the woodshed. Griffo demonstrates how to remove all the fur in one action, peeling it back from the body like a glove, inside out. Beneath their skin the rabbits are startlingly red. On their shiny bodies, small as foetuses and terrible in their exposure, lies a sinuous network of dark blue veins. Anna and her father clean the skins and stretch them in the sun to dry, nailing them with little tacks to planks of old wood. The shape of rabbit skins, Anna knows, is the shape of her father's sadness. The stumpy legs are like arms, reaching up to catch something missing.

Her whole world is like this: analogies, sadness, the hush evoked by a shape. She looks at her father's boots in the corner of the shed, their frayed laces tied together, their blunt toes communing, and even these seem weighted with his particular misery. She looks at his hands in the act of flensing rabbit skin. They are dirty hands, with nicks and scratches, hands ever busy with chores that do not need explanation. When he has finished Griffo wipes his knife on old newspaper and cleans his bloody hands with a scrap of rag, but through neglect or distraction or self-preoccupation does not, not once, meet his daughter's gaze.

Victoria will say later that what is remarkable is not that they grew up in the same remote town (her epithet for which is always *blazing*), but that they both understand the power of vanished things.

Vanished things, she proclaims, *are the basis of all art.*

Yet Anna secretly disagrees. It is presence she finds entirely compelling. The red bodies of skinned rabbits: their absoluteness, their quiddity. The memory of blood on her fingertips, her father's quick knife, and the small stain, a dark ruby, left at the end of the day.

4

After her first meeting with Victoria, Anna took key number three from Mrs Dooley, who smiled with her Irish eyes and nodded ratification at such a pleasant lodger, so quiet, so clean, so methodically coming and going, Australian, too, where her nephew lived, with that heat and all, and the no-snow Christmases, and the kangaroos, and the desert, and the black people with pointy spears, and does he write to his dear Aunt, his closest living relative, who loves him like her own, does he give a toss or care at all, such a fine lad, really, and a good-looker too, and a bit of a boy, and cheeky, but so very far away, so far far away. Anna smiled back politely, made excuses for men, then took her brass key upstairs to room number three, entered, sighed and threw herself on the bed. She lay there beneath the window which comprised two rectangles of floral lace, so that it cast vague netted shapes across the surface of her body, as though she were a bride, or a fish, or a freshly skinned rabbit. And in this state of shadow-play, this blurry transformation, she thought about her very first interview with Victoria. Her room was filled with the noise of London traffic — motorbikes accelerating, buses decelerating, honks, screeches, bald tyres on a wet surface — and Anna lay with her eyes closed, feeling depressed. She had flown twelve thousand miles around the curve of the globe to meet a woman wearing swans who did not want to talk to her. They had drunk tea, eaten cake, and engaged in shallow conversation about the English weather. Victoria was polite, evasive and having second thoughts; she dismissed her visitor after only twenty minutes.

At first Anna was tempted to give up her task. She knew in her heart the crankish ambition of biography, its overweening possessiveness, its latent collusions, its disrespect for the irreducibly copious life. Yet she was drawn to assert — unprofessionally — her personal connection; she wanted to relocate herself as the twelve-year-old girl who had pressed a library book of reproductions against her chest as though claiming a lover, the girl who saw in a glorified moment the scattered atoms of her baffled life reassemble as paintings. Anna decided she would write a letter and reveal that they grew up in the same town.

We share images, she will write. What could be more intimate? The desert. The mines. The search in darkness for gold. Do you realise how fantastic and implausible and ordained is our meeting?

Seduction, she thinks; so much depends on the right words.

Tell me about Jules, said Anna. (She pronounced the name carefully.) Tell me something about Jules.

Ah Jewels, me Jewels, me darlin' Jewels, Victoria chanted.

She affected a broad accent to remind Anna of their new understanding. *Jewels, Jewels.*

She met him in London, early in 1936. She was almost twenty-six years old and in flight from her brother and father. A colonial. Lost. Still believing in Mother-countries. Victoria was a student at the Amédée Ozenfant Academy, posing as an artist. She had classical aspirations and enjoyed the ritual of it all, the artists-in-studios, arranged in an equidistant circle around a shivering model, leaning forward, daubing, leaning back, squinting, wiping fingers on rags stuffed down the front of childish calico smocks. This effete choreography. This slow-motion dance of spectatorship. The decorously whispered encouragements and emendations. One day, in their smoking break, she was seized with impatience, and left the studio to walk across the city to visit the British Museum. It was a rainy spring day and she made her way briskly, without an umbrella, through the backstreets of strewn garbage and swimming shadows. The British Museum was, and still is, her favourite London site; its Surrealism, she claimed, consisted in its presumption of peep-showing the world's everything. The combination of universalism and incongruity thoroughly delighted her; she thought of it comically, as worlds-in-collision.

Victoria moved through Manuscripts and Medievalism, through Glassware and Chinoiserie; but she was heading as usual for the rooms of Egyptian antiquities. She liked to roam among the forest of standing sarcophagi in that tombish atmosphere in which everything old is rendered entrancing and serious. The light was umber, dull, but there were illuminated showcases of glass with exquisite trinkets and oddities — perfume jars from the Middle Kingdom, small toys of eroded ivory, tiny Anubises, Thoths, statuettes of Isis. Jewellery of carnelian and lapis was arranged in the bodily configuration of wearing, with looped necklaces and earrings where necks and ears should have been, amulets and rings indicating invisible arms and fingers. Something in this decorative advertent logic, Victoria found immensely sad. She had not yet discovered her own aesthetic, or developed her own comprehension of things. She would simply stare into the cabinets, moved and perturbed, and only later realised that she wanted something *implied*.

On that rainy spring day, the day she met Jules, Victoria was wandering in a desultory fashion past seated granite statues of dynastic families, when she saw a young man standing beside an upright mummy case, his face resting gently at the wooden chest. He blushed as he saw her approach, and sprang away.

A foolish impulse, he said, to listen for a heartbeat.

His accent was French and his manner endearingly abashed; he smoothed back his hair in a nervous attempt to recompose.

You must think me a madman, the poor fellow added.

Victoria chatted about something to cover the awkwardness, and then they walked together, like a couple, past the profiled friezes. She remembers that she glanced up at him and saw his face glide among images of kings and gods, dancers, musicians, slaves feeding oryxes. In this context he carried an aura of antiquarian gravity.

Jules Levy was a photographer from Lyon on a working holiday in London. He specialised in weddings. Most of his time was spent snapping at garlanded brides with orange-blossom and fussing mothers, stiff-looking grooms who fiddled with button-holed carnations, bridesmaids with laps full of cascading flowers. When Jules showed Victoria his photographs she was at once dismayed by their sameness, by the eradication in his images of love's specificity. For on that day, in that museum, she could not have guessed him capable of mechanical reproduction. He seemed to her the very figure of romantic singularity. He seemed to her *rare*.

When they parted she followed him all the way to the front entrance of the museum, and watched as he pop-opened his umbrella and moved down the steps into the rain, sealing himself off in a circle of water. Near the iron gates — yes — he turned and waved.

They had agreed to meet the next day, at 10 a.m., in front of the display of Canopic jars.

These are ceramic pots, Victoria explained, fashioned with the heads of animals and birds, within which the brain and internal organs of mummies are stored. Hearts, for instance. Canopic jars are jars of hearts, floating in the dark in a preserving fluid called natron. Jars of hearts, she said. Hearts. Just think of it.

Later she will realise that it was a quality of loneliness that attracted her. Even his photography was a way of marking himself off from the crowd, claiming the solitary safe space behind the glass wall of the viewfinder. But she had not expected the eroticism of his darkroom: bodies in such proximity, images quaking into existence, Jules' high face scarlet as a flower.

He worked with an exacting concentration and diligence. Victoria liked the way he sank and swayed the photograph in its fluid, as though the action, not the chemicals, induced its development. Photography is nothing spontaneous but pure fastidiousness, calculation, timing, the achievement of tone. Victoria loved the drip of the tap, the smothered quietness. When Jules bent with a magnifying glass to examine a detail, she placed a quick kiss on his rose-tinted neck, and he would complain that she never let him get on with his work. It was a space overtaken by instincts matrimonial.

He kissed me on the hair:

Jules leant above me and kissed me on the hair.

Strange fluids and emulsions scented the small room. In the red light his face was ardent, rich, artificial. Brides and bridegrooms were developing *en masse* around us and their images swung in hanging rows, like eccentric bunting. Veils were everywhere. Bouquets. Fixed smiles. And though the images had a formal obedient quality, and appeared in the folios as banal repetition, the effect of so many pegged precariously and still dripping wet had for me an arousing and aphrodisiac quality.

When Jules' lips touched my hair I felt a flash bright as magnesium illuminate the dark recesses of my body.

How can I say this? I lifted my face, and willed him to develop me.

The year was 1937 and they had just moved to Paris. Victoria was a fringe Surrealist, selling nothing at all, and Jules supported them both with his anti-Surrealist reproductions of marriages. They lived in the 6th arrondissement, on Rue Gît-de-Coeur, in an apartment at the top of fifty creaking steps (the concierge said she loved the sound of footfall on each and every one, and sat in a rocking-chair counting, *un, deux, trois*, into her bosom); it had a small balcony festooned with streamers of ivy, and a window-box of orange and pink pelargonium. From the balcony they could see bookshops: Henri Bonnefoi, Livres et Périodiques Anciens et Modernes, André Minos, Relieur, Libraire, as well as the École Supérieure de Musique, the Salle d'Armes and the Café Le Gît-de-Coeur —

which released plaited threads of coffee-scent and bread-scent to figure eight around their heads. At the end of the street was the stone quay and the piss-coloured Seine, and a glimpse, just a glimpse, of the Île de la Cité.

In this city of desolations and existential excitements, full of monuments and cigarette smoke and lost umbrellas and gloves, they laid down their hearts in a one room apartment, and slept together, entwined.

Even now, Victoria says, I still find the shape of his body in my bed.

Let me tell you, Anna, let me tell you about Jules.

There were two particular stories he loved to repeat. The first concerns the meeting of his parents, which he told in several versions, all inflected by the curiously fertile nostalgia that attaches to inherited family tales.

His mother was a Lyonnaise bluestocking, unusually tall and statuesque, and in 1910 she was working as a governess in London. On some kind of holiday break — Jules thinks it was in Scotland — she met his father, a young medical student, from Newcastle-upon-Tyne. From a distance she had seen him skating along a frozen canal and as a non-skater was entranced by this peculiar vision: the top-half of a man gliding swiftly and like magic through an all-white landscape. He wore a red-chequered jacket and had his blue-gloved hands cupped over his ears to keep them warm. When later Jules' mother spotted the skater

walking in the street she exclaimed, quite spontaneously: *Ah! but you have legs!* They began talking and
he offered to teach her skating, and thus, practising on
ice, learning the mechanics of glide and the suave
velocity of blades, she fell backwards, into his arms.

They would skate together in that quaint old-
fashioned way, with the woman encircled, leaning
slightly into the shape of the man's body. Together the
new couple reinvented movement; they discovered
the rapture of arcs and the simplicity of speed. Locals
would see them burst, arms linked, through enshroud-
ing fog, aiming for a fabulous fast-motioned future.

But the skater was killed in the eighth week of the
First World War. The war had sped him towards a
flaming death. Somewhere in Belgium a young English
doctor exploded and there was no recoverable body
for his French widow to claim and bury. The governess gave away her skates and returned to Lyon,
accompanied by her disconsolate three-year-old son.

Jules remembers vomiting all the way across the
English Channel, and thereafter associating the rank
smell with the toss of water. He lay on the bunk with
his face downwards, terrified by the pitch of the ocean
beneath him. And on the train to Lyon, he said, it was
the sound he remembered; the *clacker-clack* of the line
marked his safety-on-dry-land and his transport into
the realm of completely-forgetting-his-father. It was
an infant equivalence, a device, that he later regret-
ted, as though what one recalls is a matter of will or
contrivance.

Jules said that whenever he imagined his father he always imagined just a top half, as his mother had described. He thought of a torso, red-chequered and hearing-no-evil, sliding along a perpetually snowing horizon and moving with the supernatural ease of one already translated into spirit.

Whorls of ice, said Jules, marked the trail of my sliding father. That is how I see him. With whorls of flying ice . . .

The second story concerns a detail of his first visit to Paris. This too Jules told Victoria more than once:

Jules was about eight years old, confident of the future, and had decided that he would be a doctor when he grew up. He looked through old anatomy books that had belonged to his father, loving their sur-reptitious glimpses of the magical interiority of things — their line drawings of bodies rendered as systems of nerves, their depictions of bone shapes, their location of organs. He studied the symmetries and asymmetries of the inside world, and found there a clean well-lighted space, a tidy and entirely rational system. But on his first visit to Paris, something monstrous distressed him: he saw a display in the booth of the Anti-Alcoholic League on Boulevard Saint Germain. In the window were dried brains in various states of fermentation, all brown, diseased, appalling specimens, and Jules was nauseated and repulsed and subject to terrible nightmares. He dreamt that he performed operations on people's heads in which he was required to remove their mucky brains with his two bare hands. Brown matter stained his fingers and he was unable to clean them.

Jules never drank alcohol and did not become a doctor.

Nor, as it happens, did he learn the art of skating. He confessed to a superstition — that if he learnt to skate, he would die.

Victoria said: I met Jules' mother, Hélène, about a year after the war. I had hoped that she might have some news of his whereabouts. But she had been in a concentration camp, and was still exhausted and wasted. She looked nothing like the photograph that Jules had kept of her, but had white hair, pale skin and a gaunt and self-absorbed look. I thought the surface of her skin seemed dusty and moth-like, of a substance that might deposit powder if I accidentally brushed at her cheek. For some reason, too, Hélène was almost deaf, so that she curled her hand, like a bony shell, to try to catch at my words. So we spoke of her son, my lover, in a kind of emotional sign language. I gestured and gesticulated, drew diagrams in the air. At one point I found myself miming ineptly the movements of an ice-skater to show that I knew the story of her courtship. She looked puzzled for a second or two, then burst into tears.

I felt brutal. It was a mistake. Skating into her grief, like that.

5

It pleased Victoria enormously that they had grown up in the same town, and she made Anna draw a map to show exactly where she lived. Anna sketched out a clumsy filigree of streets and landmarks, and placed a tiny cross where she envisioned her house. Then Victoria seized the pen and grandly X-marked hers, and Anna realised that this X was the 'palace' of her childhood. It was the largest house in town, a huge building of sandstone behind a looming high wall. Through the iron-work gate you could glimpse camellia-bushes in brass urns and long shady verandahs with gloomy French windows: but that was all. No one she knew had ever been inside it. And Uncle Ernie, who knew everything, said he knew nothing about it. The kids at school said a loony old man lived there, one of the mine bosses, they thought, some rich old bugger; someone had seen a man in a metal wheel-chair, wild, demented, shouting obscenities at nothing. But it was generally so still and so quiet, an encapsulation of secrets, that as a child Anna imagined its only inhabitants were ghosts.

Tell me about your house, Victoria said.

There is not really all that much to tell. It was one of those miners' cottages made of weather-board and corrugated iron — just like all the others. We had geraniums out the front, and behind a shed, and a dunny, and a large pepper tree shading almost half the backyard. I spent a lot of time, at any case, at my great-uncle's house, which was much more ramshackle and very poor. The walls were all lined with filter-cloth taken from the mines, so it smelt profoundly of earth and trembled when the wind blew. Somehow I still manage to confuse the two, so that when I think of our house, where I lived with my father, I think as well of the sweet, earthy smell of the filter-cloth, and the walls stirring and fluctuating with each breath of wind.

Anna is remembering waking up there, having stayed overnight, and finding her face in the moonlight and her child-body alert. The walls were membrane and rippling: it was like sleeping inside a body. Anna found this a comfort. She lay peacefully, quietly, watching the silver screen of night shivering before her, watching the forces that play in thin air between waking and sleep.

What about your house? Anna asked.

———

So unAustralian! Victoria exclaimed. And so fucking full.

I was kept inside so much I think only of its interiors. Each room had high ceilings with plaster roses, and ornamental lights made of Venetian glass. We had Louis Seize cabinets full of curios: statuettes of Carrara marble, Bohemian bowls in amethyst, fancy objects wrought in gold and a collection of reliquaries in ivory. On the walls hung embroideries from various nunneries in Europe, and a series of ostentatious and rather ugly oil-paintings, including one of my grandmother, looking rather grim, in a décolleté gown. The furniture was heavy, of dark and exotic woods — rosewood, ebony, walnut, mahogany — and the floor was hard and shiny with polished Brussels squares. There were also, I remember, many animal skins, and on the floor of my father's study lay an entire polar bear, with a set of sharp teeth and two bright staring eyes. I was afraid of the stare and for several years of my childhood believed that the bear came alive when I slept. My brother's room contained a collection of swords, displayed in careful arrangements on the wall, and in my room there was a collection of antique dolls, some of which scared me because they had no eyes at all. The strangest object in our house was a stuffed giraffe — or at least the stuffed neck and head of a giraffe — which stood about six foot high in the corner of the drawing room. It had a friendly face which I liked to talk to. My brother boasted that he had cut off its neck with a sword, but I knew for a fact that my father had bought it, on one of his trips abroad, in London, somewhere in Portobello Road. I remember that when a governess came to the house to teach us — I was about six or seven years old — one of the very first details of French I learned was that giraffe is a feminine noun and bear is masculine. Like many children I misunderstood, and thought that the world was invisibly sexed.

Anna was silent. She thought of the sandstone house, gigantic and secretive, X marking the spot where all that treasure lay hidden. She thought of animal skins, eyes, a wall of crossed swords. Then she remembered something. She had awoken in the night afraid, suddenly afraid, to see indistinct shadows flitting across the filter-cloth, and had called out to her uncle. He came at once, treading softly in his dressing gown and slippers. A hurricane lamp blended his face with darkness.

Pray for me, Anna said, so that I can fall asleep.

He sat on the edge of the bed and whispered softly: Hey Jesus, how about it? Bring sweet sweet sleep to my darling darling Anna.

Then he kissed her lightly on the forehead and added heretically: Mathew, Mark, Luke and John, hold the horse while I get on.

I know what you're thinking, Victoria said.

No you don't, Anna replied. You really don't.

They sit together in the living room of the Hampstead house. Anna gazes at a screen Victoria claims she stole from Cocteau. It is perforated with star shapes and cloud drifts and is beautifully celestial. Nearby is a figure which apparently represents Jules; it is a shop mannequin from the 1950s, adorned with kewpie dolls sprinkled with glitter and wrapped in layers of bridal netting.

You really don't, Anna repeats.

In the loose and unreliable concatenation of tales that formed her knowledge of her father's past, Anna knew that he had grown up with Uncle Ernie; he had been adopted in the city after his parents had been killed in a car accident. The stories were incomplete and over-exposed, bright traces undetailed, bleached out by time, impressionistic, fugitive, vanishing even as they were recalled. There existed a single snapshot from someone's Box Brownie: Uncle Ernie holding a boy of three or four on his shoulder. Uncle Ernie and Griffo. The simplicity of the image was like an allegory: *I hold you; you are held*. Man and boy are both wearing similar white shirts: they are equally bedazzling, and a trick of light accentuates their radiant complicity. And though in the photograph Uncle Ernie is still quite young, his face is already ugly and disfigured by scars. This feature, beside the shirts and the unscarred child, adds to the allegory of love and light a terrible vulnerability.

Anna too could remember being carried in his arms — very young, drowsy, wounded and weak — after she had knocked herself unconscious with the returning seat of a swing. She woke to his concern and his gentle endearments. His eyes were swollen and it was clear that her uncle had been crying.

You're back, he said simply. Thank God you're back.

Anna had touched the welt on her forehead which throbbed and stung like a burn.

Don't, said Uncle Ernie. I'll see to it. I'll fix you.

His tobacco-stained fingers combed her tear-wet hair. His strong miner's arms were a cradle she rested in.

Afterwards Anna's mother raged and swore.

Stupid bastard, Ernie! You should have watched her more carefully.

Uncle Ernie was downcast. He held open his hands as if to say silently: it just happened, Maggie; I swear it just happened.

Anna felt then the cruelty of her mother's recrimination and an ungovernable surge of love for this man, this tender tobacco-stained uncle, now miserably inspecting one by one the cracked buttons of bone that linked out of sequence his mustard-coloured cardigan.

Later Anna listed out for herself the reasons she adored her Uncle Ernie.

He told stories. Like her father, Uncle Ernie worked in the mines, but unlike her father, he liked to tell stories. Murders, thefts, faulty explosions. Fortunes gambled and fortunes lost. Acts romantic and acts maniacal. Honeymoon catastrophes. Filmstar chit-chat. Maniacs. Lottery winners. Men blown out of cannons. When he was asked about his disfigured face he had no tale to tell; he became shy, averted his eyes, and Anna learned not to inquire. His face sealed over a secret that could not make itself a story.

His huge collection. Uncle Ernie, it seemed, collected everything. The world's trivia and variousness enchanted him equally. Insects. Labels. Books. Old bottles. Cards with lewd ladies in preposterous poses. Defunct mining gadgets. Matchbox lids in the thousands. Nails. Bottle tops. Redundant tickets and pamphlets. His tiny house was cluttered with curiosities. Uncle Ernie would say: Collected willy-nilly and arranged higgledy-piggledy!

The hole in his body. Apart from his damaged face Uncle Ernie had a hole in the side of his body, a kind of slit, a crevice. For as long as she could remember Anna had been invited to place her hand into this fleshy mystery. Uncle Ernie would lift up his shirt and would say: Go on, then; feel me insides. The puckered skin held an inexplicable, bizarre invitation. She would touch his warm side, and tickle him, and then they would both laugh.

She could tell him things. Uncle Ernie listened. He liked to be told the gossip of school. He was interested that her girlfriends painted their nails with 'Venetian Twilight' and kissed the hips of Elvis Presley. Anna was crazy for a boy called Eamon Ahern; even this she confessed to Uncle Ernie. He treated the knowledge formally, with respect and seriousness.

Griffo was in the yard chopping Uncle Ernie's wood.
Crack. Crack.

The axe split not only wood, but the winter air. Anna could see through the window the monumental woodpile, her father at his labours, the high-dive of the axe through a sky almost fluid. She thought how very old her father looked.

Then Uncle Ernie said: I was young once.

He slid a tray of hot currant scones from the open stove and placed them on the table in front of Anna. He was wearing a frilly white apron, had flour in his hair, and plucked each scone with his fingertips to set it quickly on a stand of wire.

Glory to behold, he announced, proudly.

Were you ever in love? Anna suddenly asked.

At eighteen. Head over heels.

What happened?

She left.

Uncle Ernie turned away.

Crack. Crack.

He took up the poker and stoked at the wood fire. Anna waited for more. When Uncle Ernie turned back to face her he had tears in his eyes.

Pathetic, he said, bloody pathetic.

Another secret that could not remake itself as story.

Head over heels.

The streets of Anna's town were chartered in the 1890s in a breadth calculated to allow for the efficient turning of camel trains. Before the romantic jacaranda, the pink stone public buildings, the working-class houses of iron and wood, before the conglomerate gold-mines began to form and dominate, the place had claimed for itself a predisposition of space. The indigenous people, the Maduwongga, had myths to account for the amplitude of the desert, its landforms and weather; but the migrant miners, mythically bereft and excommunicated, worshipped wealth and industry: *the vein*, they called it. Occasionally, in intimation of something native, they thanked the spirits spontaneously when they ascended at the end of a shift, to find the sky in its right place and the desert air clear. Above-ground was a kind of second geography, a bright other-country.

When Griffo worked day-shift Anna would wait after school to watch the miners rise up, at exactly three-thirty, in their small steel cage. She noticed from the beginning that as they took off their hard hats there were always some who looked upwards to check on the sky. She would wait outside the gate and feel the earth tremble beneath her feet. If it was not the pounding of the ore battery shuddering internally, it was subsidence somewhere, an invisible cave-in. Anna's body told her that the underground, with its no-colours and its no-sky and its no-escape collapses, was a kind of profanity. She searched among the dirty faces for the face of her father and prayed that he would be once again safe among them. In their earth masks the miners resembled a company of tragic actors; their eyes were glaring and huge, they had the look of men who are well-acquainted with rehearsals of the dreadful.

Anna sat on the crossbar as her father cycled home. She would say: *Faster! Faster!* and he would swerve and speed just to impress her. On the bicycle they were released from the fact that they had nothing to say to each other, and were united by wind and the spell of propulsion. Sometimes Griffo whistled and his notes sounded slippery and shiny as they blew up behind her. She liked the way his arms extended around her in protective brackets; she held her legs out from the spokes, braced herself against bumps and felt both grown-up and little all at once. She would imagine that they fled from the ghosts of dead miners who pursued cinematically, with arms rigid before them, fingers like tentacles and prefixed mad stares. These creatures could never catch up and always fell defeated, in a cumulus of dust.

On her ninth birthday Uncle Ernie gave Anna her own bicycle. He took her into his backyard, instructed her to close her eyes, then wheeled it in, ceremoniously.

So you can fly, Uncle Ernie said. Try it, Anna.

He steadied the back of the seat as she learned to ride, watched as by gradations her body tottered, righted and balanced itself, and then learned slowly the negotiated posture of wheels. By the evening she was confident and flew off, a little shaky, into the purplish air. She pedalled into a series of private excursions through different skies — early morning silver, high noon cobalt, the lurid sky-palettes of sunsets and storms.

How glorious the wind was, now that she owned it.

In her flights Anna re-learned the qualities of her town. To the known triangle of her school, her house and the Midas mine she added other designs: the parallel hotels beneath whose dark verandahs she snake-shaped, and the looped route between the swimming pool and the fly-specked milk bar. There was also a pentacle pointed out by particular sites: the bakery next to the stables where she bought fragrant bread, the Aphrodite brothel, where she talked over the fence to the women, Mr Paul's corner store, where she once-a-week bought mixed lollies in white paper bags, the movie theatre, that especial darkness, for Saturday afternoons, and Eamon Ahern's house, to which she bee-lined, then circled, too shy, outside. Further out in a series of stretching arcs lay the racecourse, the drive-in, the false mountains of ore tailings, larger mines with their poppet heads, the pock-patterned landscape of small shafts and claims and beyond that, more mysteriously, Aboriginal camps and the desert.

In this far-out region Anna felt transgressive. Sometimes she followed the railway line that extended to the other side of the continent, and when she reached the point at which shaft holes and machinery disappeared, she was given pause. The land flattened out, and the sky seemed so very domed and extensive that crow calls echoed, quavering, as though caught within a giant bell. It occurred to her that she could ride on her bike forever, but she always stopped. The air was scorching. Heat distortion caused trees to shimmer on the edge of invisibility. Hawks circled above and lizards skittered. Small spirals of sand lifted and spun. And so she always returned. She returned towards the noisy town which in this disturbing perspective of girlhood and reversal, also shimmered unbelievably. It was heat-wavy and barely credible in the distance before her.

Riding her bicycle seemed the antithesis to the dread she experienced at night. Against the inertia of night terrors she pitched her accelerating self. She was known for her cycling skill and entered a daredevil career in which she would challenge gangs of tough local boys for races and dares down the steep inclines of the slime dumps and over the mounds of old mines. Plunge exhilarated her. She closed her eyes and surrendered herself entirely to gravity. She was courageous and stupid. Some of the boys bet secretly for her to win. They would pose for a moment, four or five in a row, intensely ready, then launch together downwards, yelling and unstoppable. Anna Griffin rode like one heroic. Once three boys ganged together and bashed her up in the laneway, just to prove her feminine and bloody.

(*Crikey Moses!* said her father when she walked through the half-lit doorway with a broken nose and a split lip and a stinging cut above her eye. *Crikey Moses!*)

The town council banned bikes on the slime dumps when a ten-year-old boy, emulating some mad crazy girl or other, raced across a terrain of dips and black shadows, and flew in a perfect high curve straight into the mouth of a shaft. He fell through the chicken wire of its opening and leaving his bike tangled above him, continued falling. When Anna heard this story she had a vision of the boy on his back, blinking his last moments at a circle of sky — against which was embossed the triangular frame of a Malvern Star bicycle.

After that boys chucked stones at her as she rode down the street. They knew. It was her fault. The show-off bitch. The smartarse moll.

Does X mark the spot? Victoria inquired.

Inevitably, said Anna.

She cannot release herself from the free-fall into mournful memories. After all these years she still feels guilty for the ten-year-old boy who rocketed headfirst into the mouth of a mine-shaft.

Surrealist Piratical; what do you think of that for a title?

Tell me about the painting called *Black Mirror*.

No, said Victoria.

Why not?

No.

What is happening? Why is the reflected woman on fire?

No, repeated Victoria. No, no, no.

Picasso's *Crying Woman*, Anna said, in annoyed retaliation, was inspired by his lover, Dora Maar, in 1937. It's in all the books, it's history, everyone knows this.

Victoria sniffed.

Just goes to show how ignorant you are. *La Femme qui Pleure*: the woman who fell upon him in the studio the first time Jules left. Dora Maar put her arms around me, and said, *Don't cry, don't cry.* Then she kissed me three times — X X X. Me, Anna, me. It was me he painted.

Anna can imagine it: Victoria hysterical in Picasso's studio, claiming for herself, egoistically, the possession of all feelings, the origin of all images. She is not even sure if Victoria ever met Pablo Picasso. Her subject is as self-aggrandising as she is wedded to modest detail. She is unresolved and imprecise, like a photograph not properly taken.

6

London at 3 a.m. is any city; it carries the same possibilities of desolation. Anna listens to the smothered sounds of traffic ballooning up into the night, hauling her out to the stretched space that sleeplessness resides in. It is a dumb, lightheaded elevation. The air is thin and deoxygenated, the city vague and glistening. Below, interspersed cars — too many, too early — slide smoothly along their head-lit canals.

If she could see herself in the mirror she would be half-eaten by the dark. She would be negated and phantasmic.

Light from a street lamp falls arrow-like across the room; Anna rises groggily to close the curtains against its pallid glow and sees the humped shape of an old man, lying contracted, dead-still, in the narrow doorway of the building opposite.

Dead still.

Anna has fallen into wakefulness and it is futile to

stay in the dark, hoping to fall the other way. She switches on the bedlamp and blinks her room into existence: it is messy, predictable, mean and adequate. Beside her is the catalogue of Victoria's retrospective show, and Anna opens it for the consolation of the wholly familiar. She knows its contents so well that if she were struck blind tomorrow, these are the images she would most indelibly retain.

Her favourites:

— A swan with the face of a woman, flying over the ocean. The creature bears a halo of spiky poppet-heads, and its eyes are turned to the heavens, in imitation of saintly or devotional gestures. The sky is pink as fairy-floss; the ocean milky pale blue.

— A giraffe in the darkness, barely visible. It stands at a street corner, just beyond the range of the street lamp, like a detective in a movie. At its feet are a cluster of tiny comma-shaped objects; they resemble, but indistinctly, human tears. This painting has a border of human hands.

— A drawing room with a black-and-white chequered floor, and ornate old-fashioned furniture, neatly arranged. In the centre of the room is a huge hourglass, slowly emptying. And lined along the wall stand six unidentifiable trees, both green and aflame. Outside the square window the sky is the colour of fire.

— A woman naked on a bed — this painting is her best known, *Luxe, Calme, Volupté.* A darkish triangle is lodged on the woman's belly, and concentric circles, in yellow and purple, spread outwards from her shape. In each band of ripples there are floating faces, creamy and vague, of little boys and girls; and they lean into the picture beneficently, like the cherubim that blow wind from the corners of old maps. Scattered among these faces are tiny emblems: hearts, stars, hands, Eiffel towers.

Although Anna is a little obsessed with the painting called *Black Mirror*, it is this one, with its joyful wake, its sequence of ripples, that gives her most pleasure. She places the book, propped open, on the pillow beside her, leaves the bedlamp on, and studies the image carefully. By this fanciful method she will try to recapitulate it in her dreams. She will try to push back the nightmares and the night terrors with this splendid body, its fecundity, its play, its touristic joke.

Insomnia: how dull it is, how truly debilitating. There is in each of us, Anna thinks, a self that is nocturnal; mine is taking over. She has learnt to acquiesce to the claims the deep night has on her. No longer anxious or frustrated, she simply waits like a prisoner in isolation for her time-release. She knows the minute calibrations of night — creaks in furniture, the sigh of buildings, the obscure shapes in corners that melt into imaginary faces. Her bedlamp looks like a pineapple ring forked shining from a can; her books all have a limpid and oily sheen. Outside the day-hidden street-lives appear: a *dead still* man, deposited like waste, abandoned like an accident, there, just opposite, in a narrow doorway. Anna Griffin realises that she misses the moonlight. She misses Prussian-blue night-sky and clouds foaming above distant poppet heads. Here the city dark is brown and artificial.

At last they are getting to know each other.

Anna asks: Tell me, Victoria, what do you remember of your mother?

Nothing, she replies. Nothing at all.

Anna takes another sip of the cocktail Victoria has prepared for her. She is becoming tipsy and feels emboldened.

I don't believe you. You must remember something.

Victoria also looks tipsy.

She brushed my hair. I don't remember her face at all, but I remember that it was my mother who brushed my hair. After each long stroke she ran the open palm of her hand fully down the length of my hair, as though its flyaway strands needed constant smoothing. I remember that gesture. It was rhythmic and ritualistic. I remember the sensation of her hand upon my hair. And the brush. It was of bone with an inlay of emerald green stone, in a design of ivy . . . And so, what do you remember, my grand inquisitor, my sweet Anna-leptic?

Everything, says Anna. Every little thing.

What in particular?

She had a saying, when I was little. She would tuck me in bed, lean right over me, and whisper: *My what big eyes you have!* At that point I would close my eyes, and she would kiss both eyelids. It was a kind of game she invented to get me to sleep. After she left I found it hard to close my eyes at night. The absence of her kisses was almost intolerable. Sometimes I would wake in the middle of the night believing I had felt her lips in the dark, softly touching against my eyelids. Brushing, just brushing.

The two women stare silently into empty glasses. Victoria holds out her hand and Anna places her glass on it. Then, in an act of comic distraction, Victoria puts the glasses to her eyes and says in a rough and wolfish voice: *All the better to see you with.*

Anna thinks her hurtful. But then she laughs.

Anna is delighted to find that they are both entering a state of drunken hilarity. Victoria is a skilled concocter of cocktails and alcohol tips her backwards into cushiony space of tell-tale and recollection. She raves — that is the word for it — on all things French: French pastries, French letters, French tenses, French poetry; so Anna tells her the story of her adolescent introduction to the experience of French kisses:

Moira Ahern and Beryl Ray were sitting on the bed with her, bragging.

He was all over me like a rash, said Beryl Ray. Talk about a member of the Wandering Hands Society.

Moira and Anna both wanted more juicy details, so Beryl Ray obliged. They hadn't gone all the way, but had pashed on at the pictures. Pretty serious pashing. Nev had put his whole hand inside her bra and made her feel his crown jewels, hard as a rock. She said he mucked up her hairdo and only bought one drink, the mingy bloody prick.

Her boldness was delicious. The girls exchanged excited glances.

Anna was thoroughly impressed by the worldliness of her friends. They possessed an entirely different vocabulary, concerning objects and things she knew nothing about: beehive, fishnet, backless dress, Eau De Cologne Number Four-Seven-Eleven. When they spoke of gropings in the back stalls, in that muffled darkness, with the flickering of movie-light and the promise of damp and illicit proximities, she could barely contain her inexperienced interest. And then? she would ask. And then? Then?

But she was not quite accepted. Other girls tittered in corners when Anna approached. Even Moira and Beryl performed gestures of exaggerated alarm when they discovered she had never used nail varnish and had no gossip or magazines or lovey-dovey contributions. It was from them that she learned that her mother had run off with some man — But absolutely *everyone* knows *that!* they cruelly chorused — and she was so engulfed by the knowledge that she feared she would faint, there in the schoolyard, in front of everybody.

A real looker, said Beryl, by way of compensation; but Anna was contorted with misery and could not utter a word in response. This was her most private secret, her years of search for her mother. She could not bear these girl voices, the jollity ringing in their mouths. They were giggling at her ignorance and she felt stricken and ridiculous.

In the mines, said Ernie, men feared the *creeps*. The earth shifted and a rain of gravel fell, the timber cracked and strained and splintered at the stope, and for each miner there was blood-hurtling and an urgent wish to flee just as his knees buckled in pure terror and gave way under him. Once he saw a mate sucked backwards into a shaft by a sudden rush of air. For each miner this understanding: they worked in graves.

She remembered this now. The forms of collapse and burial.

She had wagged school for three weeks before she could face them again.

But now Moira Ahern has offered to teach Anna the art of French-kissing, and it is an irresistible offer — so sexy, so French.

I'll be Nev, said Moira, and you be Beryl.

They are sitting on the bed together, with Beryl instructing. Moira slides her hand to Anna's breast and places Anna's hand inside her panties, and when she kisses she makes a melancholy and moaning sound, so that Anna wonders if this is part of the act of French-kissing or some merely eccentric and cinematic addition; she wonders too at the pleasure of this hand upon her breast, which is so much more than the kiss itself, so compelling, somehow, and so sweetly furtive; and at Beryl there, watching her play-acting a second Beryl, engrossed by her own double re-performing with a simulated Nev.

Closer, said Beryl. You have to be closer.

So they wedged themselves further into the entanglement of their Australian French-kiss, found that particular curvilinear of film-star epiphany, and kissed, and kissed. When Moira at last disengaged her face was beaming.

I think you need more practice, she instantly announced.

Later they lay sideways on the bed, six-legged, thinking of England. Anna had never in her life imagined leaving her own town, but both Beryl and Moira had identical futures constructed elsewhere. First they would go to the city, where they have TV and big shops and dripping boys on the beach, and then they would go to England and become secretaries with piled hair and lethal high-heels.

London is where it all happens, Beryl declared. No more deadshits. Or gutless wonders. Or mingy bloody dickheads.

It snows all winter, added Moira, and men open car doors and have really clean fingernails because they all work in offices. Or drive red buses.

Lovely, said Beryl.

Lovely, echoed Moira.

Anna tried to triplicate, but simply could not. Instead she wondered what France was like, with kisses like that.

Kisses like that.

Victoria exploded. Kisses like that!

She was hugely entertained by Anna's story. Later, when she calmed down, she asked Anna again about her mother. But the young woman, suddenly sad, would say no more. She had surrendered to alcoholic declension; she was sliding towards sorrow.

Victoria said: Let me tell you about 1936, my alchemical year. Transubstantiation! *L'Age d'Or*! She laughed.

Reichsführer Hitler was already trampling over Europe, Spain was about to homicidally ignite, but Victoria had just met Jules and was blithely self-obsessed, and politically unaware. In June of 1936 the International Surrealist Exhibition was held in London, at the New Burlington Galleries. It was an unusually hot summer and Victoria described it mischievously, as if it were a series of scenes designed by Magritte. All across the city men in black bowlers and dark suits were crumpling, concertina-like; women were removing snow-white gloves and fanning them fingerless at crimson faces; children were entirely hectic and out-of-control. Ices were everywhere licked, drinks everywhere guzzled, and the insides of stores and public houses buzzed thick with the mosquito whine of endless complaining. Oh the heat, they would whine, the heat, the heat: Victoria mimicked an upper-class English accent with diabolical precision.

Yet her body recovered a kind of girlish mobility, and she strode through melting London, hot-housed and sizzling, intoxicated with the sweet remembrance of sweat. She thought of deserts, distances, entropic mirages. Of glimmering horizons, mirrors in the sky. She remembered salmon-coloured salt lakes and inverted trees, cradled in a precarious and unrealistic suspension. It was perhaps her only true adult moment of radical nostalgia.

And then, astonishingly, in Trafalgar Square — and she can no longer remember why she was in the centre of the city — but in Trafalgar Square, among the giant and sombre statues of lions, the imperial columns, the wandering pigeons, appeared a woman whose head was a bunch of flowers. She wore a pale satin dress, elbow-length black gloves, and had a many-coloured bouquet upon her shoulders. A bunch of roses. Photographers were darting around her, mad for a picture. *Click! Click!* In the summer-time square, bright with acrid sunshine, she was dazzlingly visible, a surplus, a monster. Victoria felt she had produced this spectacle from her own imagination. She moved towards the flower-woman, and a young man, tuxedoed, moustachioed and with the manners of a salesman, intercepted her rather rudely and offered her a handbill. The arcane word *Surrealist* rose up into vision.

Exhibition. Surrealist. New Burlington Galleries.

The bunch of roses walked away, trailing photographers. Pigeons uplifted. Overheated Englishmen glared and mumbled.

Almost immediately Victoria found Jules and took him to the exhibition. It was the opening day, and the traffic was held up in Bond Street and Piccadilly because of the crowds. Large groups had gathered to gawk and sneer: she had never before seen so many people attend an art gallery.

She remembers this morning as a kind of physical sensation; it was as though, entering the gallery, a parachute — *whoomph!* — jerked open inside her chest. She felt both fallen and upheld, strung in the aerial logic of movement in the sky, tense and excited with something straining to stay open inside her. Max Ernst's *Two Children Menaced by A Nightingale*. Meret Oppenheim's cup and saucer covered with fur. Dali's deliquescent clocks. Tanguy's weird plasma shapes. Collages. Frottages. Impossibilities.

Victoria recognised something: they had painted dreams.

Jules bent to inquire: Are you all right?

But she could not reply for all that was inside her. She was overwhelmed with a sense of providential culmination and the effect of the exhibition was less like a spectacle than a kind of syntax arranging itself, a new intelligibility.

Jules tugged at Victoria like a child, begging to leave.

It's so hot in here, he whispered.

He ran this index finger around the inside of his shirt collar, waved his neat hat and dabbed at his brow with a handkerchief.

And this . . . he gestured around him, is all so . . . stupid!

Bête! She still hears it, spat in her direction.

When finally they left, Jules was in a state of peevish

annoyance Victoria had always, perhaps meanly, associated with the French. They stood outside the New Burlington Galleries and for the first time fought. Jules' face was flushed. Blown newspaper spun around him, exemplifying his agitation.

Incroyable! he said. *Incroyable!*

Exactly! Victoria responded. Believing is seeing.

She tried to seduce him with the deep sincerity of her impressions, but Jules was unmoved, exasperated, and turned on his heel to walk away up the street. He did not turn back, nor did he entreat. Victoria strode again into the gallery, back into the supernatural atmosphere of an entire counter-world.

Representations of women seemed everywhere to confront her. There was Dali's sketch, like a rape, of the faceless woman whose whole upper half was a chest of drawers. There was Roland Penrose's *objet*, called *Captain Cook's Last Voyage*, which consisted of a mannequin torso held fast in a globe-shaped cage. And most hauntingly there was Magritte's *La Femme Introuvable*. This was a painting of an innocent-looking naked woman, who stood with one hand resting upon her right breast, and stared dreamily, impassive and in a kind of trance, straight out of the picture. Behind her was an irregular pattern of paving stones, which took up most of the painted background; but scattered on the stones were four very large hands, remnants of giants who did not appear. The hands gestured around the woman as though feeling for her presence. Yet this was not at all erotic; rather it was simply an intrigue, a *cherchez la femme.* Victoria stood before this image bearing a crown of question marks.

It is still a painting, she says to Anna, that returns to her at odd moments — in the bath, waking at night, cutting a slice of bread.

The gallery was loud with outraged discussion. Women in tilted hats tilted their bodies forward, all the better to see. They sniffed. Adjusted eyeglasses. Men leant backwards, holding their hats over their buttocks and fingering the rims in consternation. Thrilled art patrons everywhere frowned and giggled. Victoria was at last unable to bear her internal sensation and walked out into the light. She took her own hat from her head and looked upwards at the sun. The light was blinding. Mirage suns in black spotted every part of the city.

It was like a vision, says Victoria. Just like a vision.

Victoria takes a book from the bookshelf and opens it at René Magritte's image.

There. You see?

Anna is disappointed. The woman is crudely rendered. It is a plain photograph, black-and-white. A stilted looking ghost. Grey space. Clumsy hands. Hardly a revelation.

When was it then, Anna's trip to see the Vision?

Anna is thinking now of her younger self. How old was she, then? Twelve? Thirteen? And how in any case does one register or assimilate such events?

———

It was already quite hot, the sun a bubble of poured gold, when they set out together. Anna and Uncle Ernie strapped hessian water bags to the handlebars of their bicycles, checked their modest cribs and tied on hats; they stood high on their pedals to make a speedy start.

The air was burning, pure, clarified somehow. She remembers that black cockatoos — swift visitants — swooped in a criss-crossing farewell.

At first it was possible to cycle side by side. The ground was dry and firm, the paths through the old pocked diggings familiar, and they rode slowly, chattering. Gidgee Lake was only ten miles to the north, out in the desert along a disused railway line, and both anticipated an easy time of it. But as the sun rose higher they reached a territory of stones and double-gees and treacherous pits of sand, and began to cycle single file, pushing hard into the red country, their breath becoming audible, strained and tired. Anna could see Uncle Ernie's hairy legs, and the sweat beads sparkling on the back of his neck. Flies clustered in dark insignia on the checks of his damp shirt. She was secretly unsure if she could keep up with his pedalling, but wasn't a sissy or a sooky bubba or a grumble-bum slow-coach, and would die rather than complain. Yet she saw him moving further and further ahead and her thighs ached and her two lungs felt contracted and seared. She could feel sweat running in a trickle between her new little breasts. At last Ernie paused and called out:

Anna, hey; how about a spell?

And Anna shouted back: 'Bout bloody time!

Uncle Ernie smiled. He stood beside his bike as he waited for Anna to join him. Then said, mock-serious:

And don't you speak your bloody French round me, young girl.

They drank greedily, like animals, in a motley patch of shade.

Water, Ernie sighed. A bloke could get lost in it.

When they came at last upon the salt lake it was vaster than Anna had expected, but Ernie's description was true: it was like shivering glass. And it included a second dimension, a vague and spectral duplication, hanging low in the sky. Anna squinted against the glare and saw the whole world dissolve into a system of pink-coloured reflections: boundaries were indeterminate, surfaces were vitreous, no image stood alone. Tiny trees dangled upside-down beneath the floating lake, and others reached up from the earth in a twinning gesture. The air was crystalline and strange, the light gleaming as mirrors.

What a Vision! said Uncle Ernie.

Anna turned to look at his ugly scarred face. It was silver, bright. He held his hand to his brow in a squinting salute.

Yes, Anna responded. A Vision. Yes.

She had never seen so many horizons at once. Nor this precise pink tone dispersed around the sky. It was another kind of knowledge.

The air vibrated as if waves of sound moved through it. It was nothing Anna could hear. Nothing within her range. But the vibration existed. She felt it trouble the surface of her skin and enter the spaces of her body. Trees were jerking their heads in the easterly wind, smokebush trembled and salt crystals lifted and spun. Somewhere, up high, bird wings were beating and for some reason Anna felt like standing with her arms outstretched.

Ernie and Anna were quiet together for a long, long time, subordinated by awe, by loveliness, by who-knows-what.

Cycling home they stayed closer to the railway line and the going was easier. Uncle Ernie slowed his pace but was silent and preoccupied; Anna was too exhausted to speak. Her fair skin burned with salt and sun. She felt her body had been blasted by whatever it was she had seen.

When, after five miles or so, they spotted an abandoned fettlers' camp on the other side of the line, Uncle Ernie insisted that they cross over to visit his mate Chook, from the mines. Anna protested and grizzled, but knew already that old men are especially lonely, and that they share their loneliness in these casual and stringent meetings in which, it seemed to her, they talked in nothing but the past tense.

There were four single-room camps of blank austerity: a stove, a canvas bunk, and walls of rusty corrugated iron full of nail-holes and gaps. Chook was the only occupant and rose from the bunk, a lumbering figure in brown shadows, scarcely half-alive.

Anna could see that her Uncle Ernie was shocked.

I hardly reckernised ya, Chook, ya dirty old bugger.

Chook was apologetic.

Yeah, well. Put it there, Ernie.

He extended a hand for shaking and Anna saw then the terrible aspect of his condition: his flesh was loose and transparent like a man draped with cloth, and his colour deep blue and speckled, unearthly in its ruined and obvious dereliction. His voice chafed and whistled as he talked, and he was seized almost immediately by a loud fit of coughing.

Bloody hell, said Uncle Ernie. Why doncha move inta town?

Chook, abashed, wiped his dribbly mouth.

Mate, I wouldn' be anywhere else for quids. It's quiet. I do me prospecten. Boil me billy when I want. So what brings you to Paris?

Been gawken at the lake like kiddies at the pictures. Me an Anna. On the bikes.

Chook leaned over awkwardly and shook Anna's hand. She was appalled at her own sensation of disgust and almost checked to see if his skin had flaked onto hers. Then she sat down on her hand so that she wouldn't have to wipe it, and stared at the red dirt floor, feeling ashamed.

Uncle Ernie and Chook rolled narrow cigarettes and crouched on the bunk close together, smoking and yarning. Chook talked of his time on the

Perseverance mine and Ernie joked about mutual mates from the old days. They had peculiar names: Robbo, Stretch, Leftie, Sid. Anna tried not to listen. The past was another country. Old people's country. When finally they left, Uncle Ernie simply said:

Miners' complaint. The dust. Lost his ticket two years ago.

It sounded to Anna like the formal announcement of a death. They pedalled away from it, that man there, dying in the shadows. Anna's body was in a dream; her burnt legs rode and rode on without thinking. As they reconstructed their rhythm and found a side-by-side track, they began to exchange, in an instinct of mutual comfort, their small repertoire of comic songs. Anna liked all the naughty ones:

There's a place in France
Where the ladies wear no pants
And the men go around
With their dicks along the ground.

Ernie began to chuckle. Black cockatoos re-appeared and darted to greet them.

When Anna thought of the Vision later that night, she could also remember Chook, waiting for his death. The two were indissociable. She had an impulse, a shameful impulse, to wipe clean her hand. She realised too that what she had seen was incomprehensible. The place was not her place. And the sound she could not quite hear was not her sound. It was like hearing an amorous murmur or a prayer in someone else's language.

One day, out of the blue, Uncle Ernie said:

Here's another Vision, luv.

I was five years old, an out at the pits, with me dad. He was dryblowing soil, and I remember the shudder of the frame, sifting the dirt, an the dust, blowing away, an the pause as he sifted carefully in the gravel for gold specks and nuggets. We heard a sound, a rough drone, louder and louder, and no one knew quite what it was. Miners all round downed their tools or popped their heads out of shaft-holes to take a quick squiz. It was a plane, a biplane, one of the very first in Australia. I thought it was magic. I whooped for joy and started runnen all over the place, like a mad crazy thing, lookin straight up at the sky. Coulden believe me eyes. A plane. Just like in the papers. An then, guess what? A hat floated down. A little girl's bonnet. I could see green ribbons spinning, an it was slow an it was puffed, like a miniature parachute. An it floated into my hands, green ribbons an all. What a Vision it was. I was that darn thrilled.

Anna remembers her girl-self thinking: *They're everywhere, these Visions; you just have to wait; you just have to look.*

JEWELS

'Like' and 'like' and 'like' — but what is
the thing that lies beneath the semblance
of the thing?'

(Virginia Woolf, *The Waves*)

1

This is Victoria's house. It is a two-storey detached house in a leafy street in Hampstead, unremarkable on the outside — the requisite chain of roses, the heavy iron gate — and chosen for its proximity to the Underground railway.

Not for the transport, says Victoria, God forbid. But the sound and the trembles. I love the extension of space the trains seem to conjure. And the way they faintly disturb and shudder the buildings. You can feel reverberations beneath the soles of your feet.

What wish is this, Anna wonders, to cherish the sensation of lives extinguished in collapse? She thinks again of Ernie's description of the earth beginning to slip. Men leapt towards walls as stones fell over them. A *whoosh* of air and billowing dust unrolled along the shaft, indicating subsidence, or perhaps death, or perhaps a final closing in.

When Anna arrived on her first day she could not

believe that the woman she sought lived in such an ordinary house in such a complacent suburb. She stood patiently in the rain, waiting to be admitted. In the cage of her umbrella Anna was aware that her shabby shoes were filling up with water. She felt clownish. Ludicrous. But when she was at last admitted, passing under a portal hung with Indian embroidery, shaped in triangles studded with small round mirrors, she entered a collection of rooms not ordinary at all, but re-fashioned by the use of screens and props, some of which seemed to have been left over from stage sets or carnivals. It was a group of rooms which so theatricalised its tenant that she ought to have swept about in larger-than-life gestures. If she had been able, Victoria would have pirouetted like a ballerina, but she was old and frail, and mostly confined to the couch.

She indicated a screen to her left which was punctured with star shapes and covered with curling, streamer-like lines.

Cocteau, she said, and swung away again, pointing with both arms now, as though she had become a compass fixed on its invisible magnet, to a painting of her own, *Waves With Wings, Illimitable*. It was an image of orange-coloured waves, neither desert nor sea, or perhaps both desert and sea, which buoyed floating trinkets: champagne glasses, an open fan, a perambulator in which lay a sleeping black baby, a childish crown-of-gold from a fairy-tale storybook, two eyes released from a somewhere face, a tiny shape of Australia, brilliantly scarlet, and, at the very centre, a human foetus, translucent and striated with patterns of veins. Above the orange sea hung two very large dark wings, slightly indistinct, suggesting they were in fact a shadow of unseen wings, somewhere much higher, nearer the sun.

This was not a painting Anna remembered seeing before.

Then Victoria swung again, redirecting Anna's gaze. She leant sideways to embrace a shop mannequin of a man, life-sized and draped with kewpie dolls hanging from ribbons.

Jewels! she exclaimed. Meet Monsieur Jules!

She kissed the face of the mannequin and flicked at a doll, setting it swinging.

Mwah! a kiss of cocktail-hostess artifice.

And can I get you a cocktail? Tea? Cakes?

Victoria looked arch and ironical, but stood poised, her feathers shaking, fixed by a spotlight of her own imagining. The room hung around her like a gigantic decoration. Appliquéd shapes on bronze-coloured curtains. New Guinea carvings arranged in a circle. A series of bicycle wheels and machinery strung randomly from the ceiling, by different lengths of wire. In this room Victoria was large and impressive, and in the face of such display, of such habitual exhibitionism, Anna felt as if she was composed of water, leaking in slow puddles into the Persian carpet. Her saturated shoes swam at her feet. Her umbrella dangled.

You look like the wreck of the Hesperus, Victoria declared. Something the bloody cat dragged in!

———

Of those early meetings Anna remembers their performative aspect. Now, accustomed to this peculiar room, she can better disentangle the impression of circumambient screens and images from the woman who circles slowly and arthritically within them. Her head-dress of swan's feathers makes her appear tall and archaic, like some excavated goddess. And though fatigued, Victoria is also restless. Anna scrutinises the details of the old woman's body, her thin blue wrists, the folds of her neck: she has a slow but firm and definite energy. *She will go on for ever*, Anna thinks.

After the London exhibition, Victoria continued, Leonora Carrington and I went together to hear public lectures on Surrealism. She too had been at the New Burlington opening: her eyes were glossy with what she had seen. We were girlish and silly. We laughed at our own artistic inebriation, tilted our heads backwards and roared in chorus. Leonora Carrington's throat was pearl. Her long black hair swept like waves. In a teahouse, I remember, she raised up her teacup, summoned the waitress with an air of magisterial complaint, and announced in comical French-accented English:

But zis teacup, ma petit bon-bon; she is not covered with fur?

She held the object aloft seriously, just for a minute, in order to suspend the waitress in miserable confusion. Then she roared with her horsey, aristocratic laugh.

The first lecture we went to was Herbert Read's. He stood awkwardly on a spring sofa as he talked on

Art and the Unconscious. Dreams. Automatism. The rich latency of things. Later we heard Breton, Eluard and Hugh Sykes, all proclaiming.

But it is the Dali story I want to tell you.

It was early July and still very hot. Dali entered the gallery wearing a deep-sea diving suit decorated all over with plastic hands. There was a radiator cap on the top of his helmet, a fancy jewelled dagger lodged in his belt, and he led a pair of panting, unhappy Borzoi hounds. Edward James, who was Dali's English manager, followed carrying a billiard cue to serve as a pointer for the illustrations. There was a pulse in the air: *beat-beat, beat-beat*. The gallery was so sweltering and so poorly ventilated the air throbbed with the fan-beat of programs and hats. Expirations of all kinds were apparently imminent. Women mopped with handkerchiefs and put the backs of their hands against their cheeks to test their own temperatures. Men, all imitating my beloved Jules, ran their index fingers around the insides of their shirt collars or worried fussily at neck-scarves and bowties. I remember that Leonora lifted her hair from her neck, shook it breezily, then let it drop. Lifted and dropped. In retrospect I endow this gesture with ravishing grace. The necks of women and men, their points of exposure and enclosure, continue to excite me.

We sat together and watched Salvador Dali asphyxiate. Behind the circle of glass he gulped like a goldfish. His muffled voice became weaker, his face was lobster, and he began to flail, drowning in air. Wild gestures requested the removal of the helmet, and the audience was aroused by the expectation of disaster. Edward James tried to unscrew the wingnuts of the helmet but they would simply not budge. The hounds exposed enormous tongues and panicked and tangled. James tripped, Chaplinesque. When he recovered he used the billiard cue to assault the helmet, and with the assistance of another man finally released Dali's head from its deadly aquarium. The audience sat with mouths open: inhaled fish-like, collectively.

And would you believe it? Salvador Dali continued his lecture. He talked in Spanish-accented French with incomprehensible intensity on the subject of paranoia and the Surrealist rage against death. Leonora took notes. But I was distracted. A single plastic hand had detached in the flurry, and lay on the floor, orphaned, at the foot of the diver. It was white, child-size and appeared immaculate.

This body-piece, my Anna-tomical, was my sign, my wonder. I saw the beauty of things in dislocation. I saw the asterix of every hand. And I saw my own hands, glimmering, white and open before me, as though for the first time. As though fabulously new.

Victoria paused.

Single-handed, she joked. I became a Surrealist single-handed.

Her laugh was throaty and full and Anna joined in. But her drifting mind had snagged on an earlier sentence: *I saw the asterix of every hand.*

The Paris Victoria arrived in: less a city of monuments, than one of marvellous conjunctions. Her own face, astonished, appearing on glass surfaces.

She bore in her eye the principle of convulsive beauty: together and correspondent existed typewriters, aeroplanes, purple hyacinths unfolding, the fur collars of large women trapping droplets of water, cigarette smoke, velotaxis, old men weighted by sandwich boards, telephone receivers (ringing loudly or sitting silent), café names writ effulgent with electric lights, marble columns, kerbside garbage, gargoyles on the verge of effacement, the lit faces of patrons leaving a crowded cinema, lampposts, stairwells, wind-blown hair, the dark and deadly-looking night-time canyon of the Seine.

She linked arms with Jules Levy, held him preciously to her, and met the city, *jamais vu*, hyperaesthetic. It was a reincarnation.

A woman passes by with a corsage of parma violets, pinned to the lapel of a dun-coloured jacket, and Victoria exclaims as though she has never seen violets before.

In front of the Hôtel de Ville, in the cloudy square, children are riding a golden and fancifully decorated carousel; their smiles flash with each up-down circle they travel in. It is incomparably festive. Victoria almost weeps.

An Algerian — she supposes — is tending with blackened gloves his brazier of chestnuts; he bends forward and blows at the coals, ever so gently, re-positions the chestnuts, one by one, and then lifts his gaze to nod inquiringly in Victoria's direction. Above him a green Metro sign is blooming. A small dog, chinchilla-like and dressed in flounces, is dragged past her, sniffing. Jules buys just one paper cone of roasted chestnuts and they share this modest meal, encased in novelty.

In Victoria's mind everything here is wrapped in cellophane: Paris crackles; it is shiny; it is her own bright faceted gift.

Later, in bed, she whispers into the night:

This city: its scent, its scent is feminine.

Perhaps Jules thinks her absurd; perhaps she is overcome by her own giddy impulse of invention. He is quiet; then he stirs.

I've always thought so, he softly replies. The Metro, too. It is yeasty, rich. Sometimes it smells of menstrual blood.

In the winter dark Jules Levy stretches sleepily to encompass her. His arm is warm and firm — it almost feels like her own — as it lies, sash-like, across her naked breast.

Did you know, Anna, that I was once hypnotised? I was so anxious to become a true *Surrealiste* that I became instead a shameless and docile body, reconstructed as medium, the object of others' intentions, a sign, a manikin. I would have lain on a table, Aztec and sacrificial, with my breasts exposed to the regarding sky, inviting knives. I wanted to be oh-so convulsively beautiful, a rose, a swan, an alabaster Venus. Breton used to say: *La beauté sera C O N V U L S I V E ou ne sera pas* — 'beauty will be convulsive, or it will not be.' I believed that maxim absolutely. I still do today.

It was a late-night party at the Eluard's apartment. The crowd was eating Swiss chocolates shaped like women, which were proffered in a teapot on a silver tray. Dali was there, smacking his lips. André Breton, with his head like a light bulb, had an organ-grinder's monkey balancing on his shoulder; Victoria watched him slide chocolate women into the animal's mouth. Everyone was enacting their own exceptionality. Under the electric apotheosis of too many lamps they were stylised and enticing. Simone. Paul. Breton's wife, Jacqueline. Leonora, she remembers, wore a violet dress with lime-green hummingbirds embroidered over the bodice, and carried in her manner a sort of party-time excitation. She was by then the lover of the German painter Max Ernst, and Victoria was beginning to discover the sensations of jealousy. The pair were together, in a corner, sucking women at each end. Leonora caught her eye, dissolved her chocolate mouthful, and mimed the words *cannibal carnival*; after which she laughed and kissed Ernst with a peck on the cheek. Then in a tender parody of her silent message, she bit at his ear lobe. Victoria experienced the misery in seeing one's object of infatuation at the far other-side of a room, animated and autonomous. Her feelings were sharp, crystal. Nusch Eluard, with her heart-shaped face, walked over to kiss the light bulb and confirmed Victoria's aloneness.

On the gramophone played Ellington's *Baby When You Ain't There*. It was Jules she was missing. *Jewels. Jewels.*

Victoria drank thimbles of Chartreuse and gobbled too many women. Smoke from Gauloises floated in the air. Jelly Roll on piano. Dali talking Hitler. Breton debating Maldoror with Dora and Jacqueline. Leonora began dancing, setting her birds in flight. A tray of trembling desserts, *crème passionelle*, circulated among the crowd, each on a paper plate cut in the shape of a hand. Eluard was singing: forked tongue, spooned tongue, knifed tongue, forked tongue . . . When someone suggested, half-serious, a demonstration of hypnosis, Victoria was so very drunk and unhappy that she offered herself immediately.

Take me. Subordinate me. Give me erasure.

André Breton, minus his monkey, assumed an air of rectitude. He unclasped from Victoria's bosom a marcasite brooch, and held it like an icon before her eyes. There is no record anywhere of his precise instructions, but Simone took a transcript of the hypnotic exchange, the questions in French and Victoria's replies in English.

What fabric are you composed of?

I am lace, lace. Mostly hollows, fancily described. Women wove me. Nets to catch bodies in.

What is your colour?

Colourless deep space. Tiny luminosities in a general dark. Moony apparitions, on special occasions.

What is the taste in your mouth?

Taste: cinerary. No sweet confection but fragments of ash.

What do you hear?

Echo-chamber of this or that narcissus. Repetition. Repetition. Repetition. Faintly.

What is your shape?

Desire makes me triangular. Hips. Smiles. Spaces to rest in . . . Invitations.

What creature are you?

Swan and not swan. Winged and wingless. Beady-eyed.

Do you have a name?

Lily-white. Midas. Ruby. Swan-Seine.

Awoken from hypnosis Victoria was lucid, revived. The party stood around her in a perfect semicircle.

Bravo! said Breton. Bravo! Bravo!

Everyone clapped.

Victoria took a bow for the performance she had been insensible of performing and when she arose, flushed, she saw before her the froth of a violet dress, and beyond that hummingbirds brilliantly distinct, Leonora's face, her smile, her absurd congratulation. Ernst peered over her shoulder, his cheek double-headed against hers, and asked in heavily accented English: Whose little triangle then are you?

Since she had no knowledge at all of what she had just disclosed Victoria felt disquieted. The whole assembly laughed out loud. As they dispersed they spoke of a Victoria she didn't know.

Most of the others left in a group for the cabaret; Victoria made her way home alone through the waking city. Nacred clear light hung over the buildings. On Rue Valette a black man played harmonica mournfully and she threw francs at his jacket which rested on the pavement like a corpse.

Merci, cygne, merci.

His smile was a triangle. He nodded at her feathers.

Then Victoria followed, eavesdropping, two early-morning risers, who apparently worked together in an automobile factory. She heard of deaths, and poor machinery, and the misery of mechanised labour, she heard of a worker electrocuted, and another with fingers severed, and a third with hair torn out by a drilling machine.

A cyclist wove between them, halting the list of accidents. Stella Renaults zoomed past on the road.

The two men resumed their casual lamentation, and it was one of those moments in which vocation seems entirely presumptuous. Victoria saw Paris darken and believed her artistry despicable. The feathers on her head were mere stupidity; her paintings excrescences. Notes from the harmonica drifted from behind, and before, flowing towards her, the voices of workers.

What am I doing here?

And when at last she slept she dreamt of the Midas mine, but on awaking could not remember any details. Perhaps it had been a dream of death or dismemberment. Or a dream of sex. Even dreams had no definition or message that would make her less alien.

———

So what do you dream of? demanded Victoria.

Anna knew this was a test. She summoned her courage and told Victoria her recurrent dream. She began:

When I was a child my father worked as a gold-miner in the Midas mine, and I often imagined following him underground. But the dream I have is always about my mother . . . it is always about searching for my mother in the mine. I hate it down there, under the earth. It is scary and cold. In my dream I have a torch but it always dims and fails, so I must bang it against my thigh to revive the batteries . . .

This was the first time Anna had told this dream and she wondered if her voice betrayed a quality of confession. She attempted to produce a disinterested tone, but heard her words emerge with a fragile inflection, like infirmity, or guilt. When she finished Victoria had tears in her eyes.

My father, Henry Morrell, owned the Midas mine.

I know, Anna admitted. I knew that already.

And I dream of it too. And in my dream, like yours, I am always searching.

Anna raised an eyebrow. If Victoria had not, at that point, had a trail of tears on her cheeks she would have disbelieved. But the old woman began to sob and search for a handkerchief, so that Anna was compelled sympathetically to lean forward and embrace her, and to feel that beneath the artist's extravagant and multi-layered clothes, beneath the feathers and the jewellery, she was a brittle shape, breakable as a bird. Victoria allowed herself to be held. When she had finished her weeping she shook herself slightly and rearranged her crown in its clever fan, quite as though nothing at all had transpired.

Victoria said distractedly: They were shits, some of those men, some of those Parisian Surrealists. Late one night Peret rang Cocteau's mother to tell her of her son's fictitious death in an automobile accident. Breton stood behind him, giggling, as they made the lie more and more convincing and elaborate. Poor Madame Cocteau; I've often thought of her.

Let me make you a cocktail. A Martian? A Mary-Magdalene?

2

Anna hates the Underground, especially at night. She cannot imagine why Londoners choose to traverse their city in these roaring, fearsome pitch-dark tunnels. As she descends the steps beneath the city she feels she is entering an infernal space; heat flames up at her; noise beastly and mechanical issues from nowhere; patrons of the railway assume hopeless expressions. The air is chemical and gaseous, the tone carcereal. Buskers of little talent sing or play plaintively. A young woman with a child on her lap and a ticket saying *Homeless* pleads in silence at the foot of the stairs. As Anna passes money to her hand the woman says, God bless you; her voice has a confined and fainthearted aspect.

God bless you.

Here, Anna thinks cynically, benedictions do not alleviate.

She rides unhappily. The doors hiss and *shoosh*, sealing her in. She experiences a sharp apprehension of suffocation. Her body clenches. Her lungs contract. Then she is plunged into the darkness, she and the men with briefcases, the Sikh with his turban, the three black boys in smart leather jackets, the woman with a hairstyle, the shopgirls tarted up, the assortment of cross-class, post-colonial and tired-out humanity. They are all locked together in a strange and lonely union. Velocity embraces them. Through the window lit platforms and figures slide away, billboards blur, then there is black-out and the close echoing walls of the tunnel, swerving at the train or bending around it. Sparks. A flash of light bulb. The details of things annihilated. And such a roar. Anna closes her eyes against this fiendish transport. When she arrives at her station she discovers that her hands are wet with sweat.

The Comedy of Errors at the Barbican, performed by the Royal Shakespeare Company. Anna has been living on bread and cheese so that she can afford London theatre tickets. She is the only woman alone in the lobby of the theatre. Other women are accompanied by partners or friends, and flap expensive programs as they bend towards each other and intimately speak. Elocuted voices scroll upwards into the air. Anna stares with fanatic intensity at photographs of old productions; she wishes to appear as if her singularity is entirely deliberate. Yet she feels — it is inescapable — working-class and conspicuous. Her clothes are poor. She fingers a hole in the pocket of her second-hand jacket, and looks down, like a schoolgirl, at her unfashionable shoes which are lined with cardboard and unevenly down-at-heel. Over the past few months she has seen half a dozen fringe performances of extravagant experimentation and unmemorable titles, and tonight she feels more than ever in need of theatrical vision, those bodies fixed artificial in a spot-lit square, proclaiming learnable lines at the tops of their voices, moving with exaggerated and purified gestures. Tonight she requires the drastic consolation of dramatic pronunciation and hearty applause. The lights dim and her heartbeat suddenly quickens, and she watches the unwrapping of a radiant faked world, there, impressively close, on the stage before her. Curtains. Sets. Auras of large lives. The audience like sunflowers, their faces heliotropic.

As Anna leaves the theatre she sees in the chattering crowd a man who also — she is sure of it — lives at Mrs Dooley's. She has only glimpsed him before, leaving the tenants' bathroom at the end of the hallway and ducking with his towel into doorway seven, and is disconcerted to see that he has an independent existence that includes her choice of entertainment. He walks off quickly in the direction of the Underground station, and Anna follows discreetly, at a detective's distance. He too is alone but seems secure in that state, moving through the night with bold and untentative steps. When he boards the train she enters the carriage behind him, then follows again as he makes his way along the streets to their shared lodging house. The full moon drifts with them, at walking pace.

———

Later, when they become lovers, she will lie in the warm hollow of this man's beautiful black arm, and he will confess that he knew, that night, that she was following behind him all the way from the theatre, but that he was much too shy to turn and acknowledge her presence. He will also concede a terror of the roaring Underground, and the familiar symptom of sweating hands. And gradually they will begin to tell each other stories of their childhoods: in bed together, both released from loneliness, they wish to learn every small detail of each other. Anecdotes are precious, tiny tales intercept and punctuate their lovemaking, they narrativise everything. When first he said, in his deep voice, the word *Jamaica*, it carried the strange profundity of a spell. *Australia*, said Anna in rhyming reciprocation, as if that word too was newly sonorous.

They join their two faraway and respective countries. They improvise an international pact of diplomacy, trade, negotiate, exchange consignments of raw and valuable materials, sign with the wordless movements of their bodies some document or other of treaty and concord. The earth's globe dissolves and is reformed to their design; in this upheaval both lovers become tropical and dark.

This is the metaphor they share, this is their jokey extrapolation.

Much later, when he is angry, he will say to hurt her: *I will not be your dark fucking continent.*

But now, resting enlaced, their metaphors are still comic. They lie together in bed and speak of

Shakespeare. They send the name like a special code, like a vow or a password, back and forth between them. In his mouth it sounds not like a name but like a Jamaican noun: *shakespeare, shakespeare.* Anna kisses the broad-lipped mouth that speaks it. She adores the night of his skin with her moon face, full, resting gently upon it.

My new-found land, she whispers, my new-found land.

Insulting him gently. Providing herself with stinging memories of her own insensitivity.

In the bland light of morning Anna handed Mrs Dooley a reproduction of *Black Mirror* and asked her what she thought.

So this is it, eh, exclaimed less-than-curious Mrs Dooley, who said she was not at all arty herself but her nephew-in-Australia, the one who never wrote, made cathedrals out of matchsticks, could stuff ships inside bottles, and fix a chair? — never you mind, fix anything he could, with his magic hands and his girl-crazy smile and his cheekiness and how she missed him, and he was such a clever lad really, could av done anything, doctor, engineer, aeroplane pilot, and just like Paddy Kernan whom she used to be sweet on, with his white skin, delicate, and his black hair and blue eyes, and they used to meet near the canal, where the water gushed through the locks, and there was a dead dog there once, and Paddy pulled it out, and all Dublin spoke of it, well all their close friends anyways, and he had hands thin as spiderwebs and slipped over one day on some phlegm on O'Connell bridge, and she had to lift him by herself, all heavy he was, and his coat and his cap smelled so strongly of peat smoke that she went misty and soppy and knew she was in love.

Is this French? asks Mrs Dooley.

She pauses in her biographical recitation and points to the words *déjà vu* and *jamais vu* that rest in each corner of the reproduced painting.

Anna cannot understand why she has not commented at all on the images: the woman-on-fire, its symbols, its curious mirrorings.

So what happened to Paddy Kernan? Anna asked.

And Mrs Dooley, who looked for a second as if someone had struck her in the chest, said that she'd thought he would follow when she came out to London to work, and she waited and wrote letters and prayed to Saint Jude and to Holy Mary the Immaculate Virgin, and heard from Sally Dignam, who'd heard from someone else, that he'd drowned himself in the Liffey, like that dog he pulled out, all mucky and dripping, and she thought of his tweed cap floating and the sorrow of it and the shame, and then heard again from Sally Dignam, bloody tart that she was, with that ass and her tarty rigmarole and her rougey cheeks and lippy lips, that someone else said he'd gone off to live in Australia, where her nephew was now, and who knows maybe they'll meet again or maybe he's dead, but she still thinks of him there, back in Dublin, in the summer, there in shady Raglan Road, with his shirtsleeves and his white skin and his two hands thin as spiders' webs.

So what do you think of the painting? Anna persisted.

That French stuff is all double-Dutch to me, lovey.

Mrs Dooley laughs at her own joke, gives Anna a rough cuddle and a smacking kiss, and drinks more tea.

Ah, Paddy Kernan, Paddy Kernan, she chants softly to herself. The first time I ever saw him, she adds to her story, he had the Spanish influenza or somesuch foreign complaint. He looked, did Paddy Kernan, like death-warmed-up. Like death-warmed-up, my poor Paddy Kernan.

Victoria asked abruptly: Do you have a lover?

The stare was a challenge. Anna pressed the off button of her tape-recorder and considered whether or not she ought to lie.

Winston. His name is Winston Field. He is a black man. From Jamaica.

Anna stared back at Victoria.

Tell me more.

He lives, like me, at Mrs Dooley's boarding house. He is a postgraduate on a scholarship, studying English Literature. Shakespeare. The Comedies. I introduced myself after I saw him alone at the theatre.

And?

I was attracted to his difference. And to his loneliness.

Ah, difference and loneliness. You must bring him to meet me. How different is he?

Completely, said Anna.

———

The truth is that at first Winston Field had not seemed interested in her at all. She arranged coffee, left him books, slipped notes under the door; and in the end he told her that he was a married man, back in Jamaica.

I'm not free, he announced; it sounded so direct and conclusive.

Anna seduced him by inviting him one night to her room, lit with three shuddering candles arranged by the window on her desk. When he entered she blew them out, tugged at his warm wrist, and said:

Teach me not to be afraid of the dark.

It will shame her later on, it will seem so contrived, and Winston will gently mock her crass poetic. She will always regret what she said, because in retrospect it can hurt him, and she wonders whom she impersonated, to act so boldly and so badly. Winston knows that from the beginning his blackness preceded him. He is a proud man, and sensitive. He is a man accustomed to racial slights and disconfirmations.

(*I will not be your dark fucking continent.*)

Yet when they lay together — she must admit it — his skin excited her. She felt exulted in his entirely unlike presence. He lay with his arm cast back, triangular, above his head, and she kissed the ticklish underarm in adoration, as one might kiss, in church, an ebony saint.

I was afraid at night, she found herself confessing.

His eyes glittered darkly in the half-light of her bedroom. His face was almost close enough to kiss.

That is not so unusual, he said in reply.

Winston spoke precisely, like a doctor, or an Englishman.

I would pray, every night:
Gentle Jesus meek and mild,
Look upon a little child.
If I die before I wake,
I pray the Lord my soul to take.
Ah, said Winston.
Gentle Jesas, meek an mile,
Look upon a trouble man,
Ease im soul and let im rest,
For im is a soul distress.
You know it, said Anna.

Of course, replied Winston. But ours is more compassionate, don't you agree? The compassion lies in the word *distress*.

He rolled onto his back and looked at Mrs Dooley's ceiling. Anna wondered which Jamaican moment had claimed him.

She asked: Do you remember much of your childhood?

And he answered, again formally: Black people — everywhere — always remember. Only the imperialist has the privilege of amnesia.

You speak in slogans.

Very well, I speak in slogans.

Silence. The silence of memorialising recall. She knew then there were things he would never tell her.

Mrs Dooley's small room was becoming flooded

with silences. Anna wished, as lovers do, to build a rescuing raft, to grasp at his hands and pull him over.

Did you, Anna began again, did you own a bike as a child?

Winston turned to face her.

I did not even imagine owning a bicycle. On the sugar plantation, on the Allfrey Estate, few had bicycles. Mr Allfrey had a car, a Cadillac from America, which kept breaking down. Red. A movie car. You could see your own face in it.

You wanted a car?

A lorry, replied Winston. The estate was a kind of ghost town for seven months while the cane was growing, then the workers would come for the cutting, setting up their lives in the tenements near the factory, and it was the possibility of lorry driving that always impressed me. Every year I wanted to drive away when the workers left, I wanted to leave the estate, forever.

Forever?

I did not want — never wanted — to become a cane cutter. I was afraid of the sadness in my mother's eyes, I was afraid of Mr Allfrey and his pink-coloured sons; I was afraid of the poor working men who had limbs cut by machetes, wounds, missing fingers.

— What get inna yuh? me mama say. Dis yo place, chile. Dy will be done, papa Jesas. Amen, amen —

I remember her crying as she smoked her pipe because she knew I would leave. I was ten, perhaps eleven, and would jump on a lorry at the end of that season. She called me to her and put my head in her lap, then sang:

Nuh cry, nuh cry, nuh cry me poo chile,
you is mine an me is yours.

As if I were the one who needed comforting. I adored the acrid dense smell of her pipe smoke, the whispery sound of the sugar cane moving at night. The lush private warmth of my mother's lap.

Winston was silent in the falling dark. Then, in a beautiful bass, he began again to sing:

Nuh cry, nuh cry, nuh cry me poo chile,
me gwan be here all day till nite.

Anna, lying quietly, ensorcelled by his voice. Which floats to her, *soul distress*, across his particular darkness.

And then?

Then I got a job, almost immediately, at a beach resort. The tourists liked boy waiters, cute and compliant. I had a white uniform, with epaulettes, a white cap with gold braid, and a pair of neat white gloves. I held the tray up high, like a waiter in a movie. I smiled and winked, brought them lizards and pineapples. The tourists lay on long chairs under the palm trees and wasted time. There were little bells, just like breasts, stuck up on the tree trunks, and they rang me for drinks. I trudged across the sand with martinis and fruit juices, drinks of all sorts decorated with tiny umbrellas. My life was entirely governed by bells. I spent all my time, every minute, listening for the ring.

Did you hate them, those people?

No, not really. I was much too busy trying to please. But every night I cried for my mother and sisters. And I had a dream, a repeated dream, that Mr Allfrey held them captive in his shiny red car.

He is so silent now that he might have stopped breathing altogether. Anna tries to miniaturise Winston and imagine him as a boy. She sees him slight and gangly; he would have been boyishly angular in his cap and uniform. She sees him holding up a golden pineapple, high on a tray, and then her imagining fans out, opening semi-circular, and summons instantly and from who-knows-where a series of post-carded and sun-bleached visions of tourist-Jamaica: conga lines, steel bands, curved and perfect beaches drenched in lurid tropical light. The inauthenticity of this fantasy dishonours the life of her lover. It is memory, not vision, Anna wishes to know him by. The fluency of her brochure-like invention appals her.

Winston whispers: I've never told anyone these things before. You're the first one.

Yes, said Anna. I know. Don't regret it, afterwards.

Their space together is now joint, hermetic. Outside city sounds crash in an arbitrary disorchestration and sleepiness sweeps over Anna like a sudden fog.

Why is it, she asks, dropping off, that you mimic your mother's voice?

It's my voice too, answers Winston. Don't you understand?

———

She dreams her lover Winston is piggy-backing her over sand. The sun is blistering and the sky is hard and remote. Abstracted palm trees lean and bend gently towards them. The sea in the far distance sounds exactly like rain; but it has none of its thunder and seems merely to sprinkle on the shore. In the middle of nowhere, like a prophecy, Victoria materialises. She waves to them both. Her breasts are exposed and she is ringing a bell. We should go to her, says Anna; we mustn't be late. Her arms link tightly, in a kind of stranglehold, around Winston's neck.

3

Within just a month, Victoria has weakened. It is as if giving up her own stories depletes her of something vital. Yet she is an avid narrator, and looks forward to Anna's coming as though her life depended on it; this contradiction is somehow at the basis of their relationship. How is it possible, Anna asks herself, that Victoria wills her own fading, just as she comes so amply into being?

Sometimes she watches the old woman sleeping and sees the delicate blue flicker of the process of her dreams. She persuades herself that biography is futile. Beneath closed eyes lies this woman's *inaccessible* complexity.

A nurse visits, once a day, to check medication: she draws the curtains, fluffs the pillows, takes her patient's temperature. Nothing serious, apparently. The women joke in French. The nurse, Cécilia, is from Quebec; she has four children, all sons, and a good-for-nothing husband who drives a lorry.

In six weeks, says Victoria, I'll be dead as a door-nail, and I want no ceremony at all. A cremation, impersonal, and no blubbering from anyone. Surrealists only believe in the future tense.

Liar, thinks Anna: this woman who inhabits remembrances with trance-like conviction.

I'll be cinders. *Cendre.* Madame Cinderella. *Madame Cendrillon.* Victoria chuckles.

Cécilia leans across to Anna, brushing her face.

Don't worry, she says softly, she'll go on forever.

Anna catches her gaze.

I mean it. There's nothing wrong with her. She's just old and stubborn.

I can hear you, calls Victoria. Plotting my demise. The sooner the better, thanks-very-much.

Anna looks across at Victoria lying on the bed, and knows that each evocation she offers, each story she tells, implicates their two separate lives in a bond.

What was that? she calls again. What did you say?

We said your place here is pretty kooky, answers Cécilia, gesturing at the Surrealist decorations around the room. Damn kooky, I say. *Fou, Madame. Fou.*

Foo, foo, fee, foo, sings Victoria, delighted.

Jules, abstemious, was out of place. He had never wanted to come to the party and stood there soberly, judging us all.

I was flirting with Ernst, who wanted a triangle.

I was wilful, cruel. Leonora, Ernst and I danced together.

Do you want to know what I wore? I wore a chiffon dress of lemon and a string of jet beads. I wore lemon stockings and lemon shoes with buckles of fake diamonds, and long gloves in creme with buttons of fake pearls. And my feathers, of course. I wore my feathers.

Ernst removed a glove with his teeth, peering down at me, commanding, blue-eyed and carnivorous; then Leonora smiled all the way to her incisors and removed the second glove. They draped them like scarves around their necks. I saw the shapes of my fingers dangling loosely at their throats; I was intoxicated and expectant, hoping for obscenities. The sound of rain, pure and black, rose above music from the gramophone, and the room revolved around me, with Jules' face in it, blurred.

I can no longer remember the sequence of events. Jules and Man Ray had been quietly discussing photography, and Salvador Dali had at some point intervened. I heard words spin out in a tone of accusation; then Dali seized — rather cinematically, as though purposeful and rehearsed — a bulbous orange vase and smashed it against Jules' temple. Water, tulips and shards flew out everywhere, and Jules fell heavily, hitting his head on a sideboard as he went. He was broken and bloodied. Dali was nauseated by the sight of blood and fled from the room with Gala alarmed and in hot pursuit. Man Ray bent above Jules, examining the wound.

Victoria pauses; she seems upset. Here her party-night jump-cuts and falls into edits and distortions.

And then? says Anna. And what happened then?

It was raining, I remember. It rained light Paris rain.

Since it was too late for the Metro we made our way to the Boulevard to find a cab. The streets shone brilliantly with rainwater and the lamps reduplicated. He leant on me, my Jules. Blood streaking from his face soaked my lemon chiffon.

In bed, later on, we lay close together. Our hair was still wet.

Your friend Dali doesn't like to be contradicted, he said in English. Nor does he like Jews, he added in French.

Juif, Jules . . . jewels, bijoux . . .

I put my hand to his face. I had patched his wound with white gauze and an incompetent bandage so that he looked like a soldier, fresh from battle. The skin at his eyes was already beginning to stretch and darken; in the morning they would be purple (*Two pansies,* he said) and his face brutally swollen.

Juif, Jules?

There were things he hadn't told me. Like his brides, knowing nothing.

My stained chiffon dress was there on the floor, quiet and formless. I thought of Baudelaire:

Je t'adore à l'égal de la voûte nocturne
O vase de tristesse, ô grande taciturne.
(I adore you as I adore the vault of the night,
O vase of sadness, you who are so silent . . .)

111

After his disappearance Jules persisted supernaturally; he was ineradicable. When she was alone Victoria thought often of Jules; over the span of absence his phantom arm still lay warmly across her breast, cupping at her heart. She knew that on her deathbed, in her very last moment, in the tiny wind of life that was her very last feeble gasp, she would still be remembering him. Sometimes she resented this everyday haunting he had bequeathed her. The stories he left behind — an entreating outline — with no body to attach them to.

When he was a child of about nine or ten years old, Jules Levy went with his mother to buy some new shoes. In the shoe shop, the best and newest in the city, was an astounding contraption; it was an X-ray for feet. Jules inserted his feet into a small dark box, and looked down from above into a narrow viewing chamber that revealed the skeleton. He saw his own rather anaemic, knobbly, misshapen feet transformed to the most delicate pattern of bones; it was a glimpse, he said, of the inner beauty of things; it was like a vision. There they were, not ordinary and everyday, but gleaming, almost glassy, designs in white marble. This machine had little to do with the sale of shoes — and it was removed from stores not long after, when the dangers of recreational X-rays became apparent — but they were for a time immensely popular. Jules lined up again and again, to peer inside his own feet. To marvel. To be astonished. To see the hidden made visible in a wand of weird light.

It was this machine, he said, that gave him an interest in photography. He loved the body on a screen, its aesthetic reproduction. He loved the world in tonalities of black and white: a face becoming mica, the negative space of any shadow. His first images, unsurprisingly, were of his mother, Hélène. He photographed her standing in front of a bright window, so that she was the mere shape of a mother, with no details at all; then he photographed her standing with the window to one side, so that she was a bright half-face, exemplified in each line and each specifically personal mark. Then, standing outside, Jules photographed Hélène through the kitchen window: she was here complete, and wholly visible, her face glowing like a lamp in its shady frame. This triptych seemed to the child an entire understanding. He recognised prematurely his own lifelong metaphysic.

Nearly done, he called out, crouching behind the lens.

Her face broke into a simple smile. *His mother's face.*

During his teenage years Jules photographed every single thing around him: the apartment in Lyon he shared with his mother was exposed hundreds of times, caught in prints whose lunar shine he kept stored, with fastidious care, inserted between layers of dark-coloured tissue paper. The almond tree in the square was also endlessly photographed; it was a tree proliferated and divided and remade like no other, captured in every angle, every light, every state of bloom or non-bloom. The old man who slept each day by the Tabac, at a perfect angle to the open doorway. Bicycles leaning against the wall at school. Garbage. Flowers. Girls eating ices. The large toothless woman who cheerlessly served them. For Jules the photograph retrieved something from death, something unidentifiable but nevertheless essential. He felt an elation, a quickening, with every click of the shutter.

At night he polished his camera as if it were Aladdin's lamp. Then he kissed it, wrapped it, and placed it carefully under his bed.

Jules was lying beneath the piano, photographing his mother's feet as they worked the brass pedals, when he had his first attack of an ailment he would describe as his shiver of mortality. He felt a sensation of constriction in the chest; his pulse began to beat at double its rate, and his pounding heart was so forceful that his whole body began wildly to tilt and sway. The attack lasted almost thirty minutes, during which time both Hélène and Jules were convinced he would die.

The doctor diagnosed tachycardia — unusual speeding of the heart — and said that he should learn to live with it, that nothing much could be done. It was an ailment that would assail him, like a seizure, at unexpected moments, and each time his heart accelerated Jules wondered what secret parallel life he might elsewhere be leading. He wished too that there was a viewing device, something like the foot X-ray, by which he might examine from above his convulsing heart. This way, he felt sure, he would be less afraid.

On the day of his first attack Hélène had been practising a Ravel piano concerto written for the left hand. She sat on her right hand, so that she could master this difficult piece without acceding to the organic temptation to play with both. Jules remembers seizing the wrist of her right hand to signal his distress, because he felt he was dying, because his whole body was pulsing, and because his mother, undistracted, was blithely preoccupied with playing the piano. The music halted abruptly and Hélène bent down; she saw her son open-mouthed, quaking, his whole face distressed.

Single-handed, Jules Levy would joke to Victoria; I learnt about mortality with an accompaniment, single-handed.

In the darkroom Victoria watched images of herself emerging. In a chemical revelation she floated into being, silver and shiny. Jules swayed her face and her body in the developing emulsion, and then hung her, dripping, among the rows of brides. She saw herself reversed, whitened, immobilised, etherealised, shrunken and wholly contained within rectangles. She was almost unrecognisable to herself. That moonstone flesh. That objectivity.

In the dark-room light his skin was varnished bright red: her ruby jewels.

Kiss me, she said.

She stood on tiptoe to reach him and Jules bent obediently for a kiss.

Victoria slid her hands into his trousers and asked him to undress her. He fumbled at the fake pearl buttons of her blouse, and one pearl pinged off, rolling somewhere into the darkness. She placed his slender hand directly on her breast: *This is my heartbeat, heartbeat, heartbeat, heartbeat, uncontained in any rectangle.* She slid her two hands around to his belly, and peeled away his trousers, slowly releasing him, then rubbed against his thighs and fondled his penis. With the force of her whole body she willed him to develop.

Above them lustrous images swung. Beyond his shoulders she could see herself naked in miniatures. Upside-down and downside-up. He had made print after print, so that she was a multiplication.

Drops of fluid fell, and she wiped them from his body with her blouse.

It was only afterwards that Victoria noticed that they were both partially dressed: Jules still had his shirt on and she still had her skirt on.

They were like the two fitting halves of some mythical unphotographed creature.

And it was only afterwards she pondered his casual remark: 'over-exposure and under-exposure are both forms of invisibility.'

4

In the waxy beige light of late afternoon Victoria is lying asleep with her mouth wide open; a fine thread of spittle shines on her chin. She appears to be dead, but her breathing is audible. Cécilia has left a purple-coloured cyclamen on the bed-table beside her; the intensity of its colour and its pretty liveliness accentuate Victoria's pale emaciation. As Anna leans across the bed she catches a coil, as of incense, of the honeysuckle aroma of desert dust; or is it the similar scent of warm dried apricots? Old people begin to smell of all they have met, Anna thinks. They surrender to the permeability of elements. They capture time in these bodily and distillate ways.

When Victoria wakes up she believes, for a second or two, that there is a snail moving silently along the ridge of her cheek. Anna must pluck it away; she obligingly lifts the invisible creature and pretends to flick it out the window.

Is it gone? Victoria asks. Her tone is forlorn. She is still on the dreamy periphery of delusion.

Gone.

This range is difficult and Anna is still unused to it; she finds herself strung double-crossed between fussy old-womanliness and a capricious storyteller who is pleased to pronounce on the superiority of her knowledge and experience. Victoria discloses a life gaudily melodramatic and striped with punctuation marks; yet she sobs, she is depressed, she beads each narrative with ellipses.

Let me wipe your chin.

Piss off, Anaesthesia.

Anna wipes her anyway. For Victoria the hand moving the cloth at her face is her mother Lily-white, long ago. She sees a net of black fingers and gauze dabbing at a wound. It was a childhood fall, perhaps, or a scratch from a tree. Perhaps too there is a scar there, or a blemish, or a faint pearly mark. She props herself on her elbow, shaking herself awake, to feel the forgotten surface of her chin.

Fetch me a mirror, she calls. A mirror. Quicksmart.

Anna watches as half-awake Victoria, bent on confirmation, seeks herself in a face-sized circle of light. The old woman peers, disconsolate. Anna takes a broad comb and gathers her wispy thinning hair.

Tell me, demands Victoria, the plot of *The Comedy of Errors*.

It's pretty ridiculous, answers Anna.

All the better. Tell me.

Well, the plot turns on two pairs of identical twins.
Two?

Silly, isn't it? And both pairs of twins have exactly the same names. So there is Antipholus from Syracuse and Antipholus from Ephesus. Then there are identical slaves, Dromio from Syracuse and Dromio from Ephesus. Both sets of brothers have separated as infants, master with slave. They meet up again in Ephesus, together with their loving and long-parted parents, and all's well that ends well; happy ever after.

So what are the errors?

A series of misrecognitions as the masters and slaves mix up, and a legal tussle over a gold chain, a carcanet.

A carcanet?

In the end everyone is reconciled; all misunderstandings resolve . . . Winston is studying the slaves, who are beaten throughout the play — they're forever being struck around the head with comical violence — yet they are more witty, funny and intelligent than their masters. *Methinks you are my glass, not my brother,* one of them says, and finds himself handsome. In the end they head off together, hand in hand, since neither wants to be the senior brother.

Victoria is silent.

Carcanet, she repeats. You must bring Winston in to tell me properly. You've skipped too much. You can't tell a story.

I always wanted a twin, says Anna wistfully. I thought it would be a kind of inevitable companionship. I wanted to see another me, to be reassured.

Infantile, snaps Victoria. Infantile fantasy. Anyway, truly identical twins are not identical at all. They are mirror images of each other. I knew two girls once who were alike in everything, but their insides. One of the girls had her heart on the right side of her body, and every other organ the wrong way round. Vera, I think her name was, let me hear her right-sided heart. I put my ear at her chest and said yes, it is true.

True, Anna is thinking. *Vera*. She suspects that Victoria confabulates. Yet it is true that inside of things is incommensurate with surfaces. She adores the deep-bluish tone of Winston's skin; but more than that she adores the Winston-child, resting his head silently in his mother's lap, overcome by a shy and irremediable sadness. Images, outsides, do not suffice. Images do not tell their love-making propinquity or the intimate hallowing of their mutual time. Every artist knows this: the mendacity of images.

When Anna thinks about her mother, Maggie Griffin, she also conjectures inner life; she wonders what compulsion or rationalisation enabled her to leave, what drove her, years ago, from her small needy daughter.

Griffo met Maggie Winter during his annual vacation, when miners headed south for several weeks to little towns by the sea. They crossed three hundred miles of red dry desert just to see the white frill of a wave and gaze at the undulating bowl of the ocean. Groups of awkward quiet men, still carrying in their bodies the slightly bent posture of mine-work, would fish together on the jetty, or meet in hotels, to talk in huddled groups about their dark lives elsewhere. Any local could pick them: they drank too much, they swam in boyish clusters, they were always restless. If a man was spotted watching the sunset with impassioned attention, or if he commented on the glorious roar of the waves, or if he simply stopped in the street and looked up at the sky with the expression of one who has discovered the inside of a temple, then he was a dinkum miner on holiday, sure and certain.

There he was — that bloke Griffo — jagging skipjack and herring and watching the fluke of a blue whale rise and plash heavily in the cold Southern Ocean.

Griffo met Maggie Winter on the very first day of his arrival. By accident he entered the wrong door of his small hotel, and she was busy at a table, sieving flour in a poky kitchen. She reached to brush away hair that had fallen in front of her eyes and left a deposit of flour dust, a pale cloudy shadow, along the rim of her forehead. Griffo stayed, making chit-chat, as the young woman continued making cakes. She had downy freckled arms and a rather childish face — she was only seventeen — and Griffo could not shift his gaze from the flour trace that so tenderly had marked her; it seemed to him a sign, a token, the luminous signature of their fate. He became assertive, confident, and ever more talkative. The couple were engaged almost immediately, and married five weeks later.

At their wedding Maggie pushed the stiff netted veil from her face, and Griffo was reminded again of the necessity of their union. He leant forward and kissed his bride as one kisses a child: lightly, ceremoniously, just above the eyes. The congregation snickered and Maggie was disappointed. And although she had liked the idea of being married to a miner — it seemed a pure, manly, almost heroic form of labour — when she saw the town with its tin houses and the insect-looking poppet heads, when she saw the pepper trees and the shaft holes and the borderless reach of dead dust, she knew immediately that she had made a terrible mistake.

Her new town was metallic, inimical, stunningly aglint in the sun, and her new home was unlovely. The new curtains were gaudy, the new lounge chairs uncomfortable, the spokes of their new electric fan, a desolate metal star, pierced her sad and transplanted heart. The Griffins lived in a new area built over old mine leases, and just one week after their arrival a neighbour's front yard, only three doors away, subsided twenty feet into old shaft workings. The house stood teetering at the lip of a ghastly hollow. It terrified Maggie, these sudden holes. She could not laugh with the others when they described the *whoomph!* and the comic-book puff of cloudy dust. The crater of a yard-disappeared stood as a sign of her own subsidence, the windy hollow she felt in the centre of her body.

Griffo doted upon Maggie, but Maggie doted upon

film stars. She spent their housekeeping money on matinee trips to The Palace, and loved lustily the silver face of every actor she saw there. They spoke with unAustralian accents and had consequential lives. Violins and pianos endorsed their emotions. They moved in secure rectangles, invulnerably bordered, and experienced the pleasure of genuine conclusions.

It was an unusual form of loneliness, this loneliness of projections. Maggie had entered a secret and synthetic life. In the flicker of darkness she felt complete and verified, but as she emerged blinking and agog from matinee screenings she could not bear the blinding real that swept forward to claim her.

A year later, when her only daughter was born, Maggie's life was cemented in the mode of unglamorous dismay. She looked into the eyes of her infant and saw there an image of herself, incredibly diminished. She wept for days and days before Griffo realised that she would need time away, in a hospital.

He looked back, past the swift-moving, uniformed nurse, to see his wife rigid, alone, gazing fixedly at nothing. Her face was turned to the wall. A shadow consumed her.

So what does this mean?

It means that Maggie Griffin had already left. Maggie had left the goldfields even before Anna was born. The handsome visitor, an itinerant worker with slicked back hair, a steady stare and a fetching scar tilted diagonal across his cheek, offered a wise-cracking movie-tone, narrative of escape. When he spoke of riding the railway right out of the desert, when he invoked aeroplanes and ferry tickets and panoramic travel, Maggie fell, like Ingrid Bergman in shadowy Casablanca, into his waiting arms.

Years later her daughter Anna will fashion more complicated explanations, but this is simply a lonely woman, depleted and disappointed, who can no longer endure the realist insufficiencies of her life.

Anna is eavesdropping. From the corridor, out of sight, she can hear Winston reading Victoria the entire script of *The Comedy of Errors*. His voice is a theatre of dexterous impersonations: he manages different and particular voices for each character he performs. The slaves have East-Ender accents, vigorous and rude, and the two Antipholuses sound absurdly like old Etonians. Victoria laughs out loud and interjects comments and obscenities; occasionally she mimics Winston at the business of mimicking. They are frauds together, they are having a ball. At the end of the reading comes soft and modest clapping from the one-woman audience (*Bravo!* Anna hears), and some blurry muttered comments from Winston in response. Then he appears at the doorway, carrying the potted cyclamen.

Look what Victoria gave me. No one has ever given me flowers before.

Winston is delighted.

Classy lady, he says, nodding towards Victoria's room. She asked me to marry her.

This is the moment — Anna knows it — of irrevocable feeling. Her swollen heart flies out to meet him. Anna sees the integrity of his smile and his fabulous complexity. She has fallen in love with a married man from Kingston, Jamaica. A man who will leave her. A man who probably does not and would not ever reciprocate.

She moves forward and brushes grains of dirt from the potplant that have settled on his sleeve. It is a modest gesture. It is the only gesture she can think of that allows her to approach and touch him, without betraying the Shakespearian extravagance of her feelings.

The petals of the flowers look startling and vivid; Anna glances away so that she will not fall into this new facticity of things, this spell-binding world remade by the force of romance.

They catch the Underground to Drummond Street, to share an early dinner in an Indian restaurant. Winston hugs his potted cyclamen as though it is a trophy. Strangers greet and smile at him. He jokes, and play-acts. In the darkness, under the streetlight, his face is a full moon; Winston is radiant, Winston emits light.

When other children slept Anna was awake, imagining. The desert around her was a forest of symbols. Sometimes, in the summer heat, Anna stayed out on the verandah to look up at the sky. Stars trembled in their millions and wind sang in the air. In the distance she could hear the mine batteries pounding and ore rumbling along a conveyer belt in linked metal trolleys. If her father was underground she tried to imagine his location; she selected the shape of a distant tree and thought yes, he is there, exactly there; the roots of the tree feather downwards towards his head. When she thought of the tunnels and the excavations, the subterranean blackness, she thought also of the moons the miners carried before them, their reversed outerspace, their night-shaded other-world. If he is dead, she reasoned, someone's moon will find him. A splash of circular light will discover his face. The tree will then mark the place of his grave, and reach downwards, until it finds him, and feed and grow strong. She repeated her made-up prayer to protect her father:

Gentle Jesus kind and wise,
Let my father be alive.

But as the shadows gathered and the easterly wind rose in the darkness, she grew nightly more afraid.

Several times Griffo returned in the grey light of early morning to find his daughter sound asleep on the back steps, or on the verandah. She was always curled tightly in on herself, enclosed, moon-shaped. He would pick her up carefully, retaining the circle, and carry her inside.

When he woke her in the mornings, before he went to bed himself, Griffo had the dismal appearance of a corpse. His face bore a drawn and ashen quality, and Anna could smell the deep earth embedded in his skin. They moved to the kitchen where the wood stove had already been lit. Tea was brewing in its dented green enamel pot. Father and daughter ate porridge and said nothing to each other. This life, decreasing. Anna watched Griffo vacantly line up objects on the table, the teaspoons back to back, the teacups side to side. She longed for a chatterbox. She longed for something far-fetched, for something foreign, for anything at all that might awaken and enliven her.

Anna dear, let me tell you; I have just remembered.

Jules and I went once on a short holiday together. He had a large job — a wealthy family, whose wedding was spectacular — and with the payment bought rail tickets from Paris to Venice. It was low season, winter, and we booked a room somewhere in a backstreet, very near the centre, very near St Mark's. I remember mist rising from the canals and the floating buildings. The quicksilver sky. The boats riding on reflections. I had never seen anything quite so beautiful. Jules took photos and developed them by borrowing a darkroom; he photographed doorways, church spires, the dark cave-shapes of alleyways. Bits and pieces of buildings; nothing whole or complete. I remember noticing at the time that he loved incompletion. Worn walls. Rooftops. A particular pattern in the paving stones. He also took a series of portrait photographs of me. I still have them; I'll show you. Without my feathers, of course, but I was still impressive. We looked, I think, like a couple of honeymooners. Every day I powdered my face and drew scarlet on my lips; and I bought a new hat, a scarlet cloche, which I wore incessantly.

In any case, this is what I want to tell you:

On our third day in Venice it rained and rained,

and St Mark's square began to fill up and flood. We stayed all afternoon in a café reading, just wasting time, waiting for the rain to stop, and when we set out in the evening to return to the hotel, the square was inundated, completely underwater. It was extraordinarily black and shiny, like India ink. Lights reflected everywhere: twinkling stars. Jules hoisted me up like a child and piggybacked me across the water. We were both laughing, slightly hysterical; we were both very happy. The rain was still falling, and I held an umbrella, a scarlet umbrella, high above us . . .

Do you know the Surrealist game called Exquisite Corpse? Participants compose a fantastical body by contributing a drawing of some body part to a folded-over piece of paper. You can't see what the others have drawn and when the paper is opened out, there it is, a hybrid creature, something new and amazing. This is what I thought: *We compose our own exquisite corpse.* I was thrilled by the inky water, and the piggy-back, and the absurdity of it all.

The next morning, our last, it was still softly raining. Jules took one of his photographs of me, folded it into a boat shape, and set it floating upon the bright watery square of St Mark's. I can see it now, my own face, boat-shaped and marvellous, drifting slowly away from us.

Honey-moon, Anna. Why do you think they call it that?

5

Anna was reminded instantly of those paintings by Max Ernst, in which women have the peaked and almost monstrous heads of birds, and flounces of iridescent feathers streaming like cloaks down their backs. When she entered the drawing room Victoria was wearing her feathers, standing in birdlike silhouette, an optical illusion, peering out of the window. For the first time Anna wondered if other people had considered her mad, if this propensity for display, this pompous mummery, had ever enabled others to hurt or disqualify her as a crazy woman. The feathers were so dark they had an oily sheen. *Where had it come from, this head-dress?*

An hourglass, commanded Victoria. I want you to buy me an hourglass.

She was having a good day, and was up and about, alert, perky, dispensing orders.

So I can observe and calculate how much time I have left.

She moved behind her Cocteau screen — her eye appeared in a star-shape — paused for thirty seconds or so, and then reappeared.

Well? What are you waiting for? Toot sweet! Anna Griffin, toot sweet! toot sweet!

So Anna is on an errand for imperious Victoria; she sets off to scour the second-hand shops of London to find her prize.

The seasons are now in shift; the air is chill and diaphanous, but there are the beginnings at last of a spring moderation: buds have begun appearing, there is a milky quality to the light. In the past two months there were times in which Anna believed quite seriously that she would not survive the English winter. Her chest heaved with ice; her breath was frosty; she felt herself freezing inside-out. Winston had reassured her: if a Jamaican — who carries the sun of his home in his bones — can endure it, so too can a sunny Australian. They put their hands inside each other's jackets, as children do, for the swathe and the enclosure of a warming embrace.

In the first store the owner tries to sell Anna an eggtimer; and in subsequent shopping she has no luck at all. True hourglasses, it seems, no longer exist. She enters a phone booth papered over with advertisements for busty prostitutes, and begins ringing antique shops, one by one. It feels a fool's errand; yet she is anxious to placate the feathered old woman for whom the hourglass is somehow the colophon of every loss in her life. After fifteen calls Anna has almost run out of money, but one of the dealers suggests she place a request in the Antique Society newsletter. She does so with her very last coins, in a desperate measure, over the phone. When she returns to Hampstead it is late afternoon and already almost dark.

Winston was sitting with Victoria, drinking tea. The two turned together, guiltily, like co-conspirators.

Victoria says: *The Comedy of Errors*, Winston tells me, is all about identity, about hazarding loss as a premise for the possibility of redemption. That's right, isn't it?

Winston simply grinned.

And it's about error as the condition of all identity, yes?

Yes.

(Jesus, thought Anna. Now she's a literary critic.)

We've been talking about our countries, too.

She's been telling me, said Winston, about the black people, the Aborigines.

(Jesus, thought Anna. What could she possibly know?)

About spirits, persists Winston. Why have you never told me?

Anna is trying not to look exasperated.

I couldn't find one, she said. I couldn't find a fucking hourglass.

Victoria is supercilious.

Don't worry, you will, Ms-darling-Anna-chronos.

———

They sleep secretly together, in Winston's single bed, and Mrs Dooley is ignorant of the romance that has reshaped her establishment.

This ephemeral wedding, claimed against an authorised marriage. It is the cramped cosy dream of spaces more expansive.

Their couple, their star-crossing.

They are absentmindedly happy, pretending against pretence that their parting will not happen.

That night Winston awoke from a nightmare that set his whole body trembling.

I dreamt my wife and son were held captive in Mr Allfrey's red car.

Son?

My son James. They were pressing their faces to the glass and calling my name, but for some reason I couldn't move my body at all. Both my legs were completely frozen. They were cold and stiff. I was trying to use my arms to drag myself forward, but still I couldn't move. James began crying. His face distorted.

Son, Anna is thinking. *Winston has a son.*

This was not the time to ask. Yet she feels a vague, ignominious pang of jealousy. She feels excluded. And she thinks irrelevantly of the hourglass she failed to locate, its soft soft draining, its obscure symbolic claims, its empty/full, empty/full resemblance to a body. Anna stretches to enclose Winston in the compass of her arm.

Sleep, she says. It sounds like an instruction to a child.

But he rises away from her, turns on the bedlamp, and reaches, still trembling, for a cigarette. Anna watches as he fumbles with a box of matches.

Let me, she offers. These things will kill you.

In the long run, as Keynes says, we're all dead.

Some consolation!

Winston turns now and looks at Anna for the first time since awakening; for her benefit he manages a wry half smile.

I'm sorry. It upsets me. It's pathetic, I know.

They are moving closer. The more we say to each other, Anna is thinking, the harder it will be to part later on.

Winston switches off the light and smokes hidden in the darkness. The shawl of night wraps them protectively, as though they have become lovers in a fairytale.

I should have told you about James, I'm sorry. It just seemed so private.

Yes. Private.

But it is already forgiven. Anna is so in love with this man that even his firmest secrets, even what he will not share, have become of inestimable value to her. A spotlight of red ash tracks the route of his hand.

Sleep, she says again, this time more tenderly.

In Victoria's memory it was a day towards the end of winter, just as the seasons were beginning to change. She and Jules were walking together along the quays, along the right bank. The Seine was churned up, swift, and brown. They crossed to the Île St Louis, then to the Île de la Cité, and sat on the small ironwork seats arranged in rows at the back of the Notre Dame. Daffodil and crocus bulbs were beginning to unfurl in the garden; it was reassuring to see colour in the cold grey soil. The air was brittle and fair. A few tourists were looking up, exclaiming, snapshotting gargoyles and spires. Jules was already a soldier; soon he would leave.

It was the beginning of 1940, during the period known as the *drôle de guerre*, the phoney war. Although Britain and France had already declared war on Germany, there were at this stage few signs of wartime in Paris. Air raid sirens sometimes sounded their high nervous wail, filling Victoria with a kind of imprecise dread, and there was occasional anti-aircraft fire at German planes on reconnaissance. But over all it was a dull winter-time, a period of anxiety, boredom and existential inertia. Jules had been called up, but the exodus from Paris had not yet begun, nor had the rations, or the curfews, or the German soldiers in the street; nor too had the bombings, the terror, the forced wearing of yellow stars. The season was changing, lighting up, but history was veiling France — this was how Victoria thought of it — in deeper shadow.

Jules and Victoria were having a friendly argument about painting. Beneath the dreary façade of the Notre Dame, Victoria was railing against conservatism and romanticism as the twin enemies of art.

Beauty must be *convulsive*, Victoria pronounced, or not at all.

Merde, responded Jules. Surrealists are tricksters, frauds.

He favoured art that was still, contemplative and above all, luminous. He adored the paintings of Claude Monet; each bold pastel daub on each gorgeous waterlily was an act, he claimed, of spiritualised concentration.

Victoria sneered: How conservative, how predictable.

Surrealists! I hate them all, said Jules good-humouredly. He leant forward and kissed Victoria playfully on the lips.

Jules remembers going as a child with his mother to see a Monet exhibition. He says he stood before a painting of the Gare Saint-Lazare, and saw only an incomprehensible haze. Hélène explained that this was a painting of the effects of steam; the obscured train at the station, hidden almost entirely by clouds of blotchy paint, was the consequence of an artist enchanted by steam.

That was what she had said: *enchanted by steam*.

The mystery, Hélène continued, is that not everything we see is altogether clear; some things present themselves as nebulous instances of the beautiful.

Nebulous instances of the beautiful.

Jules still remembers his mother's words because it was an occasion of understanding. He had looked into the painting and seen the train, there at the station, heavy, formidable, heading directly towards him, even though it was barely visible as an impasto smear. He still remembers, too, exactly what his mother was wearing: she wore a tawny belted dress with a white lace collar, and shoes with sequences of buttons, covered in leather. She carried a coral pink embroidered handbag, which rested at her hip.

Soon, said Jules, all this, all this art-talk, will be irrelevant.

Never, my Jewels.

This was the day, Victoria says, this day on the cusp of spring, the day before war-time eclipsed Paris with invading emergency, that Jules took her with him to see something special.

A *transparent instance*, he joked, of the beautiful.

He was both pleased and annoyed by his Anglicised nickname, but said that if Victoria would persist with it she must see the real Parisian jewels. So after their talk on the ironwork seats behind the Notre Dame, Jules led her a little further along the Île de la Cité to the Palais de Justice. There, inside its crudely formal, strict and ugly boundaries, they came upon the church of Sainte Chapelle. Jules led Victoria inside, first to the lower chapel, and then to the upper. The lower was lovely enough — gilded groined buttresses, rich orange columns decorated with fleur-de-lys and the towers of Castille, a statue of the Virgin, faded and thoughtful-looking, in a lapis robe — but it was the upper level which invoked the experience of entering a jewel. The upper chapel had walls entirely of stained glass, mostly in tones of azure and rose. With the light, even in winter, even just before war, it was a space of pure refracted brightness. In lancets reaching upwards were depictions of Bible stories, rendered in garnet, emerald, sapphire, gold, and they cast a flush of coloured light into the chapel chamber.

For the King, explained Jules. For Louis the Ninth. This is his palatine chapel. It was completed in 1248 and built to house the holy relic of the Crown of Thorns.

Victoria turned towards him; he was looking up at the ceiling, which was covered in thousands of fine gold stars.

What? You think a Jew shouldn't know such places?

Victoria took his hand. He led her around the chapel, naming each of the Apostles, pointing out special details, whispering the Bible stories.

What you see here are mostly Old Testament, he said with a smile. My stories, too.

His face was enamelled by the heavenly tones of stained glass.

Not as beautiful, of course, as the main Synagogue of Paris.

Jules was still smiling.

This place makes you happy.

Yes, how could it not? There are no shadows, have you noticed? And there is Isaiah and the Jesse tree. A sign of God's faithfulness. The Israelites were worshipping idols and falling into sin, but he ordained a tree of which King David was the fruit. *He shall not judge according to the sight of his eyes, nor reprove according to the hearing of his ears*. Book of Isaiah, chapter eleven. Out of desolation, promise.

That was what he had said: *Out of desolation, promise*. Victoria still remembers, since it was an occasion of understanding.

Coloured light shone down on them. Light from trifoils, quadrifoils, diamonds and rectangles. Victoria stretched her hand into a beam of violet, then Jules, like a medieval courtier, bent forward and kissed it.

There *are* shadows, she said.

You Surrealists, he replied, so damn literal-minded.

Jules once argued that photography takes its power from attention to shadow, rather than the mere capture or registration of light. The placement of shadow, he claimed, is what produces the image. Shadow is no reduction but the adjective of the image. The transfer, the mysterious transfer, of ambient accentuation. Like ice whorling upwards, he said, from a skater's bright path.

Within a week Anna had a phone call, offering her an hourglass. It was a splendid thing, an eighteenth-century specimen from Avignon, in France. The ampoules were bulbous and firm, and of a glass which had within it traces of bubbles and imperfections; and the frame was of ornate brass fashioned with two phoenixes, one facing up and one down, curved slenderly and protectively around the phials. The stands were heavy circles of blood-veined marble, slightly chipped. Inside was not sand, but finely ground egg-shells, sieved so that each grain was exactly the same size. The old man in Covent Garden who held it before her said that hourglass 'sand' was often difficult to manufacture: sometimes it was marble dust from the quarries of Carrara; sometimes it was lead, or tin, or even river sand; sometimes it was the black saw-dust from the carving of marble tombs. In each case it had to be dried, rid of impurities and rendered in grains the same size. Often these substances were boiled in wine, skimmed, dried, then boiled again, up to nine times. The phoenix hourglass contained its original egg-shell.

Anna took the glass, upended it, and watched grains speed through the aperture. She paid the enormous sum that Victoria had entrusted to her, and purchased the hourglass.

On the Underground she held it in her lap, like a baby, afraid it would drop. Afraid time would break open and irretrievably spill.

6

Tour Eiffel, Palais Royal, Notre Dame, Jardin des Tuileries, Père Lachaise, Montmartre, Le Tour Saint Jacques: these sites existed as tokens of tour-guided knowledge, as plastic currency exchanged endlessly in the feverish acquisition of Paris.

This was a city Victoria knew both as an Antipodean stranger (her Plan de Paris fluttering open before her) and as a dedicated Surrealist. Famous spots on the map, touristic X-marks of simplified and summarised attractions, seen already by everybody and already over-encoded, were in the end less charged than the circuitries she felt on her skin; the tiny streets of the Marais that hid sparky alliances, the ac/dc of market stalls and noisy bars. Not the blue-guided or Baedekkered *monuments illuminés*, but the golden colour of faces that emerged lit from any doorway, the Chinese lanterns swaying like hips in cafés, like the abdomens of women composed of rose-water light, strung there in a smile shape, to shine on lovers below. The plate-glass refractions from zinc-countered brasseries. The glint off a saxophone somewhere smoky. Light rays shot, iris to iris, in the electric moment of seduction.

When Jules left Rue Gît le Coeur, he took Victoria's heart with him, so she re-learned the city at night and with heartless promiscuity. Paris was a vessel of ink with all messages still merged. A well of darkness, totally fluid.

Victoria donned a jacket of spangles, so that she wore a cover of stars, and carried her own milky-way out into the streets, strolling down boulevards, along the quays and into cafés, shining. She spoke imperfect French to perfect strangers, and seduced them with her air of abandonment and desolation. A man's hand entered under her dress as she sat over her Pernod, and she let him explore there, his face yellow with desire. She brushed against priests and old men riding home on the Metro and blew kisses to small children and rich ladies in hats. In the tunnelled spaces along the Seine she saw the twin moons of eyeglasses slide eerily towards her, and matches flare to cigarettes protruding from half-faces, to resolve in punctuations of smouldering orange. Chestnut sellers stood over braziers that exhaled sparks in the wind, little spurts of red stars, flying upwards.

Victoria was unafraid: she was waiting to be murdered. She sought out darkness. She chose the danger of shadows. She fucked standing up with her dress hitched around her. She thought she saw a hand drift over the river and trace a line in the sky, a kind of script of her death, a prognostication.

(But I will be no-body's Nadja, she thought to herself.)

On such a night, dressed as galaxies and desperate for a kiss, Victoria, *tenebrous, bereft, disconsolate*, took a cab-ride to the Parc des Buttes Chaumont. It was almost midnight as she entered and walked along its curved paths, paths lined with hoops and sulphurous lamps and tall trembling trees, paths leading, every one, to the Bridge of Suicides. She was like the swan which floated quietly on the ornamental lakes; she was silver, a mythology, and bent on reversal. She was like a figure in a story-book, condemned to live with no heart. She made her way to the suspension bridge linking the artificial rocks with the artificial island, and looked across at the belvedere, lit from below so that its dome was a skull in the sky, and then she stepped onto the space of suspended mortality. The metal grille was surmountable and the foothold nervous. The space below was inviting; it was pure black silk. But something in her paused. Morbid romance repelled her. Wanting obliteration she did not want a death others might retell as café talk.

So Victoria instead crossed, and mounted the rock, and sat alone beneath the high bright skull of the belvedere. The hole in her chest banged with what had been possible.

From this elevation she could see faint trails of

white paths, and lamplight in small spheres arcing
away into the woods. There was water somewhere,
and the sound of a waterfall, and somewhere too a
white swan, a proper sign, untrespassing, cruised with
its blond reflection across deep black water.

And it was then — as though, after all, she had suc-
cessfully summoned something to destroy her — that
a man appeared from nowhere and flung himself upon
her. It was so quick that Victoria took a moment to
realise she was being attacked; she was grappling with
a male-shape saturated with the odour of vodka; he
was pressing his thumbs at her yielding throat.

Not like this. Not like this.

Victoria raised her knee sharply to his testicles, with
just enough force to disturb him, then taking advantage
of his confusion and the dislodgment of his hands,
kneed again, much harder. The man toppled sideways,
groaning, and she scrambled and rose and kicked twice
at his ribs, all the time imagining another murderous
scenario — that she might push him, her substitute,
from the Bridge of Suicides. No one would know.

But Victoria saw her own sequins decorating the
prone body. In their struggle metal stars had released
from her jacket and sprinkled her assailant with stip-
ples of light. And now he was crying, in loud sobs, and
the light patterns bobbed, so that she was seized with
love-of-life and an urge simply to flee. She hurled herself into the darkness, back along the narrow walkway

of the Bridge of Suicides, back down into the woods and along the pale pathways, past statuary and monuments, and ornate lamps casting light poorly, and ran like a criminal who was fleeing a crime-gone-terribly-wrong. As though she were the guilty party.

When she emerged from Parc des Buttes Chaumont Victoria had to run forever down the shadowy street — outlines flashed past her, yellow headlights stunned — before she came across a cab that would take her to safety . . .

What a cliché, said Leonora. The Bridge of Suicides.

She rubbed arnica cream tenderly on her friend's wounded throat. The man had left his thumb-marks there — two mauve and yellow pansies.

Leonora bent and kissed the spot where death had almost happened. Max Ernst entered in his dressing gown; he kissed her too.

Because she wore the breathtaking pansies her assistant gave her, because Jules had taken away her heart and left her a heartless automaton, because it was 1938 and Fascism was rising and fear was a web in the air that brushed everyone's faces, Victoria was more than usually absorbed in Surrealist distraction. She strolled to the Café Le Chien qui Fume to hear Breton's lucubrations: he extolled revolution in art and sexuality in all things; he spoke as though the marvellous alone would defeat Hitler and collage would demoralise the bourgeoisie. He speculated on primitivist urges and waxed racist on Black Venuses.

Their cunts, Breton declared, are our mystery, our homecoming. They are the darkest most unconscious places we know. Nature with no lights on. (At which point, for dramatic effect, he put his hand over his eyes.)

Josephine Baker, he continued, is a Surrealist *par excellence* in her pitch-black nakedness. Her skirt of bananas is the exemplary girdle, the phallic containment of convulsive womanliness. When she dances, Africa wakes in us.

Bullshit, Victoria thought. She saw his head, like a dirigible, floating in smoke. Pink light from *nouveaux* lanterns played erratically across his face.

She was fascinated and appalled.

But somehow André Breton signified Paris itself. He was what Victoria wanted, and also what repelled her. He was Europe. He was Surrealism. He was high-aestheticism. Victoria had carried her own nationality like an inferiority complex, convinced of the superiority of all-things-European. Sometimes she felt like a person who had grown up in a country with no mirrors, so that she knew herself from the chest down but had no familiar face. She felt unknown to herself. Lost in Paris. And when she said out loud the word *Australian* — perhaps it was like this too for *Canadian, Jamaican, Indian* — she heard resident in her own voice an apology and deviation. The accent was wrong. The vowels sour, uncouth.

Nusch Eluard, with her heart-shaped face, hailed Victoria and came over to kiss her on both cheeks, but she was kissing anonymity. She inclined her head and said in a hushed wispy voice:

He's such a bore when he starts on black women, don't you think? So arrogant. So dumb.

Her eyes were flecked with lights and she wore a collar of broderie anglaise, so that her face was on a plate with a doily, almost consumable.

Victoria kissed her doubly in return.

Your neck, Nusch asked. Which bastard lover was that?

And then for some reason Victoria began to weep. In the Café Le Chien qui Fume whole oceans opened up in her, and she drowned Breton, and his wife Jacqueline, and Paul Eluard and Nusch, she drowned the waiters in long aprons and the men with cigars, she drowned the accountants and the schoolteachers, and the idle gossipers and the travelling salesmen, she drowned junkies and musicians and Don Juans and kleptomaniacs, she drowned poets and prostitutes and *agents provocateurs*. She wept for herself because she was a body others pressed their intentions on. She wept for her own loneliness and her depatriation.

Victoria was a hodge-podge of surfaces and angles. When later she saw Picasso's *Crying Woman* at Rue Des Grands Augustins, she saw her own portrait. Her shattered face, in his studio, at number seven.

But now she was still caught up in oceanic thrall, and still deliquescent. Nusch's arm was around her shoulder and she was being guided outside. Zinc furniture winked at her, faces drifted past. In the pink light everyone had achieved tints of porphyry and coral. A glass door swung away and night flooded to meet her. She pushed forward with the blunt heaviness of somebody moving underwater.

She was — what was she? — the starfish others gazed at.

Why did Jules leave?

Victoria had closed her eyes; she was still locked in that flood-lit moment of weeping.

During this time Victoria went often to the movies, and always to the same movie-house, just to sit in fake darkness. In the daytime, half-empty and with a kind of fusty air, it was precisely the smothering occlusion she required. A box to pour her sadness in. A public *camera obscura*.

The building itself was a kind of vault. A high ceiling, like a theatre. Neo-classical cartoons. Corbelling. Buttresses. Shaded lamps on the cornices. It felt very safe and entirely de-temporalised. Victoria descended the tiers of steps guided by a no-nonsense usher who wore a cap and a brocaded jacket and carried a small bright torch which sent thin searching rays into the smoky auditorium. Faces turned, in unison, to watch the two women as they passed.

Victoria sat in the front row, so that she could believe that what appeared was for herself alone.

There were claret velvet curtains that parted with

the audible creak of rollers, and then the magnifying glass, into which Victoria fell. So many flawless women with pearly faces. So many taller men bending to kiss. Victoria listened to couples making love and the usher descending with her ray. She could hear raised voices and swearing and saw the torchlight flash. But she loved it, this amorous darkness, in which she was wholly alone, with her own face, silver, flickering in and out of visibility . . .

So why did Jules leave?

Jules left twice. Once because I was a bitch. Once because of the war. I was mean and cruel. I mocked his photography. I was infatuated with Leonora. And Max Ernst, and Breton. And I flirted and fucked around.

Why?

Desire panicked me. I was overwhelmed.

You, Victoria, can do better than that.

I can't, truly. It was a kind of panic. Mad love — that's what they called it — mad love was a panic. *Amour fou.*

Victoria went silent and stared at the rings on her hands.

I went crazy after he left. You know that, don't you. Crazy with grief.

Yes, said Anna. I know. *Amour fou.*

Secretly Anna is judging Victoria Morrell. This woman speaks in the register of the hyperbolic; she is unsubtle, she exaggerates, she commemorates her own life with self-conscious fuss.

I know what you're thinking, Victoria says.
No. No you don't.

In her depression everyone existed as though behind glass. They were all remote and coldly removed. She almost believed that if she reached out she would touch not a person or a human body but some inflexible, taut and intervening surface. Victoria spent her days in the cinema and her nights roaming or attending parties. She drank and became lost. She scandalised herself. She ringed her eyes with night-shaded kohl and donned black feathers and white stars, and thus in showy weeds dragged herself into the glassy city, the city in which surfaces reflected not her but her miserable shadow. There she was in blurred versions in the front of cafés and brasseries, estranged, self-haunting, her reflection diasporic. Once it occurred to her — glimpsing some fleeting and evasive copy — that just as her swan was the wrong colour so her stars were asterisks for noth-ing, referring to meanings that had drifted away and without which some crucial meaning was inexplicable.

And each time she re-entered their apartment on Rue Gît le Coeur, she expected to find her Jules returned. The bed still bore his shape and the curtains waved as they had when he was there. There were the garlic bulbs on the windowsill he had assiduously cultivated. There were potted plants she had purchased that he had undertaken to keep watered: a particularly vivid pelargonium, African violets, ivy. There was the window shape that had framed him, since he liked to gaze down at the street, and its rectangle hung like a portrait of what explicitly was not there. The double bed they had slept in was entirely mnemonic; Victoria could hardly bring herself to climb under its covers only to find his persistent scent, and her own heart in quick-time, and her own erogenous rush. Sometimes she woke from dreams thinking he had returned and was beside her, but she found herself, empty-handed, embracing only air.

There on the wall was a trace in chalk of his profile. And there, his Turkish slippers, still nestling aligned under the bed. Superstition prevented her from moving and disposing of them, and they rested, twin boats and ridiculously long, beneath the green fringe of the emerald coverlet they had married their milky bodies on.

Victoria could not paint: half-finished images littered her apartment and were propped abandoned against walls. She was useless and unmotivated. She ate hashish, which burnt her throat, and then drank to excess, and tried violently to vomit out all of her sorrows.

One night Victoria dreamt of a network of kissing of which she was the centre. Nets of kiss patterns tessellated, lips meeting lips, kiss-cross, kiss-cross, until a kiss that had begun with her arrived at last with Jules. In this dream her desire travelled Surrealistically to find him, stretching out into night-space, travelling down half-lit streets and in the bellies of heaving trains, across fields reaching in long stripes under glaring full moonlight, into laneways, into briny ports, all the way — in a zoom effect — around head-shaped France, finally finding the bed upon which he now lay separately sleeping, his brown eyes closed.

Anna searched in Victoria's drawers while she slept.

Victoria possessed an enormous number of gloves, in every colour, some paired and some single. They were something she collected, a kind of obsession. The pairs were pinned at the wrists with small golden pins and the singles formed their own piles, neat and multi-coloured. There were also scarves and assorted beads; and secreted away, wrapped in tissue paper, was a fossilised starfish, perfectly preserved. A few dozen French post-cards, none of which was addressed to Victoria, lay tied with lengths of sepia-coloured ribbon. There was also a photograph, cracked and stained: Victoria with her arm around Pablo Picasso.

At the back of the dressing-table drawer was a box of ancient items — an opalescent buckle shaped as a broad-petalled flower, buttons of bone and of pearl-shell, small coin-shapes of amber, and a single satin shoe that was ash-smeared and smelt of smoke. There too rested Victoria's mother's journal, and Anna could not resist peering inside. Small fragments were legible, but for the most part it was written in an unfamiliar script; it looked furtive, illegible. Only ampersands, their filigrees, were at all familiar, but connection was clearly the least of its meanings.

Victoria woke suddenly.

I dreamt my brother was above my bed, swinging his swords. Here I am, an old woman, and still afraid of him, she said, in a voice quiet and tiny like that of someone dying.

Anna held the journal behind her back.

THE SWAN

Cygne, oiseau des marges
Swan, bird of the margins

(Edward Jabés, *Le Livre des Questions*)

There is a stringency to writing biography that Anna seems unable to observe. She had imagined a process of solidification, like the building of an identifiable face out of clay: the slow, careful achievement of feature and definition. But the more Anna knew of her subject the more imprecise she began to seem, the more dispersed in story, the more *disincarnated.* She assembled her notes and transcriptions in a chain before her, and saw not the neat confirmation of a life, but its meagre supplement. Not attestation, but its barest trace. Biography works, she thought, as reliquary does, investing in fragments. She remembered seeing the index finger of Galileo mounted in a small ivory and gold tower in the science museum in Florence, as though it signified something other than the adoration of his acolytes. The finger pointed to heaven, recapitulating cartoon-like his cosmic imaginings. And when Anna tried to take a photograph a museum attendant appeared from nowhere to sweep down and prohibit her — *no! no! no! no!* the woman shouted. She gestured at a poster depicting a camera cancelled by a huge black cross.

What black crosses operate now, to prevent one person knowing another? What X-marked cancellations?

Anna is striving against the treason of images that Victoria has presented her with, to try to impose order on her information. She writes the words *skeleton plan* in the centre of the page. She will build the body anew. She will start with the parents.

It is a ludicrous reduction, but Anna Griffin begins to try to meet Victoria Morrell once again. Novelistically.

(i)

Victoria May Morrell was born in Melbourne, Australia, in 1910, to Herbert and Rose (née Boyle). Herbert was a banker and investor, fabulously rich, and Rose a society beauty of the hourglass, peaches-and-cream and rose-budded variety. This implies a parental species of cardboard cutouts — indeed one can almost see the spherical belly alongside an amphora of womanliness — but in fact both parents were unconventional, even eccentric.

Herbert Arthur Morrell had a passion for collecting — such as only the truly wealthy can indulge — and sought out objects on a criterion of radical unAustralianness. Contemptuous of the local, he

chased with laborious effort and at foolish expense
exotic knick-knacks, gewgaws, art-works and curiosities. *Foreign* was a word he loved to roll in his
over-dentistried mouth. He wore suits of Assam silk
and smoked Havana cigars; his shoes were English and
French and his hats inevitably Spanish. He was both
lavishly multinational and stubbornly monocultural,
and believed that the millionaires of the world had a
duty to destroy nations in the interests of laissez-faire
capitalism, so that in the end the Universal Marketplace would mother-succour all (his own chosen
phrase, it must be added, garnered from the
Melbourne *Argus*).

No more nations! Herbert declaimed, rather
grandiloquently, in boardrooms — to the alarm of
bewhiskered men with kangaroo-and-emu shaped tie
pins and investments in wheat-and-sheep, some of
whom thought him traitorous (though a damned
spunky fellow) — and he would go on digressively to
describe the features of this or that new taxidermic
acquisition, a falcon in a bell-jar from the Royal collection in Persia, prized as much, he explained, for the
scimitar particularity of its shiny beak as for its hunting
prowess and general nastiness. The Persians are a race,
he went on, for whom everything is symbolic: they
cannot see a beak but think sword; they cannot see a
woman but think honey. (Here the board-roomed men
exchanged baffled glances and conferred.) They are by
habit indolent, effeminate, untrustworthy and sly, but
have arts of the highest distinction and calligraphic

genius. *Why I have myself* . . . and here Herbert would extrapolate with an authenticating traveller's tale, concerning adventures connoisseurish, gustatory or haremesque, that disclosed once and for all the pan-symbolic nature of Persians.

His utterances were legendary and widely reported, and no board meeting, apparently, was ever dull.

Herbert Morrell had opinions on every race and nation on earth and had systematically ranked them. At the top of the list, at one hundred per cent, he placed Great Britain, Great Britain the incomparable. This was a nation he considered peerless in its qualities and achievements. He thought of steam engines, country manors and Westminster Bridge, of butlers with white gloves bringing letters on a silver tray, and tier on tier of cakes and sweetmeats at Fortnum and Mason. He thought of dead Queen Victoria and her inestimable bosom. Her regal perpendicular. That nose. That chin. Of the words *British Empire*, which excited him, economistically.

Other races and nations (for he mentally conflated them) fell away in the steep declension of imperfection — the US at ninety-five per cent and Germany at ninety — right down to the Javans, the Peruvians and the lowly Hottentots. At the bottom of his scale were the Australian Aborigines, a people whom Herbert considered despicable since they were without markets, commodities and evidence of artistry, and moreover refused all the blandishments of Civilisation.

Australia would advance, he believed, only when the extirpation of the Aborigine was complete. In his utopian moments he imagined the nation renamed New Britain and the landscape converted entirely by hedgerows and elms, the final stage before an ultimate decomposition of all nations, whereupon the global marketplace would replace all known systems of government. He had written and self-published a volume on this topic, entitled *Whither History?*, and had performed numerous speaking engagements, the most prestigious of which were at the Melbourne and Empire Clubs. He considered himself ahead of his time, and was undaunted by a lack of official interest in his schemes. In the meantime he devoted himself to collecting objects and making money, and strode down Collins Street, his belly before him, knowing that wealth alone remained the incontestable index of worth.

Rose Mary Morrell, the woman before whom suitors grovelled and swooned, dissolving, weak at the knees, in truly disabling desire, was not interested at all in the construction of racial rankings or the envisioning of global markets. Born of a different class — her parents were indigent Irish, a farm labourer and a housemaid — she knew secretly but surely that wealth is always undeserved, and that value is always a perverse and calculating endowment. The invisible preciousness of things was never accounted for. Her father's meticulous memories. The bravery of crossing oceans. Threads of her mother's grey hair left in the creases of a pillow. She adored all her brothers and sisters and mourned daily for her parents, and it was perhaps this grieving disposition that gave her an elusive and ambiguous quality, so that even in conditions most social and pleasantly extrovert she seemed distracted by some inner and private contemplation. As she listened to yet another of her husband's mercantile monologues — he was engaged by profit, regulation, the delights of trade surplus — she thought of the unprofitable and unregulated aspects of things, the shape of her baby son's head, the bitten fingernails of her lover, the Melbourne rain, so Irish, so soft-dripping on the plane trees, and the relic of her dead mother's hair, curled Celtic and fraily intricate in the Whitby jet brooch she wore nestling against her heart.

This disproportion in the value of things was known to both husband and wife; but Rose was more ideologically divergent than Herbert would ever discover. Persuaded to the cause of International Socialism by her lover, the chauffeur, she read inflammatory tracts and workers' papers with idealist avidity, and made generous donations, anonymously, to a dozen worthy causes. Her beauty, she knew, designated her ornamental, so that she was beyond suspicion with regard to having ideas. If in company she forgot herself and produced an insight or a witticism, this was regarded as an instance of charming aberrancy. Men and women gazed at her gorgeous face and thought only one thing.

Rose Morrell, that is to say, was a clandestine

woman. Their enormous house in Kew filled up with strange and valuable objects, but she cherished investments of a more occulted kind. The concealed. The unseen. The barely-in-existence. Secrecy enchanted her. She was drawn to dreams and varieties of inner space. She gazed into the centre of roses and composed verses about water. She kept a journal written partly in her own coded language and copied lines of other people's poetry whose heartiness she delighted in:

Cushion me soft, rock me in billowy drowse,
Dash me with amorous wet, I can repay you . . .

(Her favourite: Whitman.) And she cultivated, most especially, her love for the tall thin man who stood out there in the cold in his rained-on cap and white kid gloves, the man who stamped at the ground with his feet and rubbed his freezing hands together, who blew visible currents of breath and hugged himself against the wind, and who in a repeated simple action she found entirely affecting, would lean forward to take an umbrella from the elephant's foot stand, pop it open before her and hold it up in a steady dome — her own little baptistery, her own holy place — so that she might be sealed in his compass from the driving rain.

The cabin of the car was pre-occupied by their sweet complicity. It was the core of something, a cushioned centre.

When the second baby was born Herbert Morrell

announced in a loud and gaudy newspaper advertise-
ment the Auspicious Arrival of Victoria May, sister of
Henry Edward, and Scion Additional of the Eminent
and Ever-expanding Morrells; but his wife was more
than usually elusive and quiet. Rose read in her daughter's face the immanent presence of her lover:
figments of his mouth appeared, the intimation of his
nose; her body was long with his gangly and unself-
conscious length, and her two tiny little hands looked
like the hands of workers, like hands reddened and
chafed and too much rubbed together. The baby was a
reinstatement, a bundle of *déjà vu*. Rose rocked her
and kissed gently the diamond-shaped fontanelle. She
peered and itemised, thought how unMorrell. And
when she awoke to attend Victoria at night — for she
had dismissed the nanny from all night-time duties —
when she stumbled with a flickering candle towards
the beribboned and lacy cradle (hypnagogic, dazed,
following a cry through the darkness), it might have
been her chauffeur she was stumbling to embrace. She
raised up the baby and held it against her, sexually
overcome. Its scent flooded over her. Its signification.

This Secret, Rose wrote in code in her journal, *is a
concentrated version of all my other secrets: 'the palpable in
its place and the impalpable in its place'* — since she
could never resist quoting a line of dear Walt
Whitman — *'O unspeakable passionate love.'*

*W and I were today in the Daimler together & he whis-
pered, as he does, sweet'eart, sweet'eart, & he held our baby
for the very first time. I thought he would faint away, his*

features were so very ghosted & so intense, but instead he lifted Victoria's gown & blew noisily on her navel, as I had seen my own father do, in that comical way, with a blubbery blow, like an uncontrollable kiss, & then he smiled, & then he laughed, & then we laughed together, & it was a truly wonderful moment, in our dwarf house, the car, with our baby, Victoria, the palpable hieroglyph of all our impalpable combinations, of all that rests between us & by which I celebrate myself . . .

We almost hit a tram, returning, we were so altogether distracted . . .

It continues to rain & Victoria inflates with my milk. H wants to employ a wetnurse but I adore my own breasts & their melony roundness. Her mouth is sweetness itself. She suckles like a lover.

Herbert Morrell was by most accounts obtuse to the obvious and seems never to have noticed Rose Morrell's truant affections, nor the chauffeur's overzealous and particular attentiveness. He continued braggadocio and monumental: detailing the varieties of his means of accumulating wealth, rejoicing in the peculiarities of lesser nations, and unpacking crates of impedimenta that arrived on globe-encircling ships. As he clipped cigars in the Melbourne Club, he told of his Cuban cigar clipper fashioned from the teeth of wild animals which was reputed to confer on the act of smoking obscure sexual potentialities; then he railed against the new Fisher Labor government, against miners-who-were-always-on-strike, against reprobates,

Aborigines, Henry George and the IWW. He also announced his intention to purchase as soon as possible a Voisin biplane, exactly like the one magician Harry Houdini had just flown at Digger's Rest to the wild acclamation of the Australian press. He would fly, he said, and nations would blur beneath him. He began, Houdini-like, to lust for exaggeration.

It was in 1913 that Herbert Morrell's family — minus the chauffeur and most of the house-staff but complete with a brand-new Voisin biplane — moved to the Western Australian goldfields in a relocation that was meant initially to last just one year. Herbert had decided to expand his large interests in gold exploration and believed — in a symptom others would later interpret as the beginnings of his paranoia — that his current managers were untrustworthy and in the service of a Jewish conspiracy. He would simply intervene and take over, and set things aright. Rose was stricken. She pleaded her case, to no avail, to remain in Melbourne, and in the end consented to follow her husband to the other side of the nation.

I am to be carted away into the desert. W weeps in his car & is inconsolable. He says he will hang himself, but I have made him promise not to. It is one year, I tell him. One single year. Then I will return & we will re-establish our lives, & in the meantime I shall write in my secret way, & I shall not contort my heart nor allow any forgetting; in candlelight I shall think of you, in that quivering circle in the darkness, in that mystic visibility which I carry to light our child, pushing away

at the swallowing shadows with the globe of my coming, tak-
ing her up, infolding her, kissing both of you at once . . .
Think of this, my love, kissing both of you at once.

(ii)

In a photograph of the Morrell household posed a week
before their departure Herbert Morrell has already
acquired — as though he paid cash for it — the look
of a man with a serious mission. He is seated solidly
with his legs astride and hands on his knees, his enormous belly appears upholstered like a horsehair couch,
and his face has that imperturbable and resolute look
common in fact to the faces of all men with thick black
moustaches and granite stares. Standing behind him is
his extraordinarily beautiful wife, famously hour-
glassed and dressed in a white satin gown and puffy hat
of tulle. She rests one hand on the back of Herbert's
chair and the other dangles casually a dainty parasol.
Her look is melancholy and completely remote; her
eyes are a light anaesthetic surface. In the foreground,
seated, are the children Henry and Victoria, clothed in
identical sailor suits of no known navy, and at the side,
flanking like wings, stand two neat rows of house staff,
all impersonalised in black uniforms with white
starched bibs. At the very back of the scene, depleted
by distance, there is a chauffeur in livery. Leaf shadows
speckle his face like smallpox. He is leaning on the
round shiny fender of a polished-up Daimler.

The magnesium flash has penetrated the grey

Melbourne air: faces are pearly and brightened, caught in an instant of false flashlight, and everyone, even the children, has achieved the requisite immobility, posed stock-still and unblinking — mortified, one might say — for the man with his head beneath the cloth and his single time-stopping, imperative, Medusan, glass eye.

Pose, the cloth commanded. And they all *posed*, inexpressively.

In this only known photograph of Victoria's whole family, so preternaturally lit and deadly still, the father is already absorbing all the life around him; his substance subtracts from everyone else, presence condenses to where he is, his aura is unmistakably totalitarian.

Rose, by contrast, looks almost lifeless; her hourglass is emptying. She has less than one year to live and her eyes seem to know it.

It is a photograph tinted by ruinous premonition.

(iii)

This Melbourne, this mother, this lover-chauffeur, will be lost to Victoria. It is packed away in a dark-room, with no images emerging. She will carry to her grave only a generic and eerily incomplete entrance hall, a cinematic compilation of columns, chairs and a chequered floor, together with the simple phrase *flame tree* drifting inexplicably within it. There will be no resolution to the mystery of these words. Victoria will greet her death still waiting for meaning as a bride awaits her lover.

Her first complete memory is governed by the will of her father. She is there, in the Voisin, squeezed onto her father's lap and rising steeply: it must have been an occasion only months after Rose's death. The Voisin was a biplane constructed of struts and boxes, with an engine and propeller behind and a steering wheel at the front, and as it ascended the wing fabrics tensed and relaxed, like the inhalations and exhalations of an ingenious automaton. It vibrated and heaved and was exceedingly noisy, and it seemed even to a three-year-old child too frail to buoy and carry their breakable bodies. Victoria could see wings above and wings below, stretched and translucent. She could feel her father's thighs move up and down as he worked the pedals. She loved the shape of his bracketing arms around her, his mechanical excitement, his voice distorted by speed. And as she rose up carefully to look over the side — feeling such a force of wind against her face that her bonnet blew off into the sky — she gazed down upon the earth and saw it sliding away. It was vermilion in the late light and pocked with mine-shafts, and little men — prospectors — left their labours to wave. Ahead and below the shape of wings skimmed over the ground and Victoria understood that this was their own projected shadow, their inhuman shape cast over an altered geography. She was thrilled and terrified. She peed in her underpants. As they lowered to the intersection that served as a runway, the black wing shadows grew to meet them, larger and larger.

Had the Voisin been able to fly higher than its meagre fifty feet and stay in the air a little longer than its mere ten minutes, Victoria would have seen not the outskirts but the centre of this town, this town gold-rushed into the desert and left there booming. In panorama it was a kind of anti-Melbourne, indecorous and hotch-potch, infernally heat-blasted, and also rendered mirage-like by suspensions of smoke and red dust. Solidity and dissolution were oddly combined. It both drifted and settled, wavered and fixed. Poppet heads poked up everywhere indicating major shafts; then there were boilers, chimney stacks, crushers and furnaces, as well as timber yards, tailing dumps, workers' shacks, and hotels. Not to mention condensers, cyanide plants, brothels and churches; railways, electric trams, horses and carts. Over everything, too, hung a prodigious din, since this was reputedly the noisiest town in Australia. There were already four hundred stampers and fifty crushing mills, and the sound of numerous air-compressors continually throbbed. Moreover each mine marked its own particular timetable — with a large degree of asynchronous variance — by systems of whistles, hoots, blasts and sirens.

The town was rip-roaring and uproarious, a greedy myth made visible. Its magnitude was as imprecise as it was megaphonic, and it would take something larger than a Voisin to chart its dimensions.

Victoria cannot locate the moment, or indeed even the year, when she realised that beneath the ostensible

town lay an entire underground. She thinks that perhaps she saw a map of the Midas mine or overheard her
father's all-time and favourite analogy — that travelling to the bottom of the main shaft was to make a
journey in darkness and upside down, as it were, three
times the height of the Eiffel Tower. On the mine map
the underground was a safe-looking geometry, an
upended skyscraper of neat chambers and levels; but as
men were lowered hundreds of feet into the stinking
ever-darkness, with the frail paisleys of candle-flame as
protective illumination, they carried those verticals
and horizontals inscribed in their brains; they were all
superstitious; they all sought to trick mapless death.
Down there existed a magnification of every man's
shadow; terrible shapes slid like assassins along the
walls of the tunnels. Anamorphic non-humans, hints of
negation. Down there geometry was their hope of
retrieval. Sometimes miners waited for the cage to
stop at their level to find that it had missed its mark by
almost two or three feet, so that they had to leap or
climb towards it with a shaft of nothing below them.

The space of terror did not appear on longitudinal
sections. Nor the caved-in sites of accident or
entombment.

As a small girl Victoria had no details at all; the underground was a mysterious, generalised configuration,
something to do with descent. She had heard vaguely
of catastrophe, and knew that her mother was somewhere buried. She had seen widows buying lengths of

black sateen and blue men doubled over coughing up gobs of red blood; and she had felt the earth shift and shudder as something exploded or collapsed. When as a young woman she learned of the leap towards the cage — that appalling gap, that cruel mismeasure — she felt her own heart leap, hoisted on their fear. But for now she was mostly unknowing and unafraid. The underground was a riddle she was considering, strange as the world from a Voisin and the black cross of its wing-shadow slipping like a symbol over the earth.

After the death of his famously lovely wife, Herbert Morrell postponed his return to Melbourne and became megalomaniacally intent on gaining more gold. Dividends obsessed him. Apart from his tin mine in Cornwall and his rubber plantation in Ceylon, apart from his shares in railways, steel production and the building of sea-going ships, the goldfields seemed to offer the prospect of truly world-dominating wealth. Herbert Morrell acquired a controlling interest in the Midas mine (and lesser shares in the Croesus, the Perseverance and the Lake View and Star), and felt for the first time the direct thrill of owning the labour of others. He governed timbermen, drillers, boilermen, blacksmiths, carpenters, millmen, miners, platmen, pitmen, tracemen, engine drivers, masons, feeders, tool sharpeners and battery men. He rested his fat cigar on his belly, copying the caricatures of himself beginning to appear in the *Weekly Miner*, and tried to calculate, with finicky pleasure, exactly how many workers he possessed. He theorised and imagined his own capitalistic enhancement, and saw himself unoriginally as a kind of European monarch, with his subjects arranged in a reverent pyramid, midget-sized beneath him.

Herbert Morrell opened and spread out the mine map for his son's perusal.

The Eiffel Tower, he said, is 985 feet high; this mine is 2,954 feet deep. The Tower produces nothing; it is a foolish French experiment, a white elephant, a stupid joke, a mere decoration, but this mine produces wealth, employment and national stability, and contributes daily to the Australian Gross National Product.

Whenever Herbert spoke of the underground he experienced an ever-so-slight sensation of choking, and remembered the workers who donned zinc-coloured, ill-fitting, macrocephalic suits, and then descended, looking hideous, to test the underground air. In a nightmare one of them came stumbling out of a dark tunnel towards him, whispering the word *ventilation* in a stertorous accusation.

So Herbert studied the Midas mine map for its unclaustrophobic simplicity. He ran his ring-studded finger down the length of the main shaft, trying to impress his son Henry with the full magnitude of his investment. Henry Morrell picked at his nose and asked not a single question. The boy was a buffoon:

Herbert cuffed his head. Then he hit again, and harder, until Henry flew sideways, toppled and fell. A wail rang out, and a sobbing gurgle. Blood appeared on the child's cracked upper lip.

Herbert Morrell examined his gold-nugget cuff-links, made in the current conspicuous fashion, and wished that his daughter Victoria was a boy.

(iv)

In the first year after Rose's death the children lived in perplexion. In that rowdy rude town with its subterranean rumours, they were tiny and unknown. In the streets, Nurse Tilly held their hands very tightly and they could feel her anxieties bloom around them like a summer storm. Tilly could not believe the boldness of the women and the men: they hailed her familiarly and talked to the children. She held her charges in the deep itchy clefts of her gown, and bruised them with the intensity of her fear of kidnap. Tilly cried at night, missing her home.

My Melbourne, she would say, claiming the whole city. I hate it here, she confided. I hate this noisy place.

A sneer, a sullen sneer, and a look crumpled by complaint. She flung her face into her pillow, operatically extravagant, and called on the children to witness the genuineness of her misery and prostration.

Henry and Victoria felt somehow that they should cry too, but the form of their loss was more imprecise than homesickness. When they wept it was for nothing that Tilly described, for nothing as locatable as a certain shady street in Fitzroy, or a house with pickets and a mulberry tree, or the slimy green Yarra, or the aqueous city cold. But *Melbourne* came to signify whatever it was that had gone: it sounded like a bell as they said it, *Mel-bourne, Mel-bourne*; it echoed with emptiness. *Mel-bourne, Mel-bourne.* It was a word that gaped in the middle, leaving something tender exposed.

Motherless, Henry Edward grew mean and morose, and was almost wholly inactive, but for the sport of pinching and biting his younger sister, and his habit of stabbing at mice and lizards with his antique swords. But Victoria, aviatrix, seer of vermilion dimensions, unfolded as a fantasist. Like a new-improved Voisin she flew about the house — her arms outstretched, her voice a ratchetty racket — and landed unladylike on couches of red velvet plush and *chaises* of preposterous and artificed elongation. She accompanied her own dramatics on the walnut organ and lit its curly candelabra when no one was looking. The house and everything in it furnished her own flighty imaginings. Secret rooms inside Victoria opened up like a screen — like their Japanese screen with its panels of pearlshell herons, treading carefully, one knee raised, in a black lacquer lake — a screen she could fold away again if a stickybeak like Henry Edward, or a cry-baby like Nurse Tilly, or a bossy-boots like the housekeeper Mrs Bossy Boots Murphy, ever dared to ask. Victoria's special place was in the curtain folds near the decapitated giraffe where she retreated to commune privately with invisible friends.

She was practising Surrealism. She was a child who knew that horizons swung and that the look of things converted, and understood that marvellous conjunctions reconfigure the ordinary as excitement.

If there is a beginning to her artistry it is in these recapitulations: the windrush, the planeview, the exploration and expansion, all conjured with the cheeky mightiness possessed by a small girl.

When Victoria was five years old Nurse Tilly deserted her.

One year, Tilly said. Your father promised one year.

She had eyes perpetually strewn with filaments of blood. She was a ragged thin woman, two thousand miles dislocated. Her velvet carpet bag — large enough, Victoria thought, to hold a dead baby — was passed to her through the tight wood-framed window of the train. She wept-in-buckets, hysterically, and then she disappeared. She was carried away, holding her hat, in a south-west direction, so that she could catch a boat and travel back to the sound she left trailing behind her: *Mel-bourne, Mel-bourne.* Victoria watched the last glimpse of her hand, and the tear-stained handkerchief palely waving.

Tilly's leaving was like a memory of something else. Feelings scooped out. Some part of her was agape.

Victoria lay in bed, missing her, listening to the sound of ore crushers and air compressors rumbling in the night. Whatever unfolded now was filled with empty black light. She wondered what blindness was like. Or being buried alive. She thought about the Midas mine but found it unimaginable.

(v)

Because the whole world was at war Mr Herbert Morrell, widower, mine-owner, fat-man of absurd notions, continued to deplore nations but resented, above all, the disruption to his industry. Gold profits were in decline, good workers were daily disappearing to enlist (seduced by handsome men in khaki with plumed hats and horses), and the mines were full of Enemy Aliens all plotting revolution in conspiratorial huddles or stealing gold by the tonful in their mouths and their shoes. Dalmatians. Croatians. Hordes of soon-to-be-scourged-Hun. Herbert arranged the importation of British timber-workers from the south, but most were unsuitable for mine-work or could not be persuaded to stay. (They spat up dust and cursed; they had never seen such a darkness.) So the Enemy was invited back and Herbert postponed once again his return to Melbourne in order to guard over and secure his underground empire, three times the length — he told everyone — of the Eiffel Tower.

He woke choking at night, his sheets a winding tangle. Herbert Morrell, Voisin pilot and international capitalist, feared the unions and their incessant talk on the topic of ventilation. In the underground men advanced against the earth itself, creating air, like little gods, where none had been before. At the stope they worked with jackhammers and shovelled ore onto trolleys, or now and then planted dynamite in the rock face, and hid as it blew. Dust billowed along the tunnels, insidious and death-dealing. It embraced them like a shroud, with a perfect grey entwinement. In the poor ventilation the miners sucked up silica, and when they stopped for a smoko they hacked as they coughed. Their chests were all corruption, eroded and wounded. So there existed a whole technology of air assessment: anemometers, metometers, konimeters and flowmeters; and then there were those men in ill-fitting suits, like the residue of a nightmare, like deep-sea divers, who descended, armed with instruments, to calculate the dangers of the air. They measured dust and the possibilities of cut lungs and phthisis. They lumbered in slow motion into a darkness studded with men's eyes, and dealt with miners keeled over from poisons and fumes.

Herbert Morrell liked to stand, boss-like and imperious, and watch his workers as they stepped into the metal cage. The labourers, the skilled and semi-skilled tradesmen, the machine miners with giant forearms and backs like heavyweight boxers. Crooks and larrikins all. But he was also secretly impressed by their evident bravery. That necropolis down there. The massive threat of pure earth. And he knew too that they hated him and wished him dead. When he looked into their faces murder looked back.

It was the war, of course, everything was the war.

Somewhere else in the world was a much larger necropolis, described in gory detail and with maps in the *Weekly Miner*. The rowdy town had sent off entire divisions, and the news was of trenches, explosions and men gouged open by bayonets, their guts forever foreign. Everyone spoke of *fronts* and *casualties, the Suez, the Dardanelles*. Unspeakable barbarities blossomed like poppies in conversation. Someone's brother had his face entirely blown away. Rats the size of kelpies gnawed at the hearts of strewn corpses. There were trenches like wounds, filled to the brim with flooding blood.

When returned servicemen began to linger pitifully in the streets, men armless or legless or crazy with mustard gas, men unmanly with tears and displaying embarrassing disabilities, Herbert saw his projected economic empire on the brink of collapse. New Britain was more and more implausible, and his schemes overall more remote and futuristic. Herbert hated the way limbless men still wore their khaki uniforms, folded back, flapping and pinned up where the arm or leg used to be. Henry was fascinated, and stared after them, snidely commenting; but Victoria always averted her eyes. For her the wounded, the amputees and the distraught insane were a new order of things, intercepting her understanding. She saw damage as adult. She almost feared the future.

Herbert retreated to the Bayley Club — surrounded as it was by a thick sandstone wall — to drink gin from Italian crystal and listen to mine-managers talk money-language.

If Herbert was lonely it was only the shape of his wife that he missed. He had enjoyed encircling her waist with his arm, or finding her entrance under the covers to take his pleasure. It had been a logical marriage, two shapes in coalition. For a while he used Tilly, and then, until the workers spoke of it, he visited the Japanese brothel in Brookman Street. He was pleased by the anonymity of the women's faces; under their solemn white masks of oriental face powder, with their hair a uniform dome and their costumes full and modest, they were almost as blank and unspecific as his wife had seemed. To him women were an outline, the cipher of an equation. He pulled at the pointy corners of his Belgian waistcoat, fiddled with the brim of his Spanish felt hat, and chose a woman at random. Something in their interchangeability excited him — and the way they closed their comma-shaped eyes as he moved above them. Sealing themselves up in their own private Orient.

Now the black woman, Lily-white, whom Rose herself had hired — a mission girl, compliant, well-trained for housework and general slavery — became the outline that Herbert Morrell, mine-owner, desired. Against war-stories and dreams of dusty strangulation, against men with flapping absences and the murderous intent of his workers, he held this narrow dark body, a body in whom he imagined every uncivilised simplicity. Contemptuous of her race, he nevertheless believed Aborigines the custodians of some secret and defining essence, some nocturnal mystery. He ruminated Darwinian and relocated his misgivings. Lily-white was almost not there, a symbol he banged against. She was a vault of differences. A treasure he wanted unburied.

So it was that after Nurse Tilly suddenly departed, and the walking wounded began to appear incomplete and khakied in the streets, and everything, *everything*, carried a quality of derangement, Victoria noticed in their house the quiet presence of Lily-white. In the past the black woman had slept beneath tin in the backyard, and worked mainly in the garden, a shadow variegated by leaf-light. Then she one day appeared in Tilly's old room, apparently invited, and began to roam through the house as though it were another kind of garden.

She touched objects very lightly, as if they were petals. She sniffed at the glassware and porcelain, and looked deeply into the brittle and unstamened hearts of Venetian lamps, fashioned unnaturally in the shapes of European flowers. She scuffed at the carpet with bare feet, treating it like dirt, and found patches of each room, those least well lit and beyond the glassy stare of stuffed animals, in which to seek her rest. And at night, missing stars, Lily-white would creep from Tilly's room or Herbert Morrell's bed and lie with her head on the window-sill or stretched across an open doorway.

Victoria saw her there, and spied.

Even now she tells lovingly of their first night together, and it is a kind of dream-story, an evocation, a condensation of intuitions.

Moonlight poured in on the face of the woman, whose eyes were fully open and fluid like oil, and whose face was coated with silver so that she shone like water. She lay on her back, motionless, with her two hands splayed open on the oval mound of her belly. Formal and composed. She had thin wrists and large feet and an aura of strict inwardness, and the whole room, it seemed to Victoria, was caught up in a pause of tensely held breath. Victoria was unafraid, but still she hesitated. She stood hidden and silent, rolling the hem of her night-dress up and down in a scroll; until at last she whispered as a greeting the only word that would pop into her head:

Mel-bourne, Mel-bourne,

It was the saddest, most indefinite word that she knew.

The resting black woman turned her face slowly. She seemed to have known all along that Victoria was standing there.

Come, she said. Not even needing to beckon.

They lay together in the embrasure, looking out at the night. The sounds of the night-shift rumbled over them, the crushing, the machines. Lily-white leaned close to smell the lavender in Victoria's hair, and the little girl, without knowing why, felt an impulse to weep. But then the woman spoke softly and asked her a question:

That long-neck, she said. What animal is that?

So Victoria took a deep breath and told her all about giraffes, and about Africa, where every single person is black, and about elephants and lions and deserts and jungles, about hippos with yawning mouths and pygmies with bows and arrows. It was as though she saw it all from a Voisin, extra-vivid and with speed. Images from story-books unlocked as she spoke aloud and found, fantastically, the special words to describe them. She filled the sky with her very own African confections. Exaggerated. Lied. Spoke like a mini-imperialist, creating a whole continent to suit her fancy. And when she finished Lily-white had fallen asleep beside her. Victoria felt euphoric. She rolled and unrolled her hem and looked up at the stars.

Victoria's childhood, like all others, has jarrings, arrested moments, bright distillations, and then long grainy spaces, fast-motioned and faint. She cannot at all remember when Ruby was born — she must have been seven or so, and old enough to notice — but Lily-white's baby was suddenly alive and present, affixed to her chest in a cosy bundle. Its eyes were all ink, its placidity remarkable; it was one of those babies everyone leant towards as though drawn by a new form of magnetism. Victoria let the new infant clutch at her fingers and rest her face sideways upon her shoulder. She loved its milky musk scent and its repetitious burbling. And when Lily-white permitted her to help with bathing, she knew at once that this act was a shared celebration.

My sister, my Ruby.

The tutor, Miss Casey, was also an instant presence, possibly arriving around the same time. She was freckled and French-speaking (with a smattering of rough German), and since she refused adamantly to live in a house with a black woman and her bastard, was installed, to the children's vast relief, in a large dusty room at the Australia Hotel. Mrs Bossy Boots was forever, from before the Voisin, just as father, Herbert Morrell, Midas-owner and famously wealthy widower, was permanently petrified as an absolute and unknowable emblem.

In this household there was a tough circuitry of affections. The cook Bossy Boots Murphy seemed to hate the children — Henry for his surliness and Victoria for her evanescence — yet she had a soft-spot for Lily-white and the joined-on baby, and could be heard cooing lowly and lovingly, like the pigeons she resembled. She bobbed Ruby on her bosom, kissed the top of her head, whispered lots of feathery and bird-sounding endearments. Miss Casey, on the other hand, was smitten by Herbert Morrell — the children smirked when she blushed and went girl-silly in his presence — but she also disliked Henry and Victoria and was punitive and mean. She thought Lily-white an animal, despised the baby, and sought unsuccessfully the company and indulgence of Bossy Boots (who disapproved her evident designs on the master and would not, *over-my-dead-body*, have this *upstart girlie* elevated, *never-ever*, *never-ever*, to mistress of the house). Herbert Morrell liked his daughter, but could not abide his son. He thought him gormless, a dullard and cowardly to boot, a fact confirmed when it was only Victoria who could be persuaded to ride in the biplane. And Lily-white, whose feelings seemed otherwise wholly reserved for the ink-eyed Ruby, knew too of Victoria's specialness and grew slowly to cherish her. The boy Henry existed as an emotional isolate, his heart a stone. He spent his childhood waiting to leave for boarding school.

When she reminisced Victoria spoke above all of Lily-white. When she unfolded the screens she kept folded within her, when she peered, through perdition, at those according and disaccording surfaces, she saw again and again that particular face.

Lily-white, she said, had at first taught her the safe and dangerous spaces of the house. She was disturbed by the Morrell collection of stuffed animals, and believed white people violated any number of spiritual laws; that white people held nothing sacred; that some were actually devils. The space behind the curtain near the giraffe — Victoria's special space — was designated by Lily-white particularly safe; and they would retreat there with the baby, sometimes to sleep, all three, as though they shared one body. Miss Casey learned to seek out Victoria there, and would drag her screaming back to the world of book learning.

At some stage, when Ruby was a wobbly toddler — this is the only way Victoria can remember it — her father left for Egypt on some kind of prolonged visit. It may have been, she thinks, in 1919; in any case post-cards arrived from Cairo and images of camels and pyramids were sent to Miss Casey, who read expur-gated versions of their father's travels to the children. She told only those details she thought would amuse them: vultures shitting messily on obelisks at Karnak, her father's visit to the Crocodile Grotto at Samoun, with its mummies of snakes, crocodiles, eggs and human beings. The Red Sea. Dead camels. Amusing and stupid Arabs. Miss Casey put her hand flat to her beige blouse, and giggled and giggled.

Victoria tried to imagine exactly where her father was, and in each version, concocted from the odd assemblage of images he had sent, he became lodged in a more and more peculiar land, some place where nothing sane or ordinary ever happened; some nation of pure extravagances. But it was good to have him away; the house was altogether more spacious and altered in tone. One day she crept into her father's bedroom, hes-itating even though she knew he couldn't possibly appear, and began exploring. There were lots of men things: guns, riding boots, a cap and goggles for the old Voisin. A black belt he once told her had been created from the hide of a savage. Things with stories. Fearful things. There was a falcon in a bell-jar that followed every move. Objects made of teeth. Forlorn beasts stuffed and mounted and no longer in living existence.

Then in a wardrobe she found an entire set of women's clothes, hanging perfectly still and hidden in semi-darkness. They were elaborate garments, many with panels, embroidery and transparent attachments, and out-sized hats decorated with pink tea-roses or yellow gauze, together with shoes lined up beneath them in neat matching couples. These were her mother's clothes. They were empty, lank and smelled like death. Earwigs scurried and moths lifted up: it was a little universe of soft and crushable creatures. Victoria stared for an instant, even touched the fluted sleeve of a cornflower-patterned dress, and then slammed shut the wardrobe. As she fled she saw her own face, peaky and child-androgynous, vibrate for a second in the crown-shaped mirror above her parents' dressing table. She spoke to no one, not even Lily-white, of what she had discovered.

It was not long after this that a strange man came to the front door and asked to see her mother. Victoria watched the scene from her place tucked within the folds of the curtains. It occurred to her, and for the first time, that perhaps after all her mother was some-where still alive, and hidden away like her wardrobe of clothes. Perhaps she was in a cave, or a mine, or inside some Egyptian sarcophagus. It was an appalling thought and one which made her tremble. The man was tall, thin, and spooky pale, and insisted on speaking personally to Mrs Rose Morrell. Mrs Murphy argued at the doorstep — pushing her pudgy body towards him like a hen — but the pale man became even more distressed and agitated. He flailed his arms and raised his voice.

Rose! he called out. Rose, it's me! (As if she was hiding alive in the house.)

Please Moira, he said, begging Mrs Murphy. Please, Moira, please.

Then Lily-white, who had been listening, emerged from the house, took the visitor by the arm and guided him gently into the garden. In a gesture of tender solicitude, she sat him down beside her on the gravel. Leaning close she whispered something, and the man let out a cry. He buried his face in his hands, shuddered and wept. Victoria had never before seen a grown man weep; and would never again see a man weep with such despairing abandon. Lily-white rocked back and forth, sang a song in her own language, and eventually the man rose, turned slowly, and walked away. Lily-white stayed there, singing, in the amber light of late afternoon, and it seemed to Victoria that her voice was full of plangent Melbournes. *Mel-bourne, Mel-bourne*, Lily-white sang.

It was a world, the child found, populated with many strange men. When she walked in the town with Ruby and Lily-white, men would often hail them with incomprehensible messages, and seemed somehow always on the verge of misbehaviour. They shoved their hands deep into their miners' pockets. Winked. Leered. Sometimes they burst out laughing at their own private jokes. One day a returned soldier exposed himself in the lane: he stood absurdly at attention, with one hand cradling his genitals and the other raised in salute, and sang out:

Reckon you'd like a bit a this one, ya fuckin darkie fuckin gin?

Lily-white averted her eyes, tightened her grip on the children's hands, and pushed carefully past him. There was a guttural spitting sound behind them, and a parting obscenity.

Is he a debil-debil? Victoria had asked, fascinated by what she had seen.

Nah, said Lily-white. He's a sick man. In the head.

She touched her temple, which was moist with sweat. Her eyes were large and lustrous and inflected by fear. She raised Ruby up onto her hip and they hurried away, slowing only when they met a black man, one of Lily-white's people, further up the laneway and resting in a shadow. They spoke to each other in their special way, then Lily-white laughed and continued home. When Victoria glanced back the second man waved; he was kindly looking after them. He was wishing them well and safe.

Because Aborigines were, on the whole, banned from the centre of the town, and lived mostly in shabby camps around its outer fringes, Victoria saw them moving down laneways, traversing the town in concealment in their small friendly groups. It was as though the town possessed secret passages and a world constituted by margins. When she thought of it Victoria imagined a double cartography: the laneways were a kind of net beneath which the mine-shafts invisibly ran, but these routes did not match up and this made a complicated pattern. It pleased her to think in such terms, of enigmatic routes and spaces, of mazed complications. She loved too the dappled and penumbral aspect of the lanes, so much nicer than pitch-darkness with its doomed-looking miners, and the way you could peer through picket fences and Mexican creeper into everyone's lives, and watch people on the dunny, and find cast junk, and garbage, and sad broken things.

But there are also memories of the laneway that have always disturbed her. A butcher up the road gave away his unsaleable bits of meat, so she had seen black people pass by carrying sheep's heads and horse's heads and other objects, obscured, in dripping hessian bags. This sign of their deprivation: the mucky scraps of butchered animals. Even when Victoria helped Lily-white smuggle tea and flour over the wall to her friends — there was a lovely starburst of hands reaching upwards to receive it — this image, this grisly image, did not quite dispel. A sheep's head, under an arm, its fat eyes staring, its neck especially bloody and slimed with viscera.

And it was in a laneway, too, that Henry blinded Lily-white.

Victoria was somewhere else, sitting in the dirt with the infant Ruby, and Henry summoned Lily-white to identify the lizard he had stabbed. He had pinned it through the gullet with a stick, and left it there, squirming. As Lily-white bent down to examine the creature, Henry pulled out the stick and then suddenly pushed it, like an arrow, through Lily-white's eye. She seems not to have howled — at least Victoria and Ruby didn't hear her — but came stumbling past, holding her face, which was gushing matter and blood. Her body was already acting blind, with one arm outstretched before her, and her movements anxious and uncertain, as though the world had been redefined in an instant by its impediments and obstacles. She found her way to the kitchen, and as the screen door banged Mrs Murphy's voice rang out: *Christ-Almighty! Christ-Almighty!* Ruby, in a delayed reaction, burst into tears. Victoria took the child onto her hip, carried her inside, and there they watched Mrs Murphy — who continued murmuring, all the while, *Christ-Almighty, Christ-Almighty* — tend their wounded mother, Lily-white, whose left eye was entirely split open and gone, whose beautiful face was ruined forever, and who was so very still and submissive beneath Mrs Murphy's large mottled hands, that the girls knew this was something calamitous and wholly irremediable.

Henry entered and the screen door banged once again. He lifted a pitcher of milk from the sideboard and tipped it into his face.

That night Mrs Murphy seized Henry — though he was almost eleven years old — and dragged him to his father's room to punish and berate him. Without knowing it, she used the belt that had been made from the skin of an Aborigine's back.

Lily-white was different, after that. She grew rather solitary and silent and walked awkwardly, with a slight tilt to one side. More than blindness assailed her; half her spirit seemed gone. She was afraid of Henry and her fear conveyed itself to Ruby, who put up her hands to her eyes whenever he approached. Henry enjoyed this, and teased her, making jabbing gestures in the air, and he so swaggered with his power to intimidate and scare that even Miss Casey grew afraid of him and stopped demanding schoolwork. Through her employer she arranged to have Henry sent to boarding school early, and on the night of his departure there was such rejoicing in every female heart in the house that Victoria thought that the roof of the house would lift off, or some other bewitching sign materialise to express or betray them. No one waved at the train. And Henry spat at them from the window.

He had been gone a couple of weeks when a crate arrived one day from faraway Egypt. Mrs Murphy and Miss Casey unpacked it together, *ooh*ing and *aah*ing in chorus as each foreign object was divested of its straw. There was a framed photograph of Herbert Morrell posed in Nubian dress (looking larger and more florid than Victoria remembered him), at which Miss Casey exclaimed, and sighed, and rested her hand flatly over her bosom above her starched beige blouse; and another of the Sphinx, its effaced features eerie. There were pots with inscriptions, a leather pouch of piastres, and rolls of fabric worked finely with designs of silver and gold. And below these, in extra straw, was a series of mummified animals: a heron, a cat, a small stretched-out snake, and then finally Mrs Murphy withdrew a mummified baby. Its face and hands were revealed, and it was an inadmissible object, of quite a different order to the other souvenirs that surrounded it. It was black-skinned, almost ebony, in its extreme desiccation, and its features had sunk inwards, stretched taut on resilient bone, so that it looked truly less like a baby than some miniature adult, shrunken, or perhaps tortured, by an unknown extremity. It was sheathed in a kind of rag of disintegrating cloth, with black hands holding it like kitten claws, clenched in on themselves. Its eyes were closed tight, with tiny lashes just visible.

What a sweetie! chimed Miss Casey. How very quaint! And peculiar.

But Mrs Murphy was repelled (*Christ-Almighty*, she whispered, crossing herself, criss-cross), and Lily-white, who had been watching the unpacking from a distance by the giraffe near the curtains, closed her one remaining eye and turned away.

Later, when it was night, Lily-white came for Victoria. They stole outside — she remembers an orange full-moon resting low on the horizon — and took with them all the mummies and a large iron spade. Lily-white carried the Egyptian baby close to her body, and seemed unable to speak. They chose a spot in the lane, a little way from the back of the house, dug a hole, and buried the mummies, one by one. Lily-white lit some gum leaves and swept veils of smoke over the graves, and then sang a song in the voice that resembled sorrowful moaning. The orange moon rested in her single eye. She looked tired and altered. Fearful of debil-debils. She was worn down by these white people and their barbaric predilections.

In bed later on Victoria tried to comfort Lily-white, but was instead thinking, for some reason, of those clothes hanging bodiless in the coffin-like wardrobe, and the strange man, the visitor, calling out her mother's name. For months she had been unable to bring herself to ask. But now, lying with Lily-white and speaking very softly so as not to awaken Ruby, she put her lips close as a kiss to the woman's dark cheek.

My other mother, she said. Where is she, Lily?

Lily-white drew in a breath, half-dozing, and answered slowly.

She gone, your mother. Gone to her spirit. Somewheres. I dunno.

Is she dead, Lily?

Yeah, Viccy, yeah. Your mother dead. Maybe in whitefella heaven. Or in her spirit place. Somewheres.

It was a relief to hear it. Victoria nestled in the dark triangle Lily-white had made with her arm, and they snoozed together, very close, each exhausted by sorrow, and by burial, and by untimely grief.

(vi)

Herbert Morrell was perhaps lost somewhere in Egypt; in any case he stayed away for several years. Miss Casey, poor Miss Casey, who was faithfully waiting, and under a romantic delusion of considerable profundity, grew unhappy and tetchy and talked to herself over cups of tea; her red hair became straggly and her beige blouses less laundered. But for the rest of the household it was a peaceful time. Ruby was suddenly a feisty little girl; Victoria discovered paintbrushes and brushed open her visions; and Mrs Murphy, time-moderated, was less stern and almost lovable. Only Lily-white remained exactly as she was. Her wounding had fixed her forever in a moment of distress, and left her there, marooned.

So when was it, exactly, that Mrs Murphy began taking the girls with her to the moving pictures? She would gather up her bobbled and scalloped grey shawl, pin it in the centre with a golden brooch featuring two clasped hands, then simply announce their excursion. It was somehow always a surprise. At the Lyric Picture Palace, sitting either side of fat Mrs Murphy, cosseted by fuzzy darkness and loving every minute, the girls saw a completely new empire of signs. Faces and gestures made startling by the elimination of colour,

bodies moving about with unnatural speed and jerki-
ness, mute declarations, tormented bold posturings.
Victoria adored the laminated quality of the images,
and the intervals of printed dialogue, always flowery
and in exclamation. No one was impassive and no one
ever stayed still. Life was racy. Middles were disastrous. Endings were happy. The women were all
gorgeous and the men all handsome. They saw heroines
with large eyes swept away on ice floes, bounders and
cads grabbing women by the waist, evil men with
moustaches, zippy chases in cars, daredevils in biplanes,
trains out-of-control. They saw Rudolph Valentino kiss
smouldering brunettes with tiny dark mouths and quivering presences. How the auditorium roared: it was
such commotion! The miners in the back hooted and
stamped their feet like thunder, so that the sound of the
piano was completely inaudible, and Mrs Murphy,
overcome, put her hand up to her mouth. *Christ-
Almighty*, she declared to herself, smiling.

At home Victoria replayed the pictures. She was
always the star, and everyone fell in love with her.
Ruby was given only minor roles — she was after all
still little and easy to boss — and together they
walked around in accelerated fashion and practised
virtually their own version of cinema-melodrama.
Victoria was clever at paroxysms (of desire and
death); and Ruby was a mimic of such skill she seemed
able to be anyone, and could cry and laugh and fall
over on cue. They even copied the convention of sce-
nic punctuation: Victoria held up little cards with

dialogue and flowers drawn on them, and they both stood still for a moment while their imagined audience read.

> Rosetta: Save me, my darling Duke!
> Duke: This very minute, my darling Rosetta!

Heroine swoons. Falls into Duke's arms. Victoria embraces her sister as she rapturously crumples.

Victoria Morrell looked directly into her sister's black eyes, and saw there the answering lights of a comparable ardour.

There were many different darknesses; even Victoria knew that. There was the darkness she had heard about, deep under the ground; there was the darkness of the cinema, pierced by a cone bearing images; and there was the town at night, into which, movie-crazy and Lyrically besotted, she sought out adventures. For a time she snuck out on Saturday nights, sometimes waking up Ruby to accompany her, just to peep into lit windows and spy on other people's lives. The two girls discovered that they were completely invisible: on Saturday nights everything carried a specifically adult visibility. In the pubs sweat-stained men bent and swayed — some had been drinking since the end of their short shift which finished at noon — and they became fluid-looking and indefinite and seemed aquatically sealed there, with the rows of bright bottles and the cedar piano, and the embattled-looking barmaids with rolled-up sleeves, sealed there in a queasy dank bubble of drunkenness, broken only — and it was a kind of shattering — when someone stumbled outside into the night to vomit or cry. (The girls held their noses and felt no pity at all.) There were the houses, too, small huts of ridged tin where light streamed out in little channels from rusty perforations, huts with women left alone nursing their babies by lamplight, and a goat tethered in the backyard, or a leashed barking dog; and the larger houses, mostly quiet, but for the occasional Rexanola gramophone or an argument or bash-up. There were sheds in which men in tight circles played card games in European, and the Glide-Away Roller Rink where couples, still with their skates on, smooched in the shadows along the outside walls. Trams slid past, all rectangular illumination, and over everything hung the incessant rocky rumbling of the mines.

Beyond the main street, tucked away, were rows of tin brothels, which Victoria found particularly captivating. Some of the women sat in doorways beneath lamps shaded by scarves, and they were posed spectacularly, like criminals or film-stars. They wore flimsy garments of elaborate femininity (beads, laces, boas of feathers) and their faces were made up so that they all bore identical expressions. Ruby and Victoria watched them apply lipstick and smoke cigarettes, then flick the butts into the bushes when a man came along. Neither girl knew exactly what these women did, but they appeared rosy-coloured and splendid, hieratic as sphinxes. In Brookman Street there existed a Japanese brothel; and these women were even more fantastically strange. There were only glimpses as they opened the door to a customer or moved in the backyard with a lamp to the toilet; but Victoria was in love with their rice-powder paleness and their dark lacquered hair, and the way they shuffled in the long pleats of their rustly kimonos. She and Ruby would climb the picket fence and simply wait; and then out into the darkness one woman eventually came, her white face bobbing like a petal on a wet black bough, her small lamp guiding her and perfectly steady. The sky arching above, the round face, and the glimmering lamp. It was a lovely thing, it was an apparition.

One Saturday night, at the end of such an excursion, they heard above the regular mine noise the sound of fire bells. Everyone else was running, so they did too, Victoria holding Ruby's hand and dragging her behind, and when they came at last to the fire it was both golden and disastrous. A crowd of assorted people stood in the street, some in their pyjamas and dressing gowns and one or two in roller-skates, and before them, exploding, was the Lyric Picture Palace. Its interior was lined with Baltic pine, and this made for an opulent and irresistible conflagration; the wood cackled and spat, the piano was ablaze, curtains had disintegrated in flashy display, and as they watched the walls leaned, then fell inwards, and on top of that the pressed-tin roof, embossed with lilies-of-the-field, crumpled in a spurt of brilliantly yellow flame. The firemen had withdrawn and patiently looked on from the sidelines, their tired faces burnished and their postures defeated.

After a minute or so Victoria realised she was standing beside Mrs Murphy. The old woman was weeping quietly and clutched at her grey bobbled shawl. When they turned and left together Mrs Murphy was still too upset to scold, the girls too inflamed to settle and sleep. Victoria would have liked to sing Mrs Murphy one of Lily-white's songs, one of those songs full of the sound of *Mel-bourne, Mel-bourne*, but did not know how. So instead she contemplated the streak of incandescence still distantly visible in the sky and added another darkness to her secret list, the darkness after fire.

(vii)

When, at fourteen, she was sent to boarding school in the city, Victoria could not believe the degree of cruelty inflicted on her. They all waved at the train, and everyone cried — Ruby was dramatically inconsolable — yet they did not call her back and did not change their minds. She watched Ruby break away and chase the train the entire length of the platform, and the crowd was embarrassed by her ferocious shouts and the wretched force of her sobbing. As the train drew away she looked so very small: this sister, seven years old, her heart publicly breaking.

———

Victoria knew nothing of girls her age and nothing of school life. The daily codes of the classroom were completely unknown to her. She wore a uniform, and was given books, but this was the merest disguise; they all somehow knew beforehand that she was an interloper, and ignorant. Her French, she discovered, was peculiarly accented and in some cases simply wrong, and her history — Miss Casey's history — a handful of bizarre and disconnected stories, all romantically charged and over-supplied with red-headed lovers and tragic kings. Teachers chided her and other girls mocked. Victoria experienced the terror of social non-entity. It was the loneliest time.

She will remember this period in two specific ways. The first was her friendship with Mary Heany, the large woman in the kitchen who might have been Mrs Murphy's daughter, so neatly did she copy that body and those skills. She hung back in the shadows, outshone by her kitchen. The girls hated her too: she was a Mick, and overweight, and dumb, and a cook. Her face was coarse and ruddy, her fingers were like sausages. Victoria knew immediately that this woman would care for her.

The kitchen was downstairs and at the back of the boarders' building, and Victoria discovered one day that Mary actually lived on the premises: she had a modest room, airless and dank, and it was decorated, rather dominatively, with the Sacred Heart of Jesus. In this large-framed picture, which hung directly above her bed, Mister Jesus, miserably solemn and conspicuously underfed, pointed with a burning finger to his exposed glowing heart, which was miraculously externalised, as though he bore a kind of kitchen cupboard buried in his chest. Victoria was entranced by the oddity of the image, and by the woman, Mary Heany, who sat sideways on the bed, her chunky knees protruding, complaining of her sinfulness. (Mary had a boyfriend, a dock worker, who visited Saturday nights, just — as she put it — to bounce to heaven on her body.) In the brown light of the bedroom they traded stories of loneliness, and Victoria told her of gold-mines, and the Voisin, and Ruby and Lily-white. She told her of the blinding and the fire and the black Egyptian baby, even of the wardrobe of her mother's clothes, which had begun to enter her dreams, stirring and blowing like wraiths, billowing into woman-shapes in a vague misty glow. As she gave voice to these things she cherished them all the more; it was perhaps, Victoria thought, like opening a secret cupboard and showing off your heart. Mary understood everything. Mary was wise and thoughtful. Mary was silent when necessary and spoke when required. And she enabled some kind of restoration: that Victoria might inhabit her surer self. In the daytime she wore a uniform and was a shape behind a desk; but at night, in Mary's company, Victoria knew her own specificity.

It was an aspect of their affection that Victoria also confirmed Mary. The woman had grown up in an orphanage, hungry and ill, and spoke of her past life as though she had lived it as someone else, always once removed. But she had an elaborate fantasy of a long-lost family — a mother, a father, three sisters and two brothers, all of whom were named and detailed, and would one day, somehow, find and reclaim her. So although Mary said very little of the orphanage, she spoke a great deal of her imaginary family, so that she and Victoria, sitting comfortably sideways beneath the Heart, could be lonesome together. Their voices drifted up to Jesus, soft and wandering as candle-smoke.

By her own account Victoria made no other friends, and had no girlish recollections or school-day tattle. Or would not disclose them. Of her boarding school time she remembers — ineradicably — only the river and the swans and her own conclusive act of arson.

The boarding school stood on a promontory beside the Swan River, and beyond the clipped grass and the expensive houses nestling around it was a cliff and a wild space of undergrowth and reeds, and beyond that the ribbony river, shimmering and lucent, buoying shags and pelicans and cruising clusters of black swans. Victoria went often to the river's edge, to sit quietly and be alone. She went at night so that she could gaze into the lit windows of people's houses (so many pianos, flower arrangements, jardinieres and anti-macassars) and in the day, after school, with her pencils and drawing paper, just to sit there, looking. She possessed a wedge of cover, sheltered and hidden, and it was like the underside of something, cobwebby and damp and unavoidably muddy, but positioned not far from a group of swans' nests, and with an unimpeded view around the bay and across the river. In the distance was a boat-shed from which schoolboys daily launched rowing practice — she could hear their rhythmic grunts float over to greet her — and ahead, directly ahead, an expanse of sky-filled water. When she swam she entered that sky, diving into pure reflection. She loved subaqueous estrangement; she loved the annihilation of the school world for this cold surprising place, murky with possibility. Jellyfish, fat as faces, encircled and accompanied her. They opened and contracted, opened and contracted, rhythmically, like a heart. She saw them spotting the brown water, wafting towards her like visitants.

Victoria carries into adulthood an image of herself after bathing, still wet, spreadeagled, sleeping very peacefully with her burnt face in the sun.

These times telescope crudely to one single event, when she stumbled across two boys, stamping in the swans' nests. They had their boaters still on and their school ties straight, but were dancing in Wellington boots, crushing the eggs. Matter and egg-shell were splattered everywhere. It took a little longer to see exactly what they had done. Two adult swans were pierced though the chest with makeshift spears, and they had been plucked of their wing-feathers so that they looked exposed and violated. Their long necks were limp and their black bellies already bloated with death. One boy — ginger, mean-looking, with a practised sneer — noticed Victoria's presence and called out aggressively:

So what ya lookin at big eyes? Fancy a quick fuck?

And she fled, afraid, grazing her bare hurrying legs on brambles. When they had gone Victoria returned and buried the bodies of the birds, then gathered up the feathers, which seemed too beautiful to leave, and joined Mary, and the Heart, because there was nowhere else to go . . .

It's an abomination, Mary declared. Just like in the Bible.

She remembers that Mary Heany held her in her arms and allowed her to cry — not only for the swans but more mysteriously for Lily-white, as well. So Victoria sobbed for all the wounds that she did not understand. For the world outside her swimming sky. For her hiding memories and inchoate emotions; and for the second-sight which folded into time itself to produce and reproduce her own system of ruins. Mary told another of her family stories:

My mother, Mary said, *is a giant of a woman. She is even taller than Father Dignam, with blue eyes and black hair, blacker even than swans' feathers or the blackest, moonless night, blacker than the devil himself and the hot caverns of hell, and she is beautiful and strong and her name is also Mary, since I am her long-lost last-born and named for her especially, and my mother Mary, whose skin is all-white and smooth like egg-shell, wears combs in her hair and has brooches and beads, all of them made of moonstones and little streamers of gold, and a studded crucifix, too, like the one the bishop wears; yet she is not proud or stuck up and goes about in bare feet and wears dresses with flower patterns so that she is always in springtime, and who knows maybe she was sailing on a boat on the river, or walking out alone on the cliff in the sunshine, and saw those two boys doing their dreadful things, and put a curse on them, there and then, so that they will burn away in hellfire, and burn and burn until nothing is left but their dirty charred souls, because she might have forgiven them for the swans, but not the eggs too, so that she punishes them and hates them and sweeps past on the face of the water, looking out for her daughter Mary, who has the same name as herself, and who is waiting and waiting and waiting forever to be found.*

Amen, added Mary.

When, late at night, Victoria set fire to the boat-shed, it was a magnificent thing. Convulsive flames transformed the ordinary into a theatre of light, and she watched it from a distance, from her little wedge of darkness, begin as a small lit window flaring in the night, and become a whole cathedral, and wholly glorious. And on the shining water a second boat-shed burned, puzzled by ripples as wood fragments began to scatter and fall. By the time the roof was ablaze boats had been released across the river, and they drifted there, made of fire, arks of brilliancy. The fire-brigade didn't have a chance; like the Lyric theatre the boat-shed was of Baltic pine.

(viii)

Only Mary Heany could possibly have told them. When the school expelled Victoria Morrell for criminal acts, Mary was not present at the ritual humiliation at Assembly. Victoria, said the headmistress, was a symbol to them all, a symbol of pure wickedness. She had disgraced the good name of her family, and the excellent name of her school. Three hundred girls, six hundred eyes, looked steadily upon her, thrilled at her abasement. Two teachers loaded Victoria onto the train, and neither offered comfort, neither waved.

Her conflagration returned, again and again. Sails of flame blowing open on water of dense black. Sparks. Scintillas. The whole vision bisected, streaming in two directions at once. This doubling made it much more impressive than the Lyric. She closed her eyes and saw it still, a kind of retinal after-image, cast like a flare on the screens beneath her eyelids, persisting into vision even in the darkness after fires.

Victoria felt powerful and incorruptible. Sweetly delinquent thoughts assailed her. She considered buildings for their immanent combustibility and wondered if she could rob a bank, or even commit murder. She could not have known then the other forms of darkness that awaited her. She stepped off the hissing train into a white-hot day, and saw that only her father and brother were at the station to meet her. No Lily-white, no Ruby, no Miss Casey, no Mrs Murphy. For a moment Victoria could not comprehend what had happened. Henry was enormous, over six feet tall, and now eighteen years old, pimply, rigid-faced, with wiry brown whiskers and an Adam's apple, and her father in this company was both smaller and more corpulent, but aged not at all. (He tipped his Spanish hat, as though to a passing acquaintance.) Sometime during the three years she had been away at school they had both returned, and changed her home almost completely. Lily-white and Ruby had been banished — Victoria had no idea where and no one could inform her; Miss Casey, rejected, had returned to the city of her own accord; and only the widow Mrs Murphy remained. At the house she ran to Victoria and desperately engulfed her, crushing the young woman's body into her own. She had become thin and grizzled, a shadow of her former self.

So this was Victoria, then, caught in awful reversal and returned to a place which was no longer her home. The glassy eyes of stuffed animals followed her around the room, and she nestled in the curtain folds beside the giraffe, and experienced such extreme desolation that *Mel-bourne* was all she was, a kind of sound around an emptiness, a shape containing its own vacuity. She sang to herself in a way that recalled her lost mother, Lily-white. She cried, and forgot to eat, and was tormented by loneliness.

One day she sought out Mrs Murphy for company and a talk, and found her alone, seated at the peculiar task of cleaning a chandelier.

I wish I was made of glass, Victoria heard herself announce.

Mrs Murphy looked up from the smooth crystal petal she was polishing.

What was that, lovey? What? What?

But Victoria had fallen silent. It was not something she could repeat. It was too preposterous. She had become a girl who speaks nonsense, a girl spiritless and lost.

Mrs Murphy resumed her work, glum and uncommunicative.

Perhaps she needed some exclamation mark to show them how terrible she felt: Victoria decided to make a bonfire of her mother's clothes. She stole into her father's room and simply lit them where they were. It was impossibly easy.

But the space was too confined or her spirit too damp, because the fire was not special. Flames began and then sank almost immediately to smouldering, and the wardrobe filled up with acrid smoke. Something too had alerted and disturbed Mrs Murphy, for she ran in — crying out *Christ-Almighty, Christ-Almighty* — and then returned with a bucket of water and doused everything with one swing. Victoria was given the task of cleaning up, and made to feel ashamed.

She scooped scraps of burnt soggy fabric, holding her nose against the smell, and with these redolent remains, powdering even as she held them, wondered then what her mother, Rose Morrell, might actually have looked like. She knew her other mother Lily-white in such physical detail (she had even stared unflinchingly at the circular pit where the eye once lay, just to know her with close and loving particularity), but realised that she had no image of this Rose woman at all. She was perhaps like Mary's Mary, blue-eyed and black-haired, a woman taller even than her brother, and even more powerful. Victoria sifted small objects from the detritus of the burning: an opalescent buckle shaped as a broad petalled flower, buttons of bone and of pearl-shell, small coin-shapes of amber. These unburnable traces were precious to her. Most of the shoes were also unburned, but were ruined now, and sullied, and filled with mucky puddles of foul-smelling ash.

Les chasseurs, Victoria whispered to herself. *Feu. Coeur. Cendre. Cinderella.* She put the shoes into a box, to be taken away.

It was only when Victoria leant right into the wardrobe, tilting, on her knees, into the space of scorched darkness, that she found the hidden treasure of her dead mother's journal, tucked in a far corner. She tilted back, almost nauseated from the stench and the enclosure, with the stowed-away book in her trembly hands. Her mother's journal. Its cover was splashed but its interior dry, and when Victoria opened

it she saw immediately that her mother was more elusive than she had imagined, writing mostly not in
English, but in some cryptogrammic style. Only the
curly ampersands were at all recognisable. It was like
receiving a love letter written in the wrong language.
It was exciting and heartbreaking, all at once. Victoria
tucked the journal in her dress, and rushed to hide it in
her bedroom. Her secret. Her mother. Dragged from
the fire. Goosebumps rose on her skin, as though
marking physically her entry to a paranormal zone.

When after work Henry Morrell heard of the
wardrobe burning, he entered Victoria's room with a
savage grin, and beat his younger sister about the
head. In the morning she saw her own face swollen
and discoloured, remade in lilac and indigo, and with
two black eyes. This was almost unsurprising, to see
something so monstrously sad. The mirror held her
up, ruined and defeated, susceptible now to death-
wishes and hauntings and the flitting retreat of all her
hopes.

THE BLACK MIRROR STORIES

Music that rises out of abandoned places
Your space is under the earth, inside the earth,
inside the stars.
Where do images go?
Why does a mirror gather light for thirty years
and then hold nothing?

(Peter Boyle, *Light From Beyond*)

Victoria said:

I have several Black Mirror stories and I will give you three.

What are the Black Mirror stories, my Anna-lytical?

They are myself, unrecognisable. They are myself, writing disaster. I looked into a mirror and darkness looked back.

Black Mirror Story 1

I do not remember her death, but they say I was there.

I do not remember her funeral, but they say I was there.

My mother is everything I do not remember, a darkness with no flashes, an evacuated space, an *oubliette*. Sometimes I cannot bear so much black-coloured forgetting.

I once tried, like the artist Brauner, to paint with my eyes closed, believing this act might recover the lineaments of her lost face, or at least its vague aspect, or intimation; but there was still no consequence and no true icon. I tried too, like the poet Desnos, to speak Surrealistically at will; I imagined that a word-link, unconsciously chanced upon, would somehow reconnect us. But all contrivances failed. Art is the windowpane, the barrier, against which we press our searching faces.

———

When I was seventeen years old, I discovered my dead mother's journal in a coffin-like wardrobe, full of cinders. For several days I tried unsuccessfully to decipher it — it appeared to be written in an alien and difficult script — until one morning it accidentally fell open upside-down and I noticed that the words read this way were much more familiar. In fact the letters were cuneiform versions, upside-down and back-to-front, of the English alphabet: my mother had simply disguised them by making each more square and substantial; yet she had placed the ampersands the right way up, and by this simple trick misled intruding readers. I began at first to transcribe the shapes, but found after no time at all that I could read the words fluently.

You already know a little of what I discovered. My father, the chauffeur, seems to have been a young man of unusual patience and tenderness, or at least this is how my mother always described him. He existed to wait for her voice, to pop up the umbrella, to take her elbow and hold open the door as she stepped on the running board of the Daimler. He existed in the rain and in the car; he seems never to have entered the house. I think that perhaps my mother loved the terrible exclusion he bore. He must have known her best through the rear-view mirror — a lover in a glass box, small and rectangular; and she must have known him best by the back of his neck. And like all secret lovers they would have cherished their plaited

glances, the furtive outreaching, the hidden complici-
ties. I have thought of this often and wondered how
they sustained their secret. I picture my mother with
cupid-bow lips and a pounding heart, approaching
very slowly in one of those bulbous veiled hats, and
this man, my father, shifting from foot to foot in the
foggy cold, and tracking her motion towards him as
though he were tracking a point of perihelion. She
would have burned as she grew closer; his cold made
her blush and feel her own warmth unendurably. She
might have lowered her eyelids, only to glance up
again as his hand pulled at the door handle, to see herself, a woman in a hat, floating in the lustre of his eyes.
I imagine between my parents an enormous decorum
and restraint, since the affair was apparently never discovered, and she never ran away with him. Together
they practised an almost oriental formality, moving in
tight patterns of oblique correspondence.

When I deciphered the journal I was at first dismayed. I did not judge my mother for taking a lover,
but felt instead doubly orphaned by the long deception; Father was not my father; we had both been
hoodwinked. And where was this chauffeur, this
William, this man always shivery in the greyish light
of rain or speed?

I dreamt a car sped past that I knew he was driving,
but I saw only the back of a man's neck, in blurry retreat.

It's strange to remember it now: like all irrevocable
revelations it carried with it a certain quality of

despair. I did not, of course, tell my father or brother of my discovery, but confided in Mrs Murphy. Her liver-spotted hands flew to her face and she looked at me with a puzzled stare as though she had suddenly gone deaf and was lip-reading gibberish. She was dismayed by my knowledge and demanded I destroy Rose's journal. She answered no questions and forbade discussion on the subject. She closed shut like a door. She banged in my face. I was left unassuaged and unbeloved, and I retreated behind the curtain folds like a five-year-old girl.

But small details, once revealed, find their own routes of enlargement. One day a letter came from Tilly, addressed to Mrs Murphy. The envelope lay on the kitchen table and I noticed, with just a peep, that it contained a return address. So it was that I eventually found out what I needed to know: I wrote to Tilly who lived somewhere in mythical Melbourne and asked her all the questions Mrs Murphy had forbidden me.

Tilly's correspondence returned quickly and in two separate parts. The first part was a parcel with a note attached: Tilly had stolen a stereoscope when she left my father's employ, had always felt guilty, and was now returning it. The stereoscope looked rather like a pair of opera glasses; two shafts of silver held with a wooden handle, and arranged at an angle which endowed images with three dimensionality. There was a neat boxed set of small strips of narrative — tiny little photographs with one-line captions — that could be affixed to the viewing frame. The stereoscope Tilly returned had a story-strip already within it:

Frame one: Portly rich man in opulent drawing room, possibly American. Wallpaper, ferns, paintings, chaise longue. Rich man to servant girl, coy and pretty: 'Why my beauty, how long have you been our cook?'

Frame two: Rich man steals kiss: 'Oh you naughty man!'

Frame three: 'You bashful little creature', chucking her chin.

Frame four: 'Hands! Hands! What does she mean?'

The man's wife (one supposes), fierce, statuesque, is pointing angrily. He is looking in the mirror above the fireplace, and imprinted on his back are two floury handmarks.

Tilly wrote: *I wanted this so badly, I couldn't leave it behind. It belonged to your father.*

When I think now of Tilly's theft the word *dolorous* attaches to it; it carries the sadness of servants, heavy, righteous, saturated with bleak longing for something possessed casually by others. I wonder too about her relationship with my father: how long, how often, whether it started before my mother died. In my memory Tilly figures as woeful and shrill, with alarmed upstanding hair and red eyes like a debil-debil. But this must be unkind. In any case, her letter was rather piteous.

I also wonder whether I saw the stereoscopic stories as a child, since those hands are one of my important symbols. You see them everywhere throughout my paintings. White hands. Cameo hands. Hands like thin clouds on the verge of erasure. That Tilly was my father's mistress was unsurprising, but the line *hands, hands, what does she mean?* and those melodramatic hand prints, tell-taling something anterior, those astonished me. It was like a dream returning with spontaneous understanding: *une vague de rêve,* the Surrealists call it, a wave of dream.

The second part of Tilly's correspondence was a letter. Tilly wrote that she had known my chauffeur father well, and had always been fond of him. They lost contact when some of the household moved to the goldfields, and had not seen each other for several years. When they met again, in Melbourne, William had just returned from a trip to the goldfields, where rather belatedly he had learnt of Rose's death. He entered, Tilly said, a long period of depression; he became thin and spectre-like; his skin was blue and pallid with its lack of substance, and he had rings under his eyes so that he looked bruised and old. It was only then that she heard of the love between Rose and William, and of the child, and the severing, and the promises of reunion. At length William decided to return to London, where he had lived as a boy. He wrote to her from there, sending word of his work, and his marriage, and the birth of his new daughter. At some stage William stopped responding to Tilly's letters: she assumed he was caught up in his London life and family. She had printed out the London address boldly and underlined it.

Write! she instructed. *He will love to hear from you.*

Sometimes I wonder how indeed I resisted writing, or what fear prevented it. In all lives there are these inexplicable pauses and hesitations. Lost chances. Failed words. Untimely hush. But when I arrived in London to enrol at art college the prospect of meeting my lost father was suddenly irresistible. I took the address dear Tilly had passed into my keeping, and found the house, and the green door, and the number painted on it, and behind the green door lived a diminutive pop-eyed widow, who clearly knew who I was, but did not want to admit me. I stood at the doorstep in silvery drizzle and the woman — her name was Flora — told me blankly of my father's death.

Nine years ago now. A tram. A tram killed 'im. We 'ad a loverly funeral, all carnations and ribbons.

She spoke in an East End accent and did not blink or avert her gaze, as though she was challenging me to contradict her with refutation of William's death. Behind her, in the dim hallway, appeared a tall young girl I assumed to be my half-sister. She too stood still, watching me. Light from behind her illuminated a crescent of fuzzy curls. I could see lumpy dark-coloured furniture with crocheted covers, and a standing lamp of dirty parchment. In the low-wattage light of the front room everything looked secretive, sad and only partially disclosed.

A tram, Flora repeated. It was a tram as killed 'im.

I remember peering into the house half-expecting my father to materialise. It did not seem possible I could learn of his death on the day I had at last decided to meet him. I wanted to ask for details, or to see a photograph, but words stuck in my throat. The tall girl in the dim hallway, looking so like an apparition, drifted slowly towards me. Her face was a nest of light. Her eyes were enormous. I reached past Flora and placed my address in her daughter's open hand.

I was damp, clammy and washed yet again by grief.

You would have liked my youngest sister Frances. Flora refused all her life to see me again, but Frances and I were good friends until she died fifteen years ago of cancer of the breast. We shared sisterly secrets and the same-shaped faces. She worked as housekeeper for a Catholic priest, and never married; yet neither did she disapprove of my life or my sequence of partners. And she loved me, I think, as I loved her, with gratitude for the discovery that had rendered us each less alone. In London we met regularly for tea and shopping (and she liked it when I wore my feathers in public — the cat-called remarks, the consternation, the stares), but I could never persuade her to visit me in Paris. You're the arty one, she used to say. It was a relationship that was curiously imperturbable. Nothing unsettled it. There is a deckle-edged photograph taken on a footpath in Leicester Square, and you can see the solidarity of feeling that existed between us, the Surrealist show-off, madly feathered, and the prim-and-proper housekeeper with her handbag clutched anxiously over her crotch. We are both smiling radiantly. And we both share a glorious and sisterly likeness.

Frances once confided to me that she had a life-long ambition to appear as an extra in a Hollywood movie. She wanted to be, she said, a face carried forward into history in some incidental, irrefutable and time-defeating way; not important or even speaking, but incorrigibly visible. I loved her when she told me that. Since her death I have sometimes imagined that I spot her at the cinema, there, in a glimpse, in a brief screened resurrection. In movies we seek in the pallor of those giant faces the netherland of our own lost ghosts. We seek — don't you think? — the vehicle of the face. The transporting light.

Of our father Frances remembered a long shape in a winged armchair, and a certain, but definite, circlet of embrace. It was a memory Flora maintained she was too young to recall, but Frances insisted was true.

The shape of him, she said. Just the shape of him persists.

And I remember a man who stood outside in the front yard, called out my mother's name, and then sat on the earth with Lily-white, intently weeping. An emblem of tranced and concentrated grief. We talked often about our father with just these traces. A shape and a grief-stricken waterfall of tears.

But you are wondering, aren't you, about my mother's death? You are wondering what Tilly's letter might have revealed.

How do I tell you this? How do I unconceal?

I suppose as a child I had always assumed that my mother committed suicide. With the discovery of the journal I decided that she was lovelorn and wholly despairing, and that the silence that gathered around her death was consolidating some private or public shame. Even Henry, my brother, didn't know how she died, and spent his childhood developing more and more barbarous theories. But her death was in fact a simple accident. A simple, appalling accident.

She had leant forward to adjust her hair in the long mirror above the fireplace, and the fine fabric of her long dress had brushed into the fire. It was something gauzy and light; something very beautiful flared up and killed her. The fire swept towards her face so that she became a bell of flame.

It was sudden, Tilly wrote, all so very sudden. Mrs Murphy was there, and Tilly, and I, but none of us saved her. My mother, Rose Morrell, just ignited before us. She flew around the room in a terrible panic, fanning her own death, flapping her arms like a bird and screaming for her body. In her flight she knocked over objects and shattered a vase. The whole room responded to her agitation; she was possessed, overtaken, flames shot upwards from her shoulders and the piled dome of her hair. Mrs Murphy tore down a curtain and threw it like a net over the flaming woman, and we leapt on her, Tilly wrote; we all three leapt upon her. To smother and to save the flaming woman. The woman. Your mother. Your mother, Rose Morrell.

I remember none of this. I remember no mother ignited with sparks sweeping around the room, no mother-shape beneath a curtain, no flesh smell, no horror. It is all in darkness. Tilly claims that I cut my hand on a shard of vase and was preoccupied at the time with my own small bleeding. Perhaps this explains it. Or perhaps, even then, I was too unloving and egotistical.

My mother Rose, tended by Lily-white, lived on for three days longer, but died in extremity. Her skin was entirely burned. Her condition was wretched. Towards the end Mrs Murphy put a damp cloth to Rose's mouth to muffle her constant hopeless moaning. To close off the breath that was agony to her. To save us all from the horror of unconcluded burning. She pressed hard, with both hands, until Rose sank into silence.

(*Christ-Almighty, forgive me*, Mrs Murphy would have said.)

Lily-white sang, and cut at her forehead with a stone.

The funeral was huge, with everyone attending. Tilly wrote that I wore a new dress of black linen, which

Mrs Murphy had sat up sewing throughout the night. And that a red sand storm, a willy-willy, blew up halfway through the funeral, causing mourners to squint, and cover their mouths and cough and splutter, so that the proceedings had suddenly to be crudely hastened, and everyone fled, eyes streaming, to avoid the obliterations of dust. A morbid haste attended my mother. Just as Mrs Murphy could not wait for Rose Morrell's autonomous death, so mourners fled the ceremony of her interment before the coffin was lowered. They covered their eyes, Tilly wrote, because the grit was so blinding.

. . . Do you know, by the way, what became of Brauner and Desnos?

The painter Brauner was a strange man given to grotesque presentiments. He painted a series of self-portraits, beginning in 1931, in which he depicted himself cruelly with one mutilated eye. In 1938 his eye was in fact destroyed in a fight at a studio party. He committed suicide on exactly the day he had announced, years earlier.

Robert Desnos, who wrote Surrealistically at will, and produced love poetry of incomparable delicacy, ended up in the prison camps of Buchenwald and Terezine. He died of typhus just a few days after his release. He died unpoetically.

I mourned them both and remember both of them clearly.

And my mother, Rose Morrell? Why do I speak of her with such abraded and tired generalisation? It was like peering into the tunnels of a stereoscope, and seeing only the still, black-and-white frames Tilly had attempted to draw for me. It was unbelievable. It was a mean deception.

All my life I have tried to paint her back into existence. All these images. All these figures. I was attracted to the Surrealist promise of *figuring out*. This or that conjunction. An umbrella here. A pair of lips there. The correct superimposition or renegade object. But I learned gradually that it was a crass and over-explicit form. It was the rapture of the visible, artistry with too many, far too many, lights on.

Perhaps, after all, it was Lily-white I was missing. Am. Am missing.

Black Mirror Story 2

It was 1927, I was seventeen years old, and I had arrived back on the goldfields to discover my whole world lost. Ruby and Lily-white were gone, Miss Casey was gone, Mrs Murphy was an old woman, with nowhere to go, who sat at the kitchen table with her chin in her hands and her grey hair straggly and her eyes unalert, waiting to die. We offered each other what comfort we could, and tried to find chores and diversions to fill our long days. Mrs Murphy brewed endless cups of pale-coloured tea and sedulously attended her small garden of herbs; I took to my drawings and my paintings and my fantasies of escape.

How can I describe what altered in me with the discovery of Rose's journal? I was already an errant and lonesome young woman, a firelighter, a reprobate, a laughing-stock at school; now I felt myself newly orphaned. In her cuneiform disguises, embossed with ampersands — for somehow I apprehended her indivisible from the style in which she wrote — I both found and relinquished my mother for the very first time. The journal summoned an admixture of recovery and grief: I loved her, and I wept.

After the war I met a woman who had one arm blasted away, and who kept reaching, so she said, to brush hair from her face with the destroyed lost arm. It felt like that: impossible. It was like a phantom limb asserting lost presence. I felt spooked and disfigured by incompletion.

You must understand that I was wholly alone. In the town my family was completely despised. My father, ever-greedy, had failed to install safety equipment; he had tried to break the unions; he had hired thuggish debt collectors and armies of scabs. I had no friends at all and only Mrs Murphy to care for me. I longed for Ruby and Lily-white, but they had simply disappeared. They had simply *vanished*.

Gone bush, my father said, with a contemptuous sniff. Gone fucking walkabout.

He never spoke of them again. He returned to brothels and carried with him the air of a rejected lover.

There was despair in everything. I wanted wings, or death. I thought that my life had stalled, and that everywhere, everywhere else, the world somehow continued unclouded and bright.

And then, by strange fortune, by chance occurrence, I met them, the brothers Louis and Ernest Bell.

Together they offered me for a short time a new kind of family. They were tender-hearted miners, who worked at the stopes, two young men who already had earth so ingrained in their hands that their life-lines and fingerprints were explicit and apparent. I remember they held them up before me: four hands. Exclamations. They were beautifully detailed, like copperplate etchings.

One night I had been wandering the streets, peering into windows, trailing down laneways I had known with Ruby and Lily-white, when I forgot my spy-mode of disembodiment, and was struck by a bicycle. Louis was peddling, with Ernest sitting behind, and we all three came a cropper. I had gravel rash burning on my elbows and forehead, and a triangular tear in my cotton skirt. Louis, I remember, bent down to examine the tear, and rose up embarrassed; even under the dim streetlight I could sense his sudden arousal. Ernest was more shy; he hung back in the shadows.

We went to their house, nearby, to clean up our wounds and share a pot of tea. I had never been in someone else's house before, and I confess I was shocked by how little they had. It was a spare, iron cottage, two bedrooms and a kitchen and a small sitting room at the front; and within it cheap furniture of deal and tacks, covered over with turquoise floral-patterned cloth. There were four chairs and a lamp, with a shade of stencilled brown paper, and a shelf of plaster ornaments, a milkmaid and some dogs. A woman — their widowed mother Maude — leapt from her chair, raised up her hands in concern, then set about fussily tending our wounds. She bathed me first of all, dabbing at my forehead with strips of torn linen; then she bathed her sons. Her bowl of water grew pink with our mingled blood: the liquid tilted and swayed and caught the overhead light. A pink-looking moon. I remember this detail now because it seems so retrospectively expressive.

I decided to lie about who I was.

Ruby, I told them. I am Ruby White.

Ruby White, she's a bit of all right, Louis responded cheekily.

Louis Bell was what in those days we called a fast worker. Before I left his house he had persuaded me to meet him the following Saturday night, and we became lovers soon after.

We met in the illegal tunnels children had carved into the slime dumps. Sweethearts of the earth, Louis Bell used to say. When I raised my skirt the first time I realised that he was as inexperienced as me: so in our earth burrows we were patient and careful with each other; we rolled pressed together in our worn-out blanket, with the musty scent of the mine dirt coating our exposed skin and catching in the nets of our negligent hair. Candlelight cast our young faces in gold.

Call me Midas, I joked, moving the candle closer to his face.

Louis had never heard the myth explained, so I told him my selective and vague version of King

Midas of Phrygia, how he had won Dionysus' approval and been granted a wish, how he had wished for wealth-beyond-reason so that all he touched became gold; and how he had transformed not only his food and his famous rose garden to golden objects, but his daughter as well.

Bloody hell, said Louis in shocked response.

I told how the spell was removed by bathing in a river, and how King Midas repudiated wealth and became a worshipper of Pan, the god of the woodlands.

Excuse my French, Louis apologised.

I held his golden head between my hands. He was my very first lover and he was utterly precious. In moonlight I would climb through the window of my bedroom, elated, delirious, scented with mine dirt.

Eventually I told Louis Bell who I was. It made no difference, he said; he loved me just the same.

The Bells were a family who told funny stories about each other. They transacted their shared biographies by polishing up gems of absurd moments, which they exchanged in their own economy as inexhaustible gifts. Stupid sayings, lunatic moments, comic and tricky situations; no detail was wasted or unremarked. They joked about ancestors in ridiculous accents and invented generations in the future who continued their vaudeville temperaments. I was charmed and abashed. I thought of my unmentionable father and brother. Then I thought of my absent mothers and sister and wondered what community might yet have been possible.

On Sundays we sometimes — all four of us — went on family picnics together. We sat in spindly shade and ate corned beef and fruit cake and drank tea from a billy bubbling over a fire of sticks. Maude had come with her husband in the gold-rush, thirty years earlier, and was a buoyant and spirited woman, undefeated by grief. Her sons adored her. Their love was visible in the gestures with which they handed her food, or brushed a few crumbs from her lacy collar, or a fallen leaf from the light ruffled voile of her hat. More than sexual embrace, I yearned for this touch. I yearned for the gently confirming and the familial. The aura of veneration and simple tenderness. Ernest saw me watch as he took and flung the stray leaf, and then he reached over, as though telepathic, and touched the back of my hand. When I looked into his eyes, he blushed and looked away. Louis leant across his brother and kissed me on the cheek with a cheery smack, then kissed Ernest and Maude in exactly the same way, binding us all in a cohesive circuit of affection. We all laughed; it was joyful, this bracelet of hearty kisses.

These fluttering and subtle moments, these lovely exchanges, I have preserved against the disaster of all that followed.

When I discovered I was pregnant Louis was delighted and proposed marriage immediately. He even knelt before me and held out a ring in a velvet casket — as he had seen performed in the cinema — and offered eternal undying devotion.

Eternal Undying Devotion, he repeated, as if making a vow.

My hesitation both hurt and dismayed him. But I feared my family. I feared my dull vicious brother and my money-mad father. However, at four months I could no longer contain my secret. It was such an adventure, this body, filling up with life. I peered sideways into the looking-glass and rejoiced in my baby convex, just there, just emerging.

So I summoned my courage and told Mrs Murphy everything; and Mrs Murphy, driven by some old-fashioned code of honour, locked into servant fidelity and mixed allegiances, straightaway left and told my father. This betrayal exploded something both inside and outside: our lives, all our lives, filled up with things broken.

On the goldfields, even now, people still talk of it. People still talk of what happened to the Bell family in 1927.

Henry Morrell and two other men knocked down the door of Louis' cottage in the middle of the night. They were armed with antique swords and a metal pail of acid. One of the men flung the acid at Ernest's face, and as he fell, blinded, the other man sliced at his side with a sword. Henry himself, so the trial revealed, cut down my beloved Louis in a fit of maddened fury. The amount of blood was immense, and there in the shadows was Maude, wailing in her nightgown, aghast, bespattered, tearing at her hair.

The mutilated body of Louis Bell was dragged away, and under cover of darkness dumped in an old mine shaft. It was almost two years before it was found and recovered.

At the trial in the city Henry Morrell was pardoned. He was pronounced temporarily insane, and acting in defence of the honour of his only sister who had been violated, possibly by force, by a working man. His accomplices, on the other hand, were convicted of the murder, and both later hanged in the Fremantle gaol.

What words can tell this? Violence is somehow beyond my language. It becomes a story, told in pubs, printed in columns in newspapers, far from the unspeakable hurt of Maude, collapsing into the oval pool of her eldest son's death, or the anguish of Ernest, who reaches out before him in burning black, knowing he is feeling in the air for the shape of catastrophe. Or from Louis himself, who looks with incomprehension into the eyes of the man who hacks him, who falls unmanned, in agony, in fearful distress, astonished to be witnessing his own death at twenty-three, and thinking: *I wanted to be a father; I will never be a father.*

For myself: it is a simple summary because I had lost all feeling. I was sent to the city in the south for the period of my confinement, and the baby was born and immediately given up for adoption. Mrs Murphy attended me, but I could not endure her company and was cruel and spiteful. I addressed her as Judas, and watched with calculated indifference as her mottled old woman's face dissolved in tears. In the meantime I persuaded my father that the only hope for my virtue and my long-term marriage prospects was to send me abroad, to London, so that I could achieve the requisite female accomplishments divorced from the taint of local scandal. I can hear myself now, eloquently persuading him. He agreed to a fare, and an allowance, and I left Australia just three weeks after the birth of my baby. My womb was still open, my breasts still filled with milk. In my mouth, the deathly taste of cinders.

Louis was the most joyful man I have ever known; he carried his own body as if it had been given to him as a gift. I remember kissing the open palms of his hands. I remember saying: Works of art!

And I have just remembered something else. There is a strange tale told of the Surrealist poet I mentioned, Robert Desnos. In the prison camp he moved up and down the lines of inmates waiting for the gas chambers, reading their palms and telling their fortunes. In each case, so the story goes, he predicted long life.

Black Mirror Story 3

People in France speak of the Occupation as though it existed in parenthesis, a pause in the continuum, a sequestered curved space in the proper syntax of history. But memory breaks open such hypothetical spaces. Parentheses only appear to possess containment.

When I think now of the Occupation it is all Cubist distortion.

Even during the *drôle de guerre*, the phoney war, we felt jagged anxiety in the pits of our stomachs. There were curfews and blackouts: the city became abstracted and strangely angled; and every day there was someone, who knew someone else, who knew for sure of impending disastrous invasion; or someone's relative who had a story about dismemberment in Belgium, or a whole family casually executed, or mass starvation. Tales and rumours striated the air like strafe; one felt clammy, alert and charged with imprecise dread.

Frances wrote from England to call me Home, but this was a ludicrous suggestion; I could not even contemplate it.

At first I was preoccupied by Leonora's condition. Late in 1939 Max Ernst was interned as an enemy alien — he too carried the wrong nation in his passport and documents — and Leonora was in Paris trying to secure his release. We went together to Government offices where she railed and wept and was driven to a distraction bureaucrats considered both typically female and typically English. She had nightmares about the French earth swallowing her lover, and woke beside me, in Jules' place, shouting out at the night, her blue face staring, her long hair disarrayed. Her anguish was terrible. She saw scary shapes on the ceiling and hallucinated guns at her temple. Ernst was finally freed with the intervention of the art dealer Peggy Guggenheim, but Leonora was by then incarcerated in a hospital in Spain, believing her belly was a mirror that reflected the details of war-time.

Peggy took Max Ernst with her to America; Leonora, eventually discharged, moved to live in Mexico. I saw neither of them again; we lost all contact.

Somehow, even now, I remember the beginnings of that time as a kind of 1940s newsreel. First there is an aerial view, almost generic, I suppose, of Parisians streaming away from the threatened city: they are all heading south with piled-up bicycles and rickety pushcarts, and with mattresses and rocking chairs strapped to the tops of black shiny cars. They move with dull exhaustion at a slow-motioned pace. No one honks a horn or jumps the queue; it is a defeated procession, requiring the polite and unanimous gestures of defeat. There is a warm June sky, dappled with light puffs of cloud, and the call of birdsong, somewhere, and an illusion of rightness-with-the-world; then a swift camera sweep downwards to the square shapes of Panzer tanks lurching in equidistant formation along the boulevards; they are heavy and dark, with men in fat helmets perched like puppets on top. Swastikas flap from the Arc de Triomphe, and everywhere red and black banners drape the façades of public buildings. And there is Hitler himself, blandly murderous, his face already an icon schoolboys create with small smudges of charcoal. I never actually saw him, but in this movie-in-the-head he is ineluctably present; the famous, or infamous, bear such invasive familiarity.

So the city of Paris on a June day became a city of the Wehrmacht, and for me it was a period of shameful inertia. I closed down my responses. I became a *poupée*, a doll. Everywhere German soldiers appeared suddenly, and in packs, smuggling their evil intentions like a species of tourist. They book-browsed on the left bank and followed guides through Montmartre. They purchased perfumes, and silk stockings and miniature models of the Eiffel Tower. Officers partied at the Ritz, and enlisted men toasted and clinked beer steins in the smoky depths of the *speiselokals*. They also took a census of French Jews and deported them to death camps. And they tortured French men and women at

Rue des Saussaies, and at Rue Lauriston, and Avenue
Foch. I could not bear to think of it. Our concierge
dragged away. The fatal yellow stars. The knowledge
of nightmarish brutalities, a few streets away. It was
another kind of Surrealism, the Occupied city. Think
of the sound of seven synagogues, exploding. Think of
swastikas imposed everywhere in a spider-like montage. I had thought until then, naively, that anomaly
was above all a principle of delight.

It is difficult to describe the experience of inhabiting a
city so morally ambiguous.

Unable to sell paintings, I worked for a pittance in
the kitchen of a small restaurant near the Palais Royal,
one of many participating in the black-market economy. Guilty-looking men paid with handfuls of
foreign currency; we never asked how they came to
have these in their possession. They ate whatever
meat or cheese was available, and left drunk, and reel-
ing, scattering a few *sous* on the table behind them.
We all despised them. In the streets we waited in long
slow queues with our food coupons for a weighed
portion of bread, or yellow beans, or a few ounces of
margarine. Everyone was hungry. In the Bois de
Boulogne desperate men trapped sparrows. Other
people scavenged whatever they could. I remember
there was no soap: I felt dirty and my clothes were
worn and stained. As the Occupation continued, as
atrocity was more apparent, I felt ever more dirty.

———

It was also a kind of hollowness; I emptied out. This was in part a consequence of desolating loneliness. Most of my fellow artists were somewhere in England or America; Jules, of course, had not returned. The Eluards stayed on in Paris and were members of the Resistance: they alone sustained me.

But when my body was occupied, when I knew my own concavity, the transformation was complete. I had been walking home one night, heading along blacked-out Rue St Honoré, down one of the side streets — Rue de Bourdonnais, I think — to the river at Pont Neuf, when I was accosted by three German soldiers. They began by calling out to me from the opposite side of the road; then one was suddenly on me, and had thrust me against the wall, and was tearing ineptly with fumbling fingers at the buttons of my clothes. Two others held my arms out in a crucifixion. Each of the soldiers in turn took me, standing up: I shall not go further into any details. It was Nusch Eluard, with her heart-shaped face, who enclosed me in a diamond-patterned blanket with satin-lined edges, and whispered comfort and sympathy, and unfurled a song in my ear, and lowered my head down slowly onto a white-frilled pillow, and stayed beside me, and watched over me, so that at last I slept. I slept as though, after all, I was still whole and unwounded. As though I was invincible.

But this history has no refuge of sleep to smooth and occlude it.

When I discovered I was pregnant I was not sure what to do. I did not want to become like Leonora Carrington, maddened by the idea of the war lodged in her belly, but I also wanted the child; I wanted to be a mother. The body too has a memory, and as my breasts filled out, as I began to feel my extra gravity and my shape-shifting power, I dreamt again of darling Louis Bell in the tunnel, with his lovely hands and the candlelight gilding his face. It was a reclamation. It was a return of something lost. I was reminded, perhaps perversely, of the trembling immensity of first love.

The restaurant owner, a melancholy-looking Italian vexed by the dark times, agreed to let me stay at work in the kitchen, and for a while I believe I was almost happy. The pregnancy distended not just my body but time itself: I dreamt frequently of Louis and Jules, often in conflation, and could see them again beneath my eyelids, youthful, sexually present, ablaze with optimism. I also daydreamed in the future-tense: my child would grow up happily and light-filled in a Non-Occupied Zone. We would find Jules and Hélène and make a complete family.

But at six months the future stopped; that is how I then thought of it.

At six months I lost my baby in a night of blood; it was a still-born daughter, I called her Marie. A woman who lived upstairs helped me to gather and destroy the sheets, and I buried my Marie, my hope, late at night to avoid the German patrols, in the small iron-fenced square near St Julian de Pauvre. The moon was full, what we called a bomber's moon, so it was a dangerous burial, fraught with rush and anxiety. I remembered Lily-white singing over the body of the mummy-baby, her voice abysmal and the same moon rocking in her one liquid eye.

That night, on the floor above me, a whole family was taken away when the Nazis discovered a hidden wireless and a copy of *Combat*. I heard shouts and weeping sifting down through the ancient floorboards. The pitch of disaster. The tone of fear-of-death. A dropped object bang-banged as it bounced down the stairs outside my door.

(Someone in our building — I never learned who — received payment of two hundred francs for the act of denunciation.)

Outside ack-ack guns sounded and there were sirens and searchlights.

I was pouring out blood, and unable to cry.

It was only a month or so later when I saw a woman in an olive and peacock-feather hat throw what I thought was a baby into the Seine, and something hard within me fractured and crazed. I entered mourning by a banal process of isolation and starvation and know now that all my losses gathered together at that point. I began crying and crying and could not stop. I had not understood my own capacity for bereavement, nor uttered my long-contained distress. Waste. Dust. Rain darkening stone walls. The sheer weight of dragged memories and grief-stricken searching. I felt ransacked, inhuman. When at last I returned to life I did not recognise myself at all; I stared into the mirror and saw darkness staring back.

For many weeks no one had called me by my name. Perhaps, in any case, I would not have answered. Perhaps this too was alienated from me, since I was vacant, and lost, and without child or country.

When the Liberation came one of the women who worked with me in the Italian restaurant denounced me as a collaborator. I had confided sometime earlier that my pregnancy was 'German'. I was dragged by furious men into the street to endure public shame. My hair was shorn — rather crudely, there were nicks and bloody cuts — and I was beaten with malice about the arms and the face. Thus on Rue St Honoré, I found myself standing in a group of bruised and shorn women, *femme tondues*. We were huddled together in a kind of magnetic field, reduced to undifferentiated and anonymous symbols, the bald propitiation of national shame. An engrossed crowd circled around us, spitting and hurling abuse. The woman beside me repetitively clasped and unclasped her hands; another bit her fingernails until they bled. In this group I met again the woman Marie-Claude, the woman who had worn the olive and peacock-feather hat. At first I did not know her — since her appearance was so altered — but she embraced me and kissed me like a long-lost sister, and she wept and declared that she was only trying to earn a living. That she was a good woman. A milliner. All the way from Brittany. And that it *was* a baby, she confessed, she had thrown that day into the Seine. A German baby, she said. A German baby. You understand.

When the Nazis first entered Paris, some of the residents closed their shutters or wore black arm-bands to signify mourning. I should have known what this meant. I should have understood. Disaster begins with a few oblique and isolate signs, which gather and elucidate.

THE HEART

The human heart, beautiful as a seismograph.

(André Breton, *Nadja*)

Blood leaves are falling.
Hard pulses in the plum-dark heart.
From this dormant harp,
silently,
Grief plucks its song.

(Jean Kent, *Practising Breathing*)

1

In the London Underground Anna sees it: trains resembling strips of film. They slide past her in a string of fluorescent squares, speeding vision in lit sequences to a kind of profane illumination. Trains hurtle at the darkness and disappear with a roar. They bear, she reflects, a truly lovely transience. And when sparks arise in a spray at a curve on the line, Anna experiences a flash of genuine excitement. She knows she is now seeing as Victoria Morrell sees — this fleeting dazzlement, this random white flicker of ordinary time.

Anna ascends from the Underground, striding two steps at once. Filtered light from a sky that threatens rain touches her head, and slides down the length of her body as she emerges into the street. Her heart is pounding. She looks up at the sky in time to catch the crossed arc of two swallows, diving swiftly, neatly, in opposite directions.

Auspice, she thinks. *Divination through bird flight*.

The birds swoop and swerve as Anna once did. When she could fly. When she was a small flying child. The city air smells densely of petrol and rust, a fuming bus strains past, a bicycle, a taxi; but her heart is light and her spirits air-high. Just as she was taught by Uncle Ernie to apprehend visions, now, at the closing of an old woman's life, as Victoria talks her way rather elaborately towards the admission of death, Anna looks for omens of redemption and patterns within flight. Sometimes she wishes she were Christian: it would be so much easier, this whole business of symbols.

A child walks towards her, dragged by his mother. His three- or four-year-old face is flaring with pleasure; he drags a simple wooden duck which bobs and clacks as it moves. Anna catches his eye.

Nice duck! she offers.

Charlie, the boy responds, with a kind of scholarly gravity. His name is Charlie.

Pleased to meet you, Charlie. Have a wet day.

The mother looks up and smiles directly, as if they share a sly secret, and Anna crosses the road, unmoored now from the search-for-deeper-meanings, content with the child, and the smile, and the absence of rain. Momentarily she can forget that Victoria is leaving her. Victoria, whose life she daily sifts and examines and tries to render intelligible, Victoria who finds coherence only in what is no longer there, Victoria whom she adores and now suspects might be her grandmother. Uncle Ernie went to the city and returned with a baby; it is not impossible to imagine that he had retrieved Victoria's child. Anna clings to this hypothesis because it refuses sovereignty to loss. She is waiting for the right moment. The return of Odysseus. The birthmark. The truthful unveiling. In the diastolic and systolic spaces of Victoria's life, all these openings and closings of detail and event, all this materialising and dematerialising of things moving, so unpredictably, in and out of being, she will halt the procession of images and say simply: *I am here.* She will lean her cheek against the old woman's beautifully creased face and say: *I am here, I am yours, I am evidence of the return of vanished things.*

The sky has bright grey dimensions, like laterite. And crossing the street Anna is aware of unAustralian cold at her cheeks; she experiences stinging exhilaration; as if it were a kiss.

At Mrs Dooley's boarding house the front door is ajar. A wedge of something wrong. Anna pushes gingerly at the door, and can hear from inside a voice elevated in anger and recrimination. Winston is there, in the kitchen, standing with his back to the fireplace and his hands joined behind him, and Mrs Dooley stands before him, red-faced and shouting. When Anna enters the kitchen Mrs Dooley turns, swinging in a semi-circle to face and accuse her.

So here she is then, Lady Muck herself, fuckin' whore more like, call yourself white as driven snow and a book-learning lady, fuckin' black men like there was no tomorrow; and me a widow and all alone, with no one but my nephew in Australia, who could be dead, for all I know, with his girl-crazy ways and his arty hands and his eyes as would melt any miser's heart, and he was such a lovely kid, all gooey smiles and what-not, but he wouldn't look, he's a gentleman, wouldn't look twice at a tart like you, a fancy lady who sleeps with black men, right under my nose, in a respectable house, what's more, and comes and goes all lah-di-dah with her papers and her pencils and her fancy-arty reproductions.

Mrs Dooley pauses for a break, then begins to cry.

A crying woman. Another woman shattered by the bombshell of what is hidden inside.

She slumps into a kitchen chair and puts her rough elbows on the table.

Sorry, sorry, me love, that was a bit rough, wasn't it? It's just that I was saving you, like. For my nephew in Australia. You'd make such a lovely couple.

Winston appears ashamed. He looks down at his shoes.

I'll make some tea, Anna suggests.

And in the spirit of tentative reconciliation, she bustles around the kitchen, opening the Persian-looking tea-caddy, washing the fine-china teapot, measuring equal-sized teaspoons, one by one, and hears herself saying, there, there, now; calm yourself, to the woman who has newly and flamboyantly abused her. Mrs Dooley is still sobbing, and it occurs to Anna that she too is distressed by mutability; she resents what her own history has taken away from her.

When Mrs Dooley drinks, it is in the manner of Uncle Ernie: she pours tea into the saucer, blows on it gently, and sips. The saucer tilts to her face. She bends her grey head. It is over five years now since Uncle Ernie's death, but Anna is still susceptible to the pangs this homely gesture elicits: Ernie's face, like a mirage, behind vertical ripples of steam.

And pardon my French, Mrs Dooley adds.

She takes a large handkerchief and blows her nose loudly, then resumes her tired invertebrate slump.

I got myself carried away a bit there.

Winston leaves to pack his things, and Anna longs to follow. But instead she sits with her arm around poor Mrs Dooley, a middle-aged woman fizzing and spluttering at the tail-end of her fury, a woman seized by something unnameable that has left her stranded in anger. In this over-heated kitchen, with the mineral sky gone, and the boy with his duck, and the air of reaching a surface in resolution, there is only frayed discomposure and bleary forms of grief. Anna suppresses weeping: she is not a woman-who-cries. In fact she never cries. Yet this seems to her entirely sad — that the joy of ascending into light is so swiftly eclipsed.

There, there, she repeats. Calm yourself, now.

And she thinks of Winston's expression, wondering what Mrs Dooley said to him before she arrived.

She had gone to surprise him at the library and found him not reading, after all, not caught in that virtuous librarian quiet, composed of soft low murmurings and flipping pages, but gazing at a photograph and talking to himself. In one of those gestures of lover's licence she approached him quietly from behind and cupped her white hands over his distracted black eyes, asking him, since this was the game, to guess who? Guess who?

When he dropped the photograph, startled, she quickly retrieved it.

It was a picture of a Jamaican woman and a small happy boy. They had brilliant smiles and faced the camera with an aspect of jubilation, as though offering up to the photographer their hearts and souls. Behind their heads was a hibiscus, massed with huge yellow blooms: trumpeting love.

My wife and my son. Back in Kingston. Jamaica.

You will return to them? she asked.

But of course, no question.

(Stay, she says silently. Stay. Stay.)

They had talked together for only fifteen minutes, each reaching across the rent distance that had opened between them, and then she left. She was a woman in love with a man whose image she bore away, reversed into false whiteness, held in frail promise, as the imperishable negative of some photograph not yet developed.

She had wanted to say *stay* — her mouth close to his ear, breathing amorously, confidentially, into the warm spaces of his body — but simply could not. He had already left her.

So will he return to them? asked Victoria.

Yes, said Anna. At the end of this year.

You didn't guess?

I didn't guess about the child; I only discovered that recently. But from the beginning he had told me he was a married man.

And is she beautiful, this bride?

Yes, she is beautiful. She has — they both have — the most remarkable smiles. Their smiles make me feel pinched, mean and small. My great uncle, back home, used to say that there was something called a death-defying smile. That's what they both have. Death-defying smiles.

Victoria refilled the brandy and offered more chocolate.

I had a black man once. Played the trombone.

And did he, Anna asked, have a death-defying smile?

He was from Detroit and had wonderful fingers. I liked the shape of his head, his cheeks puffing out as he blew. It didn't last very long.

They smile at each other.

I'm sorry, said Victoria. I was sweet on him myself. Don't go crazy, she adds.

Victoria pulls up the blanket and re-balances her brandy. Anna regards her with reverent and grand-daughterly tenderness.

I won't, she responds.

Once they had come in from a wet Sunday and wanted only to go to bed. They undressed with inelegant haste, flinging their clothes on the floor and wiping their naked skins on the candlewick coverlet. As they leapt beneath the blankets Winston and Anna shivered and laughed. Their hands and their feet were so cold each was obliged to perform on the other a comical ceremony of rubbing and vigorous embrace.

There, said Winston, as he placed her cold fingers between his thighs. Warm parts. The equator.

After they made love Anna realised that her face was burning. She laid her hot cheek against his pulsing neck. She wanted again to whisper *stay*, but the word fell somewhere silent, smothered in the soft intermittences of his breathing.

There are times when the gravity of what cannot be spoken between lovers necessitates wandering and evasive digressions. They looked into each other's faces in the wavering and water-marked light and what they spoke of was rain:

Where I come from, said Anna, we have under ten inches a year. Desert country. Dust. In the early days miners were so desperate for water they forced Aborigines to eat salt and then lead them to waterholes. One set up dynamite traps at waterholes just to kill off Aborigines.

Jesus, said Winston.

When I was twelve years old, Anna went on, there was a map in my classroom which showed Australia colour-coded according to rainfall. There were bands of rich dark green in the southern corners, bands of light green and a wider, more pronounced band of yellow, and in the interior a huge pool of orangey-red. We lived inside the space of orangey-red. Somehow I believed that this was what Australia looked like, banded like that, a kind of stripey pattern. I was pleased to live inside the largest and most vivid space. At the sealed and cogent centre, not stretching in a narrow band. I remember once the teacher pointed at the red pool with the tip of her ruler: the Heart, she announced. The Dead Heart of Australia.

It was an alarming notion.

Winston smiled.

Dead Heart, he repeated. Are all Australians so melodramatic?

Yes, Anna said, hoping to provoke him. We are all melodramatic. Victoria and me: we are typical.

Where I come from, Winston added, it was a dark green centre. A green heart, you might say. The rain was dense and substantial — not this vapid English drizzle — and after downpours everything was glossy and scented. There were small lakes across the ground and channels between the cane rows, and there were fallen battered blossoms and sodden leaves. We children would shake the trees so that we could make our own showers and then rats came out and together we chased them. It was a kind of celebration — not this miserable drizzle. My mother would catch rainwater in her hands and then wash her face with it. I'm not sure why. A habit, I suppose, or some kind of custom. But rain meant that: her shining face.

You're a poet, said Anna.

I'm Jamaican, said Winston.

Jamaican Shakespearian.

No, Shakespearian Jamaican.

They paused, each reflective. Their lovemaking was often like this: confession, intermission.

Once, when I was seven, Anna continued, I saw a black cat spun in the air, way up high, flying anti-clockwise. Just outside the window of my school. There it was, magically spinning.

You're making that up.

No, not at all. Cross-my-heart-and-hope-to-die.

Winston rolled over Anna and kissed her above the heart.

Anti-clockwise, he said gently, hovering above her.

Later that night Winston leant close to Anna's face.

Me can' sleep, he said softly, in his boyhood speech. Me keep thinkin bout all them po thirsty Aborigines . . .

It is 2 a.m. She can hear the distant forlorn sound of a revving-up vehicle.

Anna thinks of Winston's hands. Of his forehead. His mouth. She is laced into the space of wherever he is and knows that when she sleeps it is the nightfall of his absence she slides into. Now, insomniac, and ago-nised by yearning, she wonders how she will live with this excess of desire. She is lying on her back, consid-ering the ceiling over which streetlight flickers and plays. Discs, shafts, the swinging beam of headlights:

this spectrum of effects appears somehow like a transparent body, or indeed like the memory of such a body, evoked in fits and starts and lit in clustered flashes that signify everything vague and uncertain. She remembers the occasion of her lover carrying a cyclamen through the streets of London, all comic benignity and Shakespearian joy; he cradled it in his hands; it was mysterious, like an offering; and then she remembers the little boy with the string-along duck, the bright particular boy, so touchingly formal, so charmingly stern, and she sees this boy now, floating on the ceiling, his round face shimmering and efflorescent, and wonders for the first time in her life if she will ever have a child.

2

Jules is shadowy, said Anna. I don't see him at all.

Yes, shadowy.

He had fallen asleep, Victoria said, on the velvet chaise longue.

He was on his back, with his hands knitted together at the centre of his body — as though he were older, somehow, since this is the sleeping posture of a man with a belly, a man holding himself against death, a man preparing to rest forever in the mean confinements of a coffin. Yet he was in lovely repose; his face was young and placid.

I closed the shutters, then gathered our four or five candles. I lit and arranged them so that the light cast Jules' silhouette in profile upon the wall, and with my box of artist's chalks traced the outline of his face and the top of his body. Thereafter the wall bore the memory of my lover — a stain was at his forehead and a tiny crack at the cheek, but I was quietly surprised at the likeness there, its uncanny quality. I was surprised at the specificity of his face, captured like that, and surprised too by my own inclination to superstition; I felt I'd trapped him, that he was mine. When I dream of Jules he sometimes appears as a shadow. A chalky shadow with a crack on one cheek . . .

He had fallen asleep after a tachycardia attack. It had shocked me, his vulnerability. We had been shopping at the market on Rue Mouffetard when suddenly his whole body began swaying and jolting, his face became livid and he was gleaming with sweat. At that stage I knew nothing about Jules' heart condition, and I was alarmed to see such utter change. His knees buckled under him and our shopping spilled — clementines went bouncing down the cobbled street — and Jules gagged on what he was unable to express. Startled shoppers scrambled around us to gather our shopping, exultant at the terrible and exciting situation. A man dying, convulsively, in front of their eyes. An event-to-talk-about. *Un spectacle.*

Think of it, Anna: a seizure of the body controlled by the racing heart, a kind of perilous extravagance, an over-supply of vivacity.

When the attack was over Jules found he had wet himself.

How humiliating, he whispered in English.

He was panting against my neck; and although his body shivered, he was hot as a flame. With my silk scarf I dabbed at the sweat that flowed from him.

I remember that Jules insisted on carrying the shopping home. It was clearly a labour; he could barely make it up the stairs. When I closed the door he had dropped our basket and was already lying down, with his eyes closed and his hands resting clasped on his belly.

I'll just rest for a minute, Jules called out softly.

His fatigue was so great, his body so persecuted, that he was instantly asleep. I drew the outline then. I drew his face and body in its almost incredible stillness, settling into the immunity and suppliance of sleep. Jules called it *Cartoon of a young man's brush with Death*, and threatened to erase it, but the image remained on the wall, long after he was gone. Even now it may be there, upstairs, faintly recalling him. In Rue Gît Le Coeur.

What happened to Jules?

(Anna can barely bring herself to ask the question.)

Jules was lost: buried treasure . . . To be honest, I don't know.

The first large round-up of Jews in Paris was in July, 1942. Thousands were herded into the Vélodrome d'Hiver, the Vél d'Hiv, we called it, and then deported to camps. Jules, I believe, was not among them. He had disappeared before that; he had not worn the yellow star with *Juif* written on it. He had not carried the sign of his own fatality.

According to Hélène — who seemed so sure — he'd last been seen at Drancy, sometime late in 1943.

Drancy was a prison camp just to the north of Paris: it was a holding point before inmates were sent to Auschwitz.

Nobody knows, Hélène said bleakly, looking into the engulfing distance, looking into uncertainty, where he went after that. In her deafness and bereavement she heard only the tremendous ringing echo of his absence.

A photographer we knew in Paris told me that he heard that Jules had been working for the Resistance. Taking secret photographs, he said. Aiding the Gaullistes and the Allies with his fluency in English. But was not sure exactly where. Or when it was. Or the unit to which he had been attached. Not sure, he said.

Someone else, an old school friend, who knew of his condition, speculated that Jules had died of a heart attack.

In these dreadful times, a natural death, he said, trying hard to comfort and console me. We both knew it was a lie. But I nodded, and said yes, of course that is possible, and he touched the back of my hand in a sympathetic gesture, as though I was a widow standing in a parlour, over a walnut and brass coffin, legitimately grieving.

One of our neighbours told me that she heard Jules had escaped to the United States, through Spain and Gibraltar.

Probably a rich man in California, photographing film stars. Probably in Beverly Hills. Probably famous.

Another fake consolation. Another net to catch nothing in, thrown over tearful darkness . . .

Something grim obsesses me: O Anna, let me tell you.

In September, 1943, a group of seventy prisoners in Drancy began building an escape tunnel. They worked in shifts, day and night, for almost two months, but were discovered by the Germans with only thirty metres to go. All those involved in the escape plan were summarily executed. I think my Jules was there. I think my Jules was there in the discovered tunnel.

This is the mystery of amorous connection at work: lovers carry each other around like shadows; they trail their phantom desires; they sense as an intuitive shape the equation of the other; and they also absorb in their lovemaking the logic of each other's images. This tunnel he entered. This corridor between us. It was surrender to the darkness that I had given him.

You think I morbidly romanticise, my darling Anna-lytical? You think me necromantic? Perhaps I morbidly romanticise. But something in me, some limit, or some propensity, perhaps, will not allow any precise imagining of the camp. Or the precise physical circumstances of his death. Only this chute of darkness, and his face there, glowing.

When the Germans fled they destroyed all the records at Drancy. So we will never know. We will never know.

———

Hélène Levy was still searching for her son, Jules Levy, photographer of faces, photographer of brides, when she died, broken-hearted, in 1950. I went to her funeral. She had asked to be buried with a yellow star and her son's portrait photograph, pinned together, intimately, over her heart. Both the star and the photograph bore the strange sheen of worn objects touched again and again.

I looked into the open coffin and saw Jules' face, young and seductive, looking back. He was sixteen years old with a boy-smile and messy hair, and he peered from his rectangle, from his pillow of star, shyly eternal.

I tore at the sleeves and the pocket of my blouse, but grief swelled and grew.

3

Victoria is sitting up in bed, wearing her feathers and demanding a cocktail.

Gin fizz! she calls out. To hasten my marvellous dying! To pickle my exquisite corpse!

Beside her, on the table where the cyclamen had been, stands the antique hourglass, emptying and filling. Victoria wakes at night, at arbitrary intervals, to reach over and turn it; and even though for her it bears no timekeeping function at all, she loves the opposed brass phoenixes, each holding their glass bubbles, and the uniform fall of grain upon grain, and the two tidy pyramids, pale triangles in the night-light, diminishing and building. Such a lovely invention.

She insists too that it is a surreal object *par excellence*: what could be stranger than time configured as twin glasses, a slim communicating passage and the transit of egg-shell? She loves its slow hypnotic regularity. She loves its *déjà vu* and its iconic outline.

Cécilia is puzzled by the disappearance of her pot of flowers, but too polite to ask. She now visits twice a day because her patient's condition has deteriorated. There are good days, like today, but Victoria has made a decision — Cécilia has seen this before — that her time is nearly over. In her years of nursing, she tells Anna, this phenomenon continues to surprise her: the degree of human will entailed in death, the purposive way in which some patients greet their end, as though they are travelling towards a loving or imperative assignation. Cécilia, a woman preoccupied with murderous thoughts about her own husband, often wonders if she will end this way, with spirit and self-possession. Together Anna and Cécilia confer: Victoria is working to some schedule, announces Cécilia, some private *liaison*, some *rendezvous*.

Yes, Anna is thinking, *liaison, rendezvous*. Her mothers. Her babies. Her perished and disappeared lovers.

She has detected in herself a sort of resentment. Victoria is speeding her death, accelerating into tunnels, indifferent to the young woman, her relative, who daily tends and attends her. Arrows of story fly out and she catches them with her body. She is merely a target. She is the destination of shot energy, expended, then unimportant.

What Anna knows now of Victoria is the variety of her calamities: her life is so racked by inordinate disfigurations of grief it might all be untrue; it might all be fabrication. There are too many gravesites, located and unlocatable, and too many fragments betokening self-magnification. These hurt Anna: both the details and her own lingering mistrust. She wants to say: *I am here, I am yours, I am evidence of the return of vanished things*, but the time is not right, Victoria is not right. She is in a labyrinth in which she hears only her own querulous voice. Victoria has entered a kind of loquacious disintegration. She chatters randomly, but with an almost demented assertiveness.

When Jules and I made love in the tunnel — no, that was Louis — when Louis and I made love in the tunnel, we came out with white-coloured dust all over our skin. Like ash. Like cremation. It was at once the return and foreshadowing of death. I carried death like a disease, like irradiation, from lover to lover . . .

Do you know what Nabokov said of Salvador Dali? That he was Norman Rockwell's lost evil twin, wreaking vengeance on the world with bucket loads of shit. Or was it bucket loads of kitsch? I despised him, Salvador Dali. That flabby world he inhabited. That moral deliquescence —

Where is Ruby?
Where is Lily-white?
Where is my carcanet?

He gave me a snakeskin, once, a shed skin, which he had discovered somewhere outside our tunnel. It was covered in brown patterns of diamonds and exquisitely light, like web. He hung it around my neck as a lover's garland. Later I pinned it to the back of my bedroom door, but Henry tore it to pieces. Because it was mine. Because it was special.

Something terrible. A woman in my building returned; she had survived the camps. Her head was shorn, like mine, and she looked only half alive. A group of men at our local bar assumed she was a collaborator and spat at her and abused her. Afterwards they apologised, their caps in their hands, their heads bowed in shame. She left for Australia. 'It is the furthest place I can think of,' she said. 'The end of the earth.'

Romance makes women histrionic. This is its chief virtue, to theatricalise desire. The lover is disponibilité: ready for the marvellous.

'I am the man with sea urchin lashes who for the first time raises his eyes on the woman who must be everything for him, in the blue streets.' *André Breton, 1937. A beautiful line, don't you think?*

I carried death like a disease, like irradiation, from lover to lover. I left tell-tale hand prints all over their bodies.

The lights of Montmartre were glass beads to guide me. I wore my feathers and a lapis gown of watered silk. Breton looked down like Odilon Redon's eye-in-a-balloon, and I realised I was afraid of him. (Float away, float away.)

I always wanted to go to Melbourne, the Capital of Sorrow . . . Mel-bourne, spell-borne . . . I never made it, you know. I never saw what the sound was.

I dream of Jules as a shadow, but I also dream him bright, outlined very sharply and with unusual definition. There is a technique in photography called solarisation, in which a partially developed print is exposed to light, so that black-and-white images emerge with heavy black borders, and their planes and their details seem luminous and unearthly. He was a solarised being; oddly exposed. The surfaces of his skin were bright and incendiary.

I looked into the mirror and darkness looked back.

The surfaces of his skin were bright and incendiary.

In the British Museum, many years after the war, I rested my face against a mummy case, to check for a heartbeat.

*   'I've dreamed of you so much, walked so much, spoken*
*   and lain with your phantom that perhaps nothing more is*
left me
*   than to be a phantom among phantoms and a hundred*
times more shadow
*   than the shadow that walks and will joyfully walk*
*   on the sundial of your life.'*
*   Robert Desnos: I've dreamed of you so much. I know the whole poem. Shall I complete the recitation?*

*   Where is Ruby?*
*   Where is Lily-white?*
*   Where is the flame tree?*

4

The catalogue description reads thus:

Black Mirror (date unknown) 122 x 122 cm. Oil on canvas. Private collection.

Black Mirror *is in many ways typical of Surrealist pictorial art of the 30s and 40s, purporting to depict dream states as allegories of unconscious desire or meaning. This painting represents the treachery of art itself. In the foreground stands a woman in a long gown, with her back to the viewer, who appears to be peering into a tripartite mirror. The centre reflection, slightly to the left, is entirely black, and has one eye, a symbol of the limits of artistic vision. Further to the left the reflection is flaming in frozen fire. This repeats the burning figure motif found elsewhere in Morrell's work, and alludes to the destructive power of the life of art. In the right-hand reflection, the figure's head has been replaced by a jewel, possibly a garnet or a ruby, and may be taken to represent the financial and spiritual rewards of artistic achievement. Suspended figures hover over the top corners of the painting: one is a fat man with donkey ears (the art dealer), the second a devil, wielding a sword (the art critic). Between these figures is a heraldic black swan, its wings outstretched, indicating the corruption and blackening of a traditional symbol of beauty. Unusually, this painting features a border of objects: down the sides and along the bottom is a pattern of beautifully rendered miniature objects against a black background. These include aeroplanes, giraffes, hourglasses and Eiffel Towers, and are merely decorative, a random selection of images suggesting the Surrealist fascination with the principle of strange and meaningless conjunction. Finally, the legends* déjà vu *(seen again) and* jamais vu *(never seen) adorn the extreme top corners of the painting, a philosophical addition that refers to the endless contest in art between originality and derivation. The tone of* Black Mirror *is sombre, and it bears a clear indebtedness to the work of Salvador Dali.*

When she opens the door it is Winston, returned, carrying a bunch of lilacs.

I heard, he said. I heard from Cécilia.

Anna steps forward and leans her cheek against his chest, and his arms enclose her like a perfect wreath.

5

The sky was bone. Anna looked up and saw not a single bird. Perhaps, she thought foolishly, death has driven them away. The quiet worlds of bird flight and seasons and flecked shadows upon a face, the transient colours of water or stone or the high dome of the sky, these shift with the special-effects of grief. On Hampstead Heath it was Sunday and families were out and about, enjoying the alleviation of severity that marked the beginning of spring. Children in eskimo parkas and with rosy cheeks flung themselves onto the grass, heedless of mud, or fought with friendly aggression over the possession of a striped ball. There was an old man in a scarf, alone, sitting and reading, and a serious track-suited jogger leading a barely controllable dog. Beneath an oak, against the trunk, two lovers, both black and both somewhere in their early teens, kissed and groped with concentrated and disciplined persistence.

Anna saw all this as if it were a film: it hung before her, remote and not quite real. She was conscious too of a slight instability to what she saw; the projection might indeed be a figment of light and shadow, held up tremblingly by an invisible mechanical contrivance, contingent, finite, illusive, false. She viewed it all, this world of light, from a dark and separate chamber.

What haunted Anna was that she had not yet said her piece. She had not said the words she had so often rehearsed: *I am here, I am yours . . .* She had imagined a ceremonial conclusion, composed of a farewell, an expression of love, and the family revelation. She had imagined saying: *Here I am: Anagnorisis.* But Victoria died in her dreaming, luxuriously alone.

When she was not in monologue Victoria had been asleep, deeply removed and inaccessible. Towards the end she slept more fitfully, and her fragments of speech shortened, but what marked them above all was self-communion. Victoria's *liaison* was with her avatars, her own other selves, and she met them in an excited time-lapsing rush, the way, Anna thought, one sees film of petals quickly opening in a magical pop, or storm clouds skidding across an inconstant sky, or the polished sun rising or falling with the confident bounce of a tennis ball. Victoria was racing through her history, swift as an animation, colliding with herself. She seemed — how to put it? — she seemed almost *busy*. Then, on the final day, Victoria at last became quiet.

She had been asleep for hours and woke only once, with a start. She said lucidly:

I dreamt I was searching for something, in the River Seine.

And then she slept again, and did not wake. It was in the end that simple; it was that exclusive. Her quietus was a slow sinking into the space of her dreams.

And now, thought Anna, Victoria is ash as she wished, mingled with her swan's feather head-dress and the bouquet of velvety flowers she and Cécilia had contributed, and the small carved wooden hourglass Winston placed upon her coffin, and the various conventional floral tributes from collectors and fans; and she has left behind her a wretched chamber, filled with elongated shadows and words unsaid. There was this intolerable grief, and there was also the task, the preposterous task — bequeathed formally by Victoria — of delivering her ashen remains to her long-lost sister, Ruby.

Hampstead Heath flickered before Anna: it had become blustery, all of a sudden. She saw the trees and the grass and the sky and the people, and it appeared not present-tense at all, but waxen and antiquated. Like one of those mute movies punctuated by a black placard bearing the pretended remnants of speech.

Beyond the trees faint smoke scrolled upwards from somewhere. Smoke. Just that. Just that prepossessing sign.

———

Anna has not been in her town on the goldfields for many years. It has altered, grown. New highways criss-cross the town where small bumpy roads had been. There are supermarkets and car-lots with bright plastic bunting. The old-timers seem to have disappeared, and the streets are full of teenagers with strappy sandals and cocky attitudes. In the distance Anna sees Beryl Ray and Moira Ahern, both pushing baby-carriages. They walk in unison, leaning forward, as though moving trolleys of ore. Anna waves, but neither Beryl nor Moira pauses or turns to acknowledge her.

She leaves the railway station carrying her small single suitcase, passes the Railway Hotel, the Commercial Hotel and the Palace Hotel, and then she stands in the main street, beside the Australia Hotel, to get her bearings. The façades of the buildings are largely unchanged since the gold-rushes: history persists in this casual architectural eccentricity, in these tall shapes with their verandahs and iron lace and iron roofs. Across the road stands the elegant Exchange Hotel, with the enigmatic sign *Rialto* fixed to a high surmounting dome. Two men are rolling barrels of beer onto a ramp and guiding them carefully into cellars beneath. One of them looks up and spontaneously waves — How ya bin, luv? he shouts — and Anna nods in his direction with no idea at all who this friendly person might be. From the window behind her a fluid orange light seeps out, smelling of stale beer. She crosses the road and then double-crosses back again, realising in the blur of her own confusion what it was after all that she had forgotten, that she would meet her father at the Australia, not at the Exchange.

Anna Griffin waits in a galvanised moment, caught by the currents of her own homecoming excitement.

The town around her looks almost completely unreal. It is a confluence of white mythologies she nowadays despises: frontier heroism, brute wealth, value measured by the size of excavation and extraction. A small boy close by idly bangs at a rusted pipe with a piece of metal and the clanging sound — more than the buildings and the street names and the earth smell carried in the wind — reminds Anna of interminable afternoons in this place, afternoons of truly funereal boredom, vast in magnitude, full of stunning glare, bleached by an absorbing and drowsy sadness, from which she retreated to the lending library of the Mechanics' Institute. There she fell into the welcoming shadows of the classics and was dragged by dead Englishmen into cold wordy spaces. There she discovered a catalogue of Victoria's early exhibition (*donator anonymous*) in which she saw, like a revelation, the brilliant authority of images. Familiar objects transmutated. The mystery of repetition. Her own landscape seen and rendered with fantastic scrutibility. Here was a seam, a claim, an alluvial outcrop.

She sat alone at an oak desk in the Mechanics' Institute library, her heart quickened in a kind of inner applause, and felt exhumed by art.

Anna? As though he is not quite sure.

Griffo.

They kiss and embrace beneath the sign of the Australia Hotel.

Hey Griffo!

The man at the Exchange waves once again.

Griffo answers his wave in a comfortable copy.

Anna is once again staying in her childhood home. She has an iron bed with a horsehair mattress on the back verandah, and a clear view of the pigeon coop, ringed by diamond wire, and neat rows of glossy corn, carefully irrigated by muddy furrows; and further back, the rust-stained shed, exactly as she remembered it, where she and her father used to skin rabbits. Above her, and more evocation than real, the corrugated iron roof heats and cracks, releasing a pungent metallic scent; and the ore crusher, immemorial, sounds its thunder across the sky.

Griffo now lives with Lola, a tiny plump Italian woman, who has transformed him to this gentle nurturer of pigeons and corn. She is a brown woman with a round face (*my lucky penny*, he nicknamed her), and anyone can tell that Griffo and Lola are precious to each other; there is a regard and solicitude in their mutual glances, and a jokey tenderness to their occasional and easy talk. Anna has never seen her father so calm and contented: he whistles and hums as he checks his corn, and Lola watches him, from time to time, through the plastic Venetian blinds at the kitchen window.

In the afternoon they sit together in the shade and drink tea. Lola hands out biscuits and pours from a teapot, her motherly movements deft and precise. She passes Anna and then Griffo a cup of tea, and when she has her own she sits back in her chair, smiling.

Well? Whadaya know? she politely asks.

It is a rhetorical question. Griffo touches her forearm and dips a pale biscuit into his drink. In this small communion, and with sunshine through the lattice falling sideways upon then, they are knitted together by patterns of light. Anna can hear the pigeons making their mournful-sounding calls, she can see her father's grey hair, and the way his face now resembles the leather of rabbit skin, she can see the woman beside him brush tiny crystals of sugar from the table. A dog barks somewhere. There is a slight breeze in the peppermint. The simplicity of her homecoming almost moves Anna to tears.

When she is settled in her bed the first night, Lola visits with a jam-jar filled with sprigs of smokebush.

So you will know that you're home, she says. So you will know where you are.

Lola places the floral offering on the wooden floor beside the bed.

You can smell it, she adds. Like a memory of something, eh?

Anna smiles and pats her blanket so that Lola sits on the edge of the bed.

Thank you.

No problem.

Well, thank you anyway.

A relaxed silence settles, a respectful hush. Lola leans over and softly kisses her step-daughter on the forehead.

Sleep now. It's late. I'll cook eggs in the morning.

And then she rises and walks into the house, switching off the verandah light as she goes.

Anna is remembering herself as a tiny child. She wore bunny-slippers with a bead clasp and a sky-blue animal-print nightie. Her mother lifted her skyward (*fly! fly!*) before she tucked her into bed.

My, what big eyes you have.

A gentle enfolding. A goodnight kiss.

The verandah is draughty and Anna curls her body against the wind. For some reason, half-asleep, she chants to herself: Matthew, Mark, Luke and John, hold the horse while I get on.

For some reason, too, she remembers once again seeing trains-as-film — bubble faces, montage, consecutive images-in-a-flash — spooled on the curves of her new imagining, electrified by all that Victoria had shown her.

About four years earlier Griffo had caught his right arm in the leather belt of mine machinery, and shattered irreparably the bones in his wrist and forearm. His flesh withered and the palm of his hand decreased in size by almost half; there was also some paralysis. No longer able to work underground, Griffo retrained as a 'numbers man', a clerk's aide, in the above-ground mine office. He taught himself to write with his left hand, to shake hands back to front, and to hold a newspaper and shuffle cards single-handed. He re-learnt the world and its activities from the left side of his body.

I got a walloping, said Griffo, and I needed a breather. But I'm all right now.

In a modest gesture, he pulled protectively at his brown cardigan with his good left hand, as though afraid he had tempted fate by his satisfaction with life.

I only think about the accident once in a blue moon. Life's different now. Lola, the pigeons, the garden.

Anna and Griffo stared at each other. Without his cloak of dirt, she thought, and with his benevolent Lola, my father is like Lazarus, returned from the grave.

Give us a hand in the garden, Anna.

They move outside, together, in concert.

Pigeons flutter against the wire and sound their welcoming *vroo vroo*. The garden is a quiet fertile place. Anna helps Griffo break open sticks of gelignite, stolen from the mines, to spread as fertiliser in the soil beneath his blooming orange tree. As a child she expected exploding oranges. Now her father pats at the earth with his good left hand, he smooths the red soil and applies a little water, and tells with his body that there will be no more accidents or explosions. His manner is ceremonious and his pace steady and patient. When the task is finished Anna and Griffo wash their hands in a bucket. The sky rests there, broken by their washing, then reassembled.

Everything Anna sees has this quality of precarious coming-together.

In the back shed, now filled up with new gardening equipment, stands Anna's childhood bicycle. It looks battered, old and surprisingly small. It leans with her into the angle of continuous past.

It was not difficult to locate Ruby Morrell. Everyone knew of her. She was almost eighty years old, vigorous, indomitable, a leader of her people, and she spent most of her time at the offices of the Centre for Aboriginal Rights, installed in a bow-shaped wicker chair which framed her head like a halo. She recalled Victoria, not in appearance, but in some distinctive air of authority and command; and when first Anna met her she felt a recurrence of the taut contractions of grief. Told of Victoria's death, Ruby became silent and inward, but did not weep.

Long time, she said. It was a long time ago, when she left.

Ruby had stiff white hair and a dignified expression. She lifted her chin when she spoke, so that she seemed to inhabit a taller and more assertive space.

So this is Ruby. The sister. The long-lost sister.

Anna placed the tin that contained Victoria's ashes into the black woman's open hands, and Ruby settled back in her wicker chair and told her story:

Me mum Lily-white, and me, we didn't *vanish* like Viccy said, but we left pretty soon after Henry

Morrell returned from boarding school. Henry — the debil-debil man, Mum used to call him — had tried to attack me, and for Mum, who was scared shitless, excuse my French, that was the last straw. We headed bush, and stayed in a blackfella camp, the Five-mile, for a coupla months, then moved back to the mission where Mum grew up. I couldn't stand all the God-bothering and the smirking nuns, but I learnt to read and write, and Mum still knew the old ways, the women's Law, so she took it all in her stride. It was better away from that house, away from the white-debil-man and his shiny swords.

We still knew what was going on because Mum and Mrs Murphy met in secret once a week. For some reason they both needed each other's company. Mrs Murphy liked my mother's stories about blackfella ways, and she had a few whitefella stories of her own too, I can tell you. Mum made her promise not to tell anyone where we were living, not even our Viccy, when she came back from school. She was that afraid of Henry Morrell. I missed Viccy like anything, but Mum had it in her head that Henry would kill me, or take me away. Under the ground, she used to say. Under the ground and into the mines.

Of course Viccy was crazy about the Bell brothers, Ernie and Louis, and she had a thing going, as you know, with the elder one, Louis. Good-looking lads they were, and very good sorts. I was sweet on Ernie myself, but after the scarring he wouldn't have anything to do with women. Broke my heart, your Ernie did.

Terrible business, that was. Terrible business.

And Mrs Bell, poor soul, left behind like that.

(Here Ruby pauses for so long that Anna thinks she may have ended her story. She is moving through a time-stretched inwardness Anna can only guess at.)

Back when Henry killed Louis Bell we thought he was a goner, that he'd be hung for sure down in Fremantle gaol, and it was pretty shocking, I can tell you, that he got off, scot free. Mum thought this showed that Henry was truly a debil-debil; to the very end of her life she was sick with fear of him. Everyone on the goldfields talked for months about the killing, and poor Mrs Bell, poor soul, she went round the twist a bit after it all happened, and died less than a year after Louis' murder. They still hadn't found the body when Mrs Bell died, and that was what got to her, I think, not knowing where he was, just wondering and wondering, every day wondering.

It's true that Ernie followed Viccy and Mrs Murphy to the city, but that's not the half of it. Ernie stole some gold — enough to buy a baby, he said — and a lot of the miners, I think, were in on it with him. There was a great deal of sympathy for Ernie Bell, and everyone for miles around hated Henry's guts. Some blokes on the mine helped Ernie smuggle out the gold, and he took off, quick as a flash, still with his bandages on, down south to follow Viccy. When he returned he had a baby boy, your dad Thomas, now Griffo, and he loved that little boy like it was his very own. But anyways the cops were onto him, quick-smart. Ernie ended up serving two years in the local gaol, on a charge of gold-stealing. I reckon it was a short sentence because you just had to look at him, you just had to see his damaged face, what all that acid had taken away, to know how much dear Ernie Bell had suffered. Yours truly took care of the baby boy; I looked after your dad while Ernie was in the clink; that's why he — and you, for that matter — have my married name, Griffin. When Thomas went back to Ernie he thought it best to keep the new name; that way, he reckoned, he could make up some story about dead parents, or famous relations, or whatever he needed to say. When your dad was a boy he asked me once if we were related, and I said, Of course we are, all Griffins are related — and he seemed to like that, cheered him up, and he used to visit and play with my own band of littlies. He's like an older brother to my eldest boy Roy; they got along together like a house on fire. Mucking around. Down at the slag dumps. On their bikes like crazy-fellas. Still mates today, him and Roy. You know my Roy, works at the Lake View and Star.

Anyways, I know what you're thinking, but that's not how it went. Viccy's not your grandma. Mrs Murphy said that Viccy gave birth to a daughter, and a family, a rich family that lived by the river, took her away immediately. Viccy's dad set it all up, the silver spoon, so to speak, and maybe so that he could keep track of her and someday meet up. His own grand-daughter, after all. Ernie was distraught when he realised he couldn't get Louis' and Viccy's baby, so he made what you call discreet inquiries, and paid the gold to someone who worked at the maternity hospital, and who acted as a go-between. Some poor lass, up the duff and with no man to support her, sold her son to Ernie Bell for a lump of gold. It made no difference, in the end, to Ernie Bell. He adored that boy, your father, and gave up work on the mines, a good paying job he had, so he could spend proper time looking after the baby. Bloody adored him, Ernie did. Excuse my French.

Mr Morrell was pretty put out, as you can imagine, by all that had happened, and after the trial and the baby he sold his share in the Midas mine and pissed off back to Melbourne. Good riddance, we all said. He left Henry in the house, all alone, because no one would have anything to do with him, the bastard. Mrs Murphy came straightaway to live with me and Mum, and she liked living with us, I think, because we were a lively bunch; but she still liked to boss us around from time to time. Bossy-Boots Murphy, Viccy and I used to call her. Hadn't changed at all. And her and Mum died, believe it or not, in the very same week, so we had a Christian funeral and a native one, and it was pretty damn miserable around here, I can tell you. Two grand old ladies. I miss them both.

A pause. Now Ruby seems to have become aware of the tin of human ashes she is cradling. She gives it a little shake as if to shake off imminent tears.

Two grand old ladies . . .

You know in those days Native Welfare used to

come and steal us light-skinned kids, but my mum always managed to hide and to save me. Coupla times we went bush, way out into the desert, and stayed there, escaping, living on love and bush-tucker.

Whitefellas always wanta take what's not theirs, Mum used to say. Whitefellas always wanting things, always wanting more and more.

I lost Viccy, you see, but I never lost my mother. She hid me, Lily-white did. I never lost my mother because she never lost me.

All those poor children, stolen away. But me, I was never stolen.

Anyways, everyone thought — Ruby changes the subject — that Henry Morrell would eventually leave, but he stayed on in the house. Some kind of riding accident, people said, put him in a wheel-chair, and he stayed on inside, getting crazier and crazier, shouting at people from behind his wall. Henry's dad paid a fortune to have nurses come and look after him; they had their work cut out for them, I can tell you, and earned every bloody cent. He was a complete loony by the end and a real handful.

What I remember most clearly is Ernie Bell, when he first returned with the brand-new baby. Before the cops got onto him he shared that early time, and it brought tears to your eyes to see how tender he was, and how loving and devoted. Adored that boy. I'll never forget how he held the baby up and kissed it on the tummy, and *ooh*ed and *aah*ed and made a fuss like any new mother. I was still in love with Ernie then, and he broke my heart. He had eyes, as they say, only for baby Thomas. Still, I met my Harry Griffin, so it was happy-ever-after. For a while there, anyways. Before the gut-rot took him.

Ernie and me got together in his last few years. When you left for boarding school, you know, he was very lonely. Missed you like crazy, he did. Talked about you all the time. Called you a smarty-pants and egg-head, but he was very very proud of that scholarship you got, and said you'd make something of yourself, and return to the goldfields some day, as a doctor maybe, or a teacher. We used to hold hands on my verandah, and share a bottle of home brew, and yarn for hours and hours about what happened in the olden days. Good yarner, was Ernie. Good listener, too. A real gentleman, your grandad.

Ruby lapsed again into private silence.

Me mum, Lily-white, she was the one. She knew all the stories. Mum knew everything.

Ruby proffered a photograph. In it she stood holding hands with her mother Lily-white in front of a building Anna did not recognise. Both women faced the camera, resembling each other, except that Lily-white bore the shadow of her absent eye.

Nice. You look like sisters, Anna said clumsily.

There was a bloke once, too. Before I was born Mum lived with an Afghan, a cameleteer, a bloke named Ali. They lived somewhere up near Ora Banda way — true love, I reckon, from the way she spoke of him. Mum said he wore a red silk turban and had skin like a blackfella. Prayed. Spoke quietly. Decent sort of bloke. Ali got stabbed in a brawl trying to help out a mate. Just one of those things, I suppose. Sad. In the old days. Like poor Louis Bell. Like Rose. Like Rose Morrell.

Me mum, she knew everything, Ruby repeated. Like she could see inside you. Like you had a special window set into your body . . .

Ruby embraced Anna when she stood to leave.

Did Viccy ever talk about me an Mum?

All the time, said Anna. All the time.

In the night Anna woke after only two hours sleep. What had she been dreaming?

It was a dream scenario in which Lily-white and Winston coexisted, as partners, perhaps, or as brother and sister. In the image fragment that remained, they were holding hands together, on a shady verandah. Lily-white was young and lovely, her two eyes preserved, and Winston was naked to the waist, as though he had just bathed or finished labouring work. Anna found this fragment completely opaque.

She lay in the darkness, remembering.

Victoria had told her once that Lily-white's totem creature was the blue-tongued lizard. She was not sure what this meant, except that Lily-white would never eat them and was careful not to harm them. She told of an occasion when they came across one in a laneway. It raised itself up, opened its mouth wide, and exposed its broad indigo throat and its dragonish face, and Lily-white had clasped it carefully behind the neck, and then gently, very gently, moved it to safety under a bush. She knew things, Victoria said. Lily-white knew everything.

Winston said once that his nickname was Makandal. His mother's family was from Haiti, and Makandal was a legendary Haitian leader who waged war against French planters in the late eighteenth century. In local stories Makandal would miraculously escape from his enemies by transforming himself into a bird, or a lizard, or fire, or a wolf.

H'm, my lil one, my Makandal, his mother used to say. Someday gwan fly. Someday gwan burn.

I didn't know him, thinks Anna. I didn't know Winston at all.

There is a humility and wisdom to her revelation. She has given him back to his family. She has returned him to Jamaica. She faces the night without imagining loss and deficiency.

Well? Whadaya know?

It was their last evening together and Anna was having dinner with Griffo and Lola. Over crumbed cutlets and white beans, and aware of the indelicacy of her task and the embarrassment she would cause him, she told her stunned father the story of his life. An inarticulate man, he was now almost speechless. He moved the food about on his plate with deep solemnity. His damaged right arm hung at his side. For a few moments Anna thought her father would weep: his chin twitched and his lip trembled and he could not meet her gaze.

Well, he said at last. I knew about that Henry Morrell business, killing Louis, an' all that. But for the rest of it . . . well . . . for crying out loud . . .

Ernie had maintained, all his life, that Griffo was the child of a young couple, Nellie and Theodore Griffin, killed in a car accident. He had supplied descriptions and heroic and detailed biographies.

There's a photo, Griffo said, of Ernie and me together. He's holding me up and he looks just like a dad with his kiddie. I really should've known that he was my dad. I should've realised then.

Poor Ernie, added Griffo. Poor Uncle Ernie.

Lola attempted to revive the dinner spirit with tiramisu. She kissed Griffo lightly on the cheek as she placed her triumphant home-cookery before him on the table.

Eat, she commanded. Both of you now. Eat.

Later that evening Griffo pressed an address into Anna's palm.

Your mum wrote to me, he said. After all these years. She's been searching for you. I wrote back saying that you were off in the Old Country for a spell. Look her up, Anna. She'd like to hear from you.

Anna caught sight of herself, at a distance, in the speckled mirror hanging on the wall behind her father's head. Under the dim light she was surprised to see herself appearing — so manifestly — a woman enveloped and contained by grief. She looked older and ragged, and the quality of sorrow that had rested incipient in her features was now evident and exaggerated. She wondered if she should have left Ernie's story undivulged.

Not yet, she told her father. No, not yet.

Grief was this strange folding in, Anna reflected, this recursion of something dark tucking under like a wave. Already Victoria's face was vanishing. Already silence was easier than words. Anna took her dark fold, this irrevocable reshaping, this crypt inside, and walked past her father, out into the noisy night.

6

The woman who levitated as a little girl, constellating her home town from the shiny sky, seeing below her the curve of the horizon, as space itself is curved, and the stellar arrangements of spinifex, and dust moving in twirling eddies, and corrugated earth, and straggly-looking trees; who saw, further in, the poppet heads like monsters and the glinting iron rooves, the landscape of pockmarks and shaft holes and slime dumps and slag heaps, and everything that, seen together from a child-glorious elevation, was profound in its quality of strange, strange loveliness; this woman is in France, in Paris in fact, preparing to descend and enter the earth.

After her brief visit home, Anna was drawn, as though tracking a ghost, back to where Victoria had been. Grief has an ambition of rematerialisation; it seeks longingly what might have been held, or seen, or spaces once inhabited. To Anna it seemed that Victoria was somewhere just ahead of her, somewhere just out of reach, trailing mysteries still, and leading her on like a drifting wraith in a creepy story. It was a movie she had seen: a plot in which a wide-eyed child is tempted out of bed into blue-tinged darkness, and then entranced into smoky clutches and inexplicable translations. She could not dispense with this intuition: that she was following some cliché or other, that her feelings, their whole system, their whole expression or non-expression, were unoriginal.

Outside the entrance to the ancient catacombs of Paris lies a large semicircular bed of pansies. They are bright pink, purple and yellow faces, all bobbing in a slight breeze and looking surprised. Anna considers plucking one, but manages to resist. She is panicky and apprehensive. She would like to tear silken petals into fine even strips. She would like to destroy a flimsy face. Her pulse is hammering in her body and her skin is flushed and hectic.

The descent is by a series of spiral steps; these are poorly illuminated and seem interminable. Then there is a chamber, open and dull, with educative plaques on the wall, and a long walk through a vaporous tunnel before reaching the ossuary. Here a sign says: *Arrêtez! Ici c'est l'empire de mort!*, and Anna almost smiles. *Stop! This is the empire of death!*: it is so melodramatic and artificial, so redolent of adventure stories, old-fashioned commandments, boys with lit torches held gleefully beneath their chins. But she is chill, and afraid. Her lungs are weighted with the fuggy air, and her breathing difficult and heavy.

What am I doing here?

Why would anyone enter earth-chambers to see six million skeletons?

In this vision before her it is the neatness of the depositions that is unexpected. Green mouldy bones, mostly skulls and thighbones, are displayed stacked geometrically or in uniform rows. Most are in diamond or triangle shapes, or layered in simple horizontal designs: everywhere is the implication of fastidious arrangement. Mortuary workers in candlelight must have handled every bone, placing it, just so, with deliberation and care, into artful exhibition. Here the empire of death is not blasted remains; it is remade as architecture. The bones are stacked higher than Anna's head, and she must traipse forward, through this dim tunnel, which opens onto a neon-lit chamber, only to close back into another narrow dim tunnel. Another shaft of bone on bone on bone on bone.

From somewhere she hears a short burst of giggling; young people in a group are making cartoonish ghost sounds — *whoo-hoo! whoo-hoo!* — and telling nervous and probably silly jokes. Then it is quiet again, but for a few echoic reverberations, and Anna becomes conscious of the crunching wet gravel beneath her, and the patches of mud underfoot, and the dripping earth ceiling.

She remembers that Ernie told her of swarms of cockroaches living in the mines, especially in the crib and toilet areas: men relieved themselves, he said, into holes alive with insects. As a child this detail had shocked her; and Anna looks about her now for scurrying life. She sees nothing, not even a mouse. Everything is still.

She remembers Victoria calling herself *a Prospector of the Marvellous*: Victoria was a woman unafraid; she would not have entered this place with a pounding heart. Victoria, she knows now, was an alchemical woman, a woman who made gold from red dirt and the many varieties of darkness.

She remembers an image she saw once, a safety poster, displayed outside the Midas mine. It was a picture of two large white hands, hanging downwards. They appeared severed and ghostly. The caption simply read: THESE ARE PRECIOUS.
  The asterix of any hand.

She remembers a boy called Eamon Ahern. When she was nine Anna Griffin had a crush on Eamon Ahern. Even now the long-ago name is adorable. Eamon Ahern died when he rode his bicycle straight into the mouth of a mine. Anna still feels responsible. She still feels guilty.

———

She remembers — but it must be false, it must be one of Victoria's memories, transmigrated — Ernie as a young man, unscarred, working in the mine. He is stripped to the waist and has a small lamp affixed at his forehead. Under the earth, shadows are so definite, and light so intense, that he appears to exist as a photographic solarisation.

She remembers Winston Field's chest: she remembers placing her ear there, listening for the drum of his heartbeat. She lifted her face to his and said: The rumour is true; you're alive. When he laughed she heard it inside him, deep in his body. His voice, it is his voice she now remembers.

Why has Anna Griffin come?

Anna has come to visit the dead woman, Victoria Morrell.

This is where she will be. This is their *rendezvous*.

A group of five teenagers, four girls and a much taller, awkward and spotted boy, pass Anna, then hesitate, and return to ask her if she will kindly photograph them here. Here, exactly here. They speak English with an accent that is possibly Dutch.

Anna peers through the viewfinder of the camera and there they are, young, vivid, undiminished by the gloomy empire of death. Their smiles are elated. One of the girls bursts into soft laughter, then places her hand over her mouth and recomposes herself. (Behind their heads, almost perfectly aligned, is a double row of skulls, the eye sockets huge, the analogy unmistakable.) In the flashlight this group is both dazzled and dazzling: Anna has never before seen faces so lunar-bright.

Moonstruck at twelve hundred.

It is as though the memorialising light has rescued or redeemed them. She hands back the camera. The group chatters and moves on. Comic ghost noises float up like streamers behind them.

So Anna is alone again, with the artful bones. She is looking for a hand to clutch. She is looking for a daughter to rescue. She would like to haul Victoria to the surface — not glancing backwards — and reanimate her, from the beginning, as a tiny child. Instead she leans her back against the cold grimy surface of the lost souls around her and whispers into the darkness:

I am here, I am yours, I am evidence of the return of vanished things.

In this enclosure her voice sounds husky and sexually charged. It falls, dissolving, into the shadowy air.

But Anna has said her piece. She has visited what she feared. She feels suddenly acutely aware of her own body; there are bubbles of spit in her mouth, a trickle of sweat on her spine, dampness in her hair where drops of water have landed. Her heart rate has — without her noticing — at some stage quietened and normalised.

And now she moves through the ancient tunnels as though in another body, and not in a grave; she imagines she tracks the artery to some larger and invisible heart. Here, where there is lime and clay and the mystery and vulgarity of bones intermingled, where there is this easy coalescence of elements and memories, this accession — what is it? — of seanced conjunctions, she marches past waste and elimination and follows in the breezy wake of the young people ahead of her. They are jesting and laughing and need no explanations at all.

Give me your hand. Give me a kiss.

Darkness sweeps over Anna with the caress of an open sky.

In the desert where they all grew, singly and together, resolving images from the imprecisions of sky and dirt, there is a spot that alone is Lily-white's. It is the place, under the earth, where she buried the placenta she gave birth to with her daughter, Ruby. She returned part of her own body, those cells that cradled her mothering life, to the site where she first felt quickening, the site Ruby began. It is a modest dip in the land, oval-shaped and simple. Whitefellas would pass by and not notice anything at all. But a small mound of gathered stones marks the generation of spirit. This place is holy. It contests all the mine-work and despoliation that is everywhere around. It is the unregarded and persisting monument of countless other stories. It is its own kind of marvellous. A secret marvellous.

Acknowledgements

This is a work of fiction which is indebted to many Surrealist texts — both print and visual — and to the work of commentators on Surrealism, particularly Mary Ann Caws, Rosalind Krauss, Whitney Otto and Hal Foster. I also draw in oblique ways on texts by Breton, Aragon, Desnos and Carrington.

The following Australian texts have been useful: Ian Templeman and Bernadette MacDonald, *The Fields* (Fremantle Arts Centre Press 1988), Geoffrey Blainey, *The Golden Mile* (Allen and Unwin 1993), Gavin Casey, *Short Shift Saturday* (Angus and Robertson 1973), AN Bingley, *Back to the Goldfields* (Hesperion Press 1988), Norma King, *Daughters of Midas: Pioneer Women of the Eastern Goldfields* (Hesperion Press 1992).

Winston's prayer and song are derived from Opal Palmer Odisa's magnificent story 'Me Man Angel' in *Bake Face and Other Guava Stories* (Flamingo 1987).

I have many friends to thank for support and discussion, particularly Susan Midalia, whose literary critical intelligence was an enormous help at a difficult time. Veronica Brady, Victoria Burrows, Trish Crawford, Hilary Fraser, Prue Kerr, Joan London, Margaret West and Terri-ann White, have all offered indispensable moral support. Beth Yahp's clever advice and good humour is gratefully acknowledged, as is Marion Campbell's continuing role as a writing mentor. Jane Southwell's scholarly work and energetic discussion did much to clarify my own ideas on surrealism. I would also like to thank my editor, Judith Lukin-Amundsen, for her patient work, Elaine Lewis, for her consistent belief in my writing, and my agent, Fran Bryson, for her general help and advice. My beloved daughter Kyra has been an inspiration from the beginning.

This project was supported by the Eleanor Dark Foundation with a writing residency at Varuna, and by the Australia Council with the gift of a writing space at the Keesing Studio in Paris. My colleagues in the Department of English, Communications and Cultural Studies at the University of Western Australia have been unfailingly generous and supportive.

I wish above all to thank my parents to whom this book is lovingly dedicated.

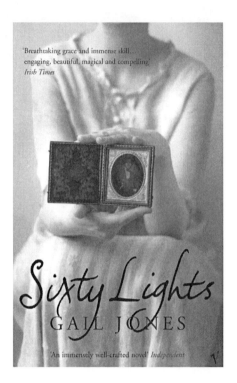

'Breathtaking grace and immense skill...
engaging, beautiful, magical and compelling'
Irish Times

Sixty Lights

GAIL JONES

'An immensely well-crafted novel' *Independent*

Sixty Lights

by Gail Jones

In 1860, Lucy Strange and her brother Thomas are orphaned. Left in the care of their uncle, the children begin slowly, frighteningly, to find their place in the world. And so begins Lucy's adolescent journey of discovery, one that will take her away from her childhood home in Australia, first to London, then to Bombay and, finally, to her death at the age of twenty-three. It is a life abbreviated, but not a life diminished. Lucy is a remarkable character, forthright, gifted and exuberant; she touches the lives of all who know her.

Written in confident, finely interwoven and intricate layers, *Sixty Lights* is the powerful chronicle of a modern and independent young woman's life in the Victorian world. Objects evoke memories and hint at the future in a narrative that flows between pleats in time. Through her observation of such objects, Lucy's photographic talent is apparent.

NOW AVAILABLE

'A superb storyteller'
Australian Bookseller & Publisher

Dreams

of

Speaking

GAIL JONES

VINTAGE

Dreams of Speaking

by Gail Jones

Alice is entranced by the aesthetics of technology. Mr Sakamoto, a survivor of the atomic bomb, is an expert on Alexander Graham Bell. This displaced pair forge an unlikely friendship sparked by the poetry of modern inventions and enriched by slowly revealed secrets and vulnerabilities.

This novel from prize-winning author Gail Jones is distinguished in its honesty and intelligence. From the boundlessness of space walking to the frustrating constrictions of one person's daily existence, *Dreams of Speaking* paints with grace and skill the experience of needing to belong despite wanting to be alone.

NOW AVAILABLE

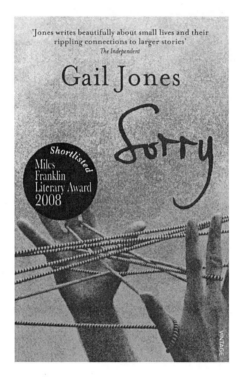

'Jones writes beautifully about small lives and their
rippling connections to larger stories'
The Independent

Gail Jones

Sorry

Shortlisted
Miles
Franklin
Literary Award
2008

Sorry

by Gail Jones

In the remote outback of Western Australia during
World War II, English anthropologist Nicholas Keene
and his wife, Stella, raise a lonely child, Perdita. Her
upbringing is far from ordinary: in a shack in the
wilderness, with a distant father burying himself in
books and an unstable mother whose knowledge of
Shakespeare forms the backbone of the girl's limited
education.

Emotionally adrift, Perdita becomes friends with a
deaf and mute boy, Billy, and an Aboriginal girl,
Mary. Perdita and Mary come to call one another
sister and share a very special bond. They are content
with life in this remote corner of the globe, until a
terrible event lays waste to their lives. Through this
exquisite story of Perdita's troubled childhood, Gail
Jones explores the values of friendship, loyalty and
sacrifice.

NOW AVAILABLE